Murder is a Family Business

Book One
In
The Alvarez Family
Murder Mystery Series

Heather Haven

The Wives of Bath Press
223 Vincent Drive
Mountain View, CA 94041

http:// www.thewivesofbath.com

Cover Art © 2013 by Heather Haven/Jeff Monaghan
Edited by Baird Nuckolls
Layout and book production by
Heather Haven and Baird Nuckolls

Print ISBN-13: 978-0-9884086-9-2
eBook ISBN-13: 978-0-9892265-0-9

First eBook edition Jan 1, 2011

Testimonials

"Heather Haven makes a stellar debut in Murder is a Family Business." **Highly recommended.** SHELDON SIEGEL. NEW YORK TIMES BEST SELLING AUTHOR OF PERFECT ALIBI.

"The writing was clever and I couldn't stop laughing. This is the perfect beach book." Laura from The 100 Romances Project

"Ms. Haven has found a new fan." Dishin' It Out, Ginger Simpson

"Wonderful! Charming! Fun." Dr. Cynthia Lea Clark, Psy.D

"It is a thoroughly enjoyable reading experience. I look forward to the next book in this series." Candy Bezner, Single Titles

"Wonderfully fresh and funny!" - Meg Waite Clayton, author of *The Wednesday Sisters* and *The Four Ms. Bradwells*

~

The Alvarez Family Murder Mystery Series:

Murder is a Family Business – Book One
A Wedding to Die For – Book Two
Death Runs in the Family – Book Three

Acknowledgements

I would like to acknowledge the United States Coast Guard for their invaluable help and information.

Dedication

I would like to dedicate this book to my Cafe Bee writing buddies, to Ellen Sussman and my fellow participants in her writing classes, especially Baird Nuckolls, friend and writing/business partner, to my supportive husband, Norman Meister, to families everywhere, and to my mother, Mary Lee, who is more like daughter, Lee, than Lila, just in case anyone asks.

Murder is a Family Business

Chapter One
The Not-So-Perfect Storm

"God, surveillance sucks," I griped aloud to a seagull languishing on a nearby, worm-eaten post, he being my only companion for the past few hours. He cocked his head and stared at me. I cocked my head and stared at him. It might have been the beginning of a beautiful friendship, but a nearby car backfired, and he took off in a huff. Watching him climb, graceful and white against the gray sky, I let out a deep sigh, feeling enormously sorry for myself. I eyeballed the dilapidated warehouse across the parking lot hanging onto the edge of the pier for any signs of life. I didn't find any.

I knew I was in trouble earlier when I discovered this was the only vantage point from which I could stay hidden and still see the "perpetrator's place of entrance," as I once heard on *Law and Order*. That meant I couldn't stay in my nice warm car listening to a Fats Waller tribute on the radio but had to be out in the elements, hunkered down next to a useless seawall.

For three lousy hours, rambunctious waves from the San Francisco Bay made a break for freedom over this wall and won. Salty foam and spray pummeled my face, mixed with mascara, and stung my eyes like nobody's business. Then the wind picked up, and the temperature dropped faster than the Dow Jones on a bad day.

Speeding up Highway 101 toward Fisherman's Wharf, I'd heard on the car radio that a storm was moving in. When I arrived, I got to experience it first-hand. Yes, it was just winter and me on the San Francisco Bay. Even Jonathan Livingston Seagull had taken a powder.

I concentrated on one of two warehouses, mirrors of each other, sitting at either side of a square parking lot containing about twenty cars and trucks. "*Dios mio*, do something," I muttered to the building, which housed the man who had caused me to age about twenty years in one afternoon.

I struggled to stay in a crouched position, gave up and sat down, thinking about the man I'd been following. I was sure he was a lot more comfortable than I, and I resented him for it. Two seconds later, I realized the cement was wet, as well as cold. Cursing my stupidity, I jumped up and stretched my cramped legs while trying to keep an eye on the door he had entered, lo those many hours before. With me being the only one on the job, I couldn't keep an eye on the cargo bay on the other side of the warehouse, but I felt pretty safe about it being a non-exit. Without a boat or a ship tied there, it emptied into the briny bay. The perp, thankfully, didn't look like much of a swimmer, even on a nice day.

I tried to focus my mind on Mr. Portor Wyler, said perpetrator, and the singular reason for all my misery. I kept coming back to this burning question:

Why the hell is a Palo Alto real estate mogul driving 42-miles roundtrip two to three times a week to a beat-up, San Francisco warehouse on the waterfront?

After that, I had an even better one:

What the hell am I doing here? Oh, yeah. Thanks, Mom.

My name is Liana Alvarez. It's Lee to my friends, but never to my mother. I am a thirty-four year old half-Latina and half-WASP PI. The latter, aforesaid relatives, drip with blue blood and blue chips and have been Bay Area fixtures for generations. Regarding the kindred Mexican half of me, they either immigrated to the good old US of A or still live in Vera

Cruz, where they fish the sea. How my mother and father ever got together is something I've been meaning to ask Cupid for some time.

However, I digress. Back to Portor Wyler or, rather, his wife, Yvette Wyler. It was because of her I was in possession of a cold, wet butt, although I'm not supposed to use language like that because Mom would be scandalized. She has this idea she raised me to be a lady and swears her big mistake was letting me read Dashiell Hammett when I was an impressionable thirteen year-old.

My mother is Lila Hamilton Alvarez, of the blue blood part of the family, and CEO of Discretionary Inquiries, Inc. She's my boss. Yvette Wyler has been a friend of my mother's since Hector was a pup, so when Mrs. Wyler came crying to her, Mom thought we should be the ones to find out what was going on. That didn't seem like a good enough reason for me to be where I was, assigned to a job so distasteful no self-respecting gumshoe I hung out with would touch it, but there you have it. Leave it to my mother to lay a guilt trip on me at one of my more vulnerable times. I don't know who I was more annoyed with, Mom or me.

Furthermore, I had no idea what my intelligent, savvy, and glamorous mother had in common with this former school buddy, who had the personality of ragweed and a face reminiscent of a Shar-Pei dog I knew once. Whenever I brought the subject up to Mom, I got claptrap about "loyalty" and "friends being friends." So naturally, my reaction to the woman made me aware of possible character flaws on my part. I mean, here Mrs. Wyler was, one of my mother's life-long chums, and I was just waiting for her to bark.

But the long and short of it was pals they were. Discretionary Inquiries, Inc. was on the job, and I was currently freezing my aforementioned butt off because of it; thank you so much.

Computer espionage in Silicon Valley is D.I.'s milieu, if you'll pardon my French. The Who, What, Where, When, and How of computer thievery is our livelihood. To elucidate, high tech companies don't appreciate staff making off with new hardware or software ideas, potentially worth millions of dollars, either to sell to the highest bidder or to use as bribery for a better, high-powered job with the competition. If you haven't heard about any of this, it's because this kind of pilfering keeps a pretty low profile in Silicon Valley. Upper management of most companies feel it's important not to give investors the shakes nor the techies any ideas. Ideas, however, are what techies are all about, and it's a rare day when somebody isn't stealing something from someone and using it for a six-figured trip to the bank, whether upper management likes it or not.

Until the recent change in copyright law, each individual company dealt with the problem by filing civil lawsuits against suspected counterfeiters. It was a long and arduous process often resulting in nothing more than a slap on the wrist for the guilty parties. Now that there are federal statutes with teeth, which include prison sentences, these companies are anxious to see the guilty parties pay to the fullest extent of the law. It's at this point that Discretionary Inquiries, Inc. is brought into the act.

D.I. is the Rolls Royce of high-tech investigation, if I must say so myself, with a success rate of over 94 percent. To say business at D.I. is brisk is an understatement. D.I. often turns away work. For me, it's exciting and challenging; I love working with the FBI's counter-intelligence division, the IRS, the U.S. Customs Service, and the "hi-tech units" of police departments.

My particular specialty is being a ferret, and I hope I'm not being too technical here. I sniff out means and opportunity *after the fact* until I have enough evidence that will stand up in court. Yes, I am a perfumed ferret, resplendent in Charles

Jordan heels, Bulgari jewelry, and Versace dresses. I sit in cushioned office chairs and have high-powered lunches drilling stricken staff members who "can't believe what happened," until I enlighten them as to how it can and did. Then everybody's happy, and I receive a nice, fat bonus when the job is done. Sometimes I'm allowed to throw a bone to the local newspapers or one of the television stations, depending on how spiteful the wounded company wants to be, so everyone loves me. And, it is my dream job.

This was my nightmare. I closed my eyes and willed it all to go away. It didn't. Just then, the sky darkened, and a gust of wind whipped up at least half the water contained in the Bay. This water joined forces with a maverick wave with a nasty disposition and impeccable timing. They both came at me like a blast from a fireman's hose. I lost my balance, and found myself flat on my back in a very unladylike position, as my mother would say.

I gurgled and spit out about a half-gallon of salt water hoping the Bay was as clean as the mayor boasted. My hair was plastered to my scalp and face in long, wet, strands that went nicely with the quivering blue lips and streaked mascara. I got to my feet and tried to zip up my black leather jacket. The teeth caught in the fabric of my sweater and refused to budge despite any amount of coercion from numb fingers. My wool slacks clung to my legs and lost whatever shape they previously had. To finish it off, my new suede boots bled their color in puddles around my feet.

"Well, at least it isn't raining yet," I said aloud, trying to remember what I'd learned about positive thinking the previous month. I had attended a three-day seminar at the Malaysian Institute of Advanced Studies in "Self-Excellence and Positive Thinking" sponsored by the Ministry of Culture. I'm not sure what I got out of it, other than great food, but the Institute has a rather unique approach to carrying out daily tasks with "dedication and integrity," as stated in their brochures. This approach is being written up on about a billion dollars worth of software right here in Silicon Valley. D.I. is their very own personal firewall against thievery, so I wanted to give these Malaysian theories a chance.

I saw the lights go out from under the door of the warehouse and wondered if it was a power outage, or was Wyler preparing to leave? Whatever, my body tensed with renewed alertness or as much alertness as I could renew. At that moment, of course, a bolt of lightning struck. Its point zero was so close by my soggy hair stood on end, and my nose twitched from the electrical charge. The flash of light illuminated everything, including the white-capped waves of the Bay hurtling in my direction. The lightning was followed by a clap of thunder, which sounded like a herd of longhorns stampeding over a tin bridge.

As if that wasn't enough, the walkway I stood on began to quiver, and I knew it was going to do something Really Big at any moment. That's when the heavens opened up. Sheets of rain, driven by the wind, hammered at my skin, and I could barely open my eyes.

"That's it! Stick a fork in me, I'm done," I yelled to the world at large. I reached inside my drenched shoulder bag for my cellphone and prayed it would work. It had been acting up lately, like everything else in my life, but I hit speed dial and ran to a nearby Plexiglas phone booth. The booth no longer contained a phone, only sodden newspapers littering the floor. Fighting the assaulting rain, I pushed the door closed and heard someone pick up on the first ring. Things were looking up. My cell phone was working.

"This is Lila," said a well-modulated voice.

My mother annoys me when she is well modulated, but now that she sounded dry on top of it, I found it maddening.

"It's me, and I feel like Noah without the ark. Get the dove ready. Find me an olive branch. The rains have come, and I am gone."

"Yes, dear. Ha ha. Now what is the matter?"

"What isn't the matter?" I wailed, forgetting I was annoyed with her. "I'm cold; I'm soaked through, and I was almost hit by a bolt of lightning."

"Where are you, Liana? Try to be more *succinct.*"

"Where am I?" I was so stunned by the question that I took a deep breath and decided not to have a tantrum. Lowering my voice several octaves, I enunciated each word. "I am where I have been for three miserable, boring, useless hours, in accordance with your wishes. Succinctly, I'm in a phone booth catty-corner to the warehouse. The lights went out maybe thirty seconds ago just as a storm hit full force. It's raining too hard to see anything more than a foot away. I'm drenched; I'm tired, and I'm freezing." The octaves began to climb again because while I was wiping the water from my face, I poked a finger in my right eye. "Son of a bitch!"

"Watch your language," Lila rebuked, ever the lady. "And don't be petulant, Liana. It doesn't become you. So, what you are saying is, you don't know whether or not Wyler is still inside the warehouse," she said, getting to the issue at hand.

"*Exactamente.* What I do I know, is it's a monsoon out here, and I'm going to catch pneumonia if I stay out in it much longer."

"Oh, stop being so dramatic, Liana. It's just a little water," the woman who gave birth to me chided. So much for mother love. "It's too bad you've lost him so late in the proceedings, though. We were doing so well," she added.

I loved the way she included herself in all of this. "Well, don't tell me you want me to go into the warehouse and look for him," I said, with an edge to my voice. An involuntary shiver ran through me, as I felt a movement of the wet papers at my feet. This wind even comes through Plexiglas, I thought.

"Absolutely not! We agreed to follow him from a safe distance, not to make contact. If we lost him, we lost him. Go on home."

"Oh." I felt the air go out of my balloon of martyrdom. "Sorry about this," I added. This may have been my third tedious day following a man who made Danny DeVito look tall, dark and handsome, but I was a professional and trained to do the job. Although, to be honest, I wasn't quite sure what that job was. His wife thought he was cheating on her. Okay, that's understandable given who she was, but once she caught him in *flagrante delecto*, what then? California has a no-fault divorce law with a fifty-fifty property split, pants up or pants down.

As far as I could see, this wasn't quite the same scenario as demanding the return of stolen property, intellectual or otherwise. I mean, what was he going to "return" here? If Wyler dropped his drawers elsewhere, literally, could he just return his private parts, figuratively, to the little wifey with a vow to never do it again?

When I thought about it that way, I guess you could make a case for it. However, if Lila considered a philandering husband in the same category as computer espionage, and if D.I. was heading in that direction, I was going to get out of the business and become a nun.

"It can't be helped," Lila replied, interrupting my mental wanderings.

"What can't be helped?" I said, still lost in my own thoughts.

"Pay attention, Liana. I'm telling you to go home. Make sure you log all the information you've got on the computer when you get to the office in the morning." She added, "We'll go over it tomorrow with Richard. By the way, have you been able to come up with the owner of the warehouse?"

"You mean in my spare time?" I retorted. "No, I've done some digging, but I can't find a company name yet. I think we're going to have to bring in the Big Guns."

"Hmmm, strange," Lila pondered. "By 'big guns,' as you've put it, I *assume* you mean Richard." Mom has an irritating way of underlining certain words of a sentence with her voice. I don't mean to complain, but it can be almost as exasperating as her modulations. And then there's her overall aversion to the use of slang words, which is too bad, because I use them all the time. Dad's side of the family.

Aside from Dashiell Hammett, my formative years were influenced by any 1940s movie on television I watched. That was whenever I wasn't being thrown outside to play. When I was ten years old, much to my mother's dismay, I fell in love with Barbara Stanwyck's portrayal of Sugarpuss O'Shea in the movie *Ball of Fire.* I imitated "jive talk" every waking moment until I got hustled off to a craft summer camp. The camp may have curtailed my jiving, but to this day, Miss Stanwyck is one of my favorite actresses, along with Selma Hayek, who I just loved in *Frida.*

Mom continued her train of thought about the warehouse, oblivious to my inner musings.

"At first, I didn't think it was important enough to tie up Richard's time, but now I'm curious as to why something as simple as finding out the ownership of a building should be so difficult. Maybe we'll ask his department to see what they can discover tomorrow. We'll talk later. Go home."

With that, she hung up without even so much as telling me to drink some hot tea when I got there or to be careful driving in this weather. It was at times like these I wondered if Mom and Medea had maternal similarities I didn't care to think about.

I threw the phone in my bag and leaned against the Plexiglas, reluctant to go out again into the storm. All of a sudden, I felt movement again at my feet and looked down.

Under the papers was a small lump, a moving one! I drew my breath in, as I opened the door to the phone booth. Water rat! There was a rat in this phone booth with me! I stepped out in the rain backward, keeping my eyes on the mass of papers. Then I thought I heard a plaintive cry. I leaned my head back into the booth ignoring the rain beating down on my back like small pebbles.

"Kitty?" I said. "Kitty, kitty, kitty?"

A meow sounded again. I pulled the wet papers from on top of the lump to reveal a small, orange and white kitten, drenched to the skin. It turned amber eyes up to me and let out a silent meow as it cowered in the corner.

"Oh, my God! Look at you." Reaching out a hand, I picked up the trembling creature. "What a little thing. And so wet. Come here." Like an idiot, I looked around for the owner until I caught myself. I tried to unzip my jacket to slip the kitten inside but the teeth still wouldn't release one of my best cashmere sweaters. The jacket's pockets were huge, so I wound up sort of stuffing the kitten inside, as gently as possible, of course. It turned itself around and stuck its head out with a puzzled stare.

"Well, I can't just leave you, and it's pouring out there. So you stay inside until we get to my car." With that pronouncement, I pushed its small head back inside the dry pocket and left my hand inside for protection and company. The kitten moved around a little and then settled down, leaning against my open palm.

Half walking, half jogging to my car in the torrential downpour, I glanced back in the direction of the warehouse and began to play the "on the other hand" game with myself.

On one hand, Wyler has to be in the warehouse. But it looks dark and deserted. Did he somehow get by me? No, no, he can't have!

On the other hand, when I was lying flat on my back swallowing half the Bay, maybe he did. Stranger things have happened.

Oh, come on, I other-handed myself again. I had the only entrance and exit under constant surveillance for the last three agonizing hours, and I was only indisposed for less than a minute. How likely is it he got away? He must be there. On the other hand, and now I was up to four hands, why aren't the lights on if he is?

This might not look so good on my resume. Uh-oh! I should check for his car. If I let him get by me, Lila will never...wait a minute!

I began to see a silver lining in all those damp clouds.

If Portor did get by me, Lila will never let me live it down. Following this line of logic, she would probably never, ever ask me to do something like this again.

I continued this new train of thought sloshing through puddles up to my ankles and almost broke out in a dance like Gene Kelly in *Singing in the Rain*.

The movements of the kitten in my jacket distracted me, and I wondered what I was going to do with it when I got back to the car.

Well, I reminded myself, *I couldn't just leave it back there to drown.*

That settled, I removed the keys from my bag, pressed the beeper to unlock the doors and slipped into its dry, comparative warmth.

This classic '57 Chevy convertible was my pride and joy, the last extravagant gift from my father shortly before his death. It contained a rebuilt engine, in addition to all the latest gewgaws offered in newer automobiles. Dad had outbid everyone at a vintage car auction for this stellar rarity still wearing the original white and turquoise paint job. He gave it to me for my thirty-first birthday, a reward for surviving a rotten marriage and a bitter divorce. I never knew what the price tag was, but the insurance premiums alone are enough to keep me working until I'm around ninety-seven.

The kitten stopped moving, and I panicked.

This is all I need, I shuddered, *a deceased kitten in my jacket to complete an already ghastly day.*

However, it rubbed up against my hand, and I could feel the fleece lining had dried it off. Then it popped its head out to stare at me with that "now-you've-gone-and-done-it-so-I'm-your-responsibility" look. It was a little unsettling.

"Well, I see you're okay, little guy, but what am I going to do with you?" I challenged, trying not to look it in the eye. Seized with an idea, I thought of my friend who was a vet and would probably take the kitten in, warm-hearted chump that she was. I checked the time. Six-thirty. She would still be at the clinic. "Let's take you to see your new mommy," I cooed. I started the car and drove down the Embarcadero now black, wet and abandoned in the storm. I felt as if I were in a film noir; there didn't seem to be a soul out besides this wet feline and me.

After the earthquake of '89, nearly everyone in San Francisco had prayed the freeway would come down, and the beauty of the bay would be revealed again. When the cement structure was razed, it revitalized a previously neglected area of the city, and man oh, man, do I wish I had been an investor in some of that waterfront property. Everybody who was anybody wanted to be in this area: living, working, shopping, walking, jogging, or running along the Bay, all the while talking or texting on cellphones. That was the latest form of multi-tasking.

The amazing part was they were willing to pay through the nose for the privilege of being crowded into this strip of territory along with a never-ending stream of tourists. Even with the foggy summers, it's probably worth more per square inch than any other place in the states.

I only drove for a couple of blocks when I began to have the gnawing feeling I had some unfinished business. I decided to check and see if Wyler's car was still around or if he had given me the slip. Ever since I started trailing him, I'd noticed he'd always left the car about three blocks away from the warehouse on a side street instead of parking right in front of it. That, in itself, I found very suspicious. He didn't strike me as a man who was into exercise for exercise's sake.

Turning on my brights, I hung a U-turn and drove back to where he parked earlier. I spotted the lone black Mercedes, a solitary car on the block. Noting the time, I hesitated to drive away. Something told me I should return to the warehouse and search for him even if Lila had given me direct orders not to make contact. I turned off the motor shivering in my wet clothes and listened to the sound of the rain drumming on the roof of my car, while I chewed at my lower lip for a time.

Oh, well, I thought as I started the engine, *this won't be the first time I haven't paid any attention to what Lila said. Or the last, either.*

I turned the car around and drove back to the warehouse. At this point, I didn't care if I blew my cover or not. I needed to know.

As far as I could see, which wasn't much, the parking lot was deserted. The lot was around one hundred and twenty feet deep stopping at the thick and ineffectual four-foot high cement wall on the Bay. A narrow walkway leading to piers directly behind each warehouse ran alongside the cement wall. Amber-colored, low-watt lampposts lit the air above the walkway between the two warehouses and the parking lot and served more as symbols than actual illumination. About five feet inside the perimeter, telephone poles lay on their sides to keep vehicles from hitting the warehouses or the seawall.

Given my vision was *nada* even with the headlights on, I relied on my memory and hoped nothing had changed within the last half hour. I aimed the car towards what I calculated was the warehouse door and waited for the feel of the wheels hitting the pole. When I felt the resistance, I stopped the car, turned off the engine, but left the lights on.

Pulling some Kleenex and a headscarf out of the glove compartment, I wiped my face with the former and tied the latter over my head to contain my dripping curls. Underneath the passenger's seat, I found a flashlight, small but powerful, and a not too dirty hand towel. With all this movement, the kitten began to wiggle inside the jacket. I hauled the critter out and wrapped it in the towel. All the while, I spoke in what I hoped was a good version of the reassuring tone of voice was used on *The Crocodile Hunter* the one time I had watched it in mute horror. Of course, this wasn't a crocodile, but the same theory should apply.

"You stay here for just a couple of minutes, little guy. I'll be right back." I placed the mummy-wrapped cat on the seat, opened the door and slid back out into the downpour. I aimed the flashlight at what I hoped was the entrance to the warehouse and was rewarded by the glint of the metal door. I ran to it, found the handle and pulled with all my might. Major locked. Rivulets of water streamed down my face, as I searched for another way to get into the building.

A far off flash of lightning struck, and out of the corner of my eye, I thought I saw something on the ground in the walkway near the water's edge. It was hard to tell by the three-watt bulb of the lamppost, so I trotted towards it, aiming the flashlight ahead of me. The closer I got, the faster I ran, because it looked like a shoe, toe pointing upwards.

Breathing hard, I rounded the corner to see what connected to the shoe. It was Portor Wyler. He lay flat on his back, arms opened wide, unseeing eyes staring up into the falling rain. The front of his once white shirt had turned a pinkish hue, blood diluted by the downpour. Three small reddish holes formed a "v" in the center of his chest.

I know I screamed, but a clap of thunder must have drowned me out. I felt the shriek reverberate inside me but never heard it. I also must have been backing up, because I tripped over one of those damned horizontal telephone poles and fell backward, flinging the flashlight up in the air. It landed near my head with a sobering, clunking sound. I retrieved it, got up, and leaned against the building fighting for control.

When I could move, I stumbled back to the car and grabbed my cellphone off the front seat. The first two times I punched in 911, nothing happened. After banging the phone against the steering wheel, I finally got a connection. My teeth chattered from shock, cold, and fear, but I gave a lucid enough report to the dispatcher before the phone went dead again, as dead as Portor Wyler. Frustrated, I threw it into the back seat as hard as I could. I turned back to face a kitten that had managed to get out of his shroud in my absence and was staring up at me, wide-eyed. I reached a shaking hand out, and it rubbed its body against my fingers. This small bit of friendship overwhelmed me, and I bit back tears.

I couldn't get the picture of Portor Wyler's face out of my mind. His mouth had been frozen open in an "oh," as if he'd been as surprised as me that he was dead. Funny what you notice when you see death for the first time.

Chapter Two
The Right Place at the Wrong Time

"Let's go over this again, Miss Alvarez." Officer Davis, a lanky African-American, glanced down at his notes. I hoped he was older than he looked, which was about thirteen.

"Listen," I said, "I don't mean to sound testy, but I have spent two hours in a parking lot and twice that in this chair, and the only two people I've seen are you and Pickles."

"Pinkerton," he corrected.

"Am I ever going to see anyone from Homicide?" I demanded. Before Dad had started D.I., he'd been a cop. I knew how it went since I'd been in diapers.

"You will," he answered without looking up. "Tell me once more what happened."

I took a deep breath and started my story. Again. Four hours before, I had been brought to the North Point Precinct, caravan style. The police originally wanted me to leave my car at the warehouse and take me in one of their cruisers. Once I'd explained I had an animal onboard, however, they insisted I follow them, flanked front and back by flashing cop cars. It was a short parade but effective.

Before ushering me into one of the interrogation rooms, I'd watched several cops gather a small cardboard carton, a blanket, a bowl of water, and a couple of sandwiches together. I thought they were for me, but soon found out where I was in the food chain. Demanding the keys to my car, they presented this bounty to the small feline temporarily in residence there. I'd noted the litter for the cardboard carton was donated by the resident long-haired calico, Snickers, who seemed to run the precinct. The police mentioned in passing they would be searching my car for any weapons, such as a gun, even though I had already told them I wasn't carrying. I was sure they would be ably assisted by one if not both of the cats.

"And that's pretty much it, as I told you a dozen times before," I said, doing a couple of shoulder rolls to relieve the muscle tension. I glanced at my watch. It was nearly one a.m. I knew Lila would be frantic wondering where I was. "And, once again, I would like to make a phone call."

"In a little while," he answered. "You had never met Portor Wyler before three days ago?" Now this was a dicey question. I didn't want to go into Yvette Wyler being a long time friend of my mother's, even though I rarely saw her. As for Portor, I did meet him once at a Bat Mitzvah many years before. I decided to go into Attack Mode.

"Look, I'm not answering any more questions until I see someone in charge. Furthermore, Captain Frank Thompson of the Palo Alto Police Department is my godfather, and I happen to know he has a few friends around here. He's not going to like it when he finds out…"

I never got to finish my half-baked threat because the door opened and an unshaven, out of shape, middle-aged man carrying two cups of coffee strode in. He set them down on the small table sitting between Davis and me, spilling much of the contents.

"Okay, Davis, thanks. I've got it now." He shot me an apologetic smile, took a couple of wrinkled paper napkins out of his shirt pocket and began to wipe up the liquid. I watched silently. Office Davis sauntered out, closing the door behind him.

"Sorry about the wait," he offered. "Most everybody's out with the flu, and we had a drive by shooting in the Tenderloin. Three kids dead. Shame."

I didn't say anything.

He went on, "I'm Detective Fenner." He reached over and extended his hand.

I shook it and said, "I'm Lee Alvarez but you already know that."

"Yes. Miss Alvarez, I'm not really assigned to this case but..."

"Everybody's out with the flu," I finished for him.

He nodded and continued. "That means that tonight I'm the only game in town, so bear with me." He rifled through the file Davis left on the table saying, "Have some coffee."

"Thanks," I said and sucked down the lukewarm paint thinner, as if it were Starbucks' finest.

"You're right about Frank having some clout around here," he said, while he read one of the handwritten reports. "He and I were at the Palo Alto Police Academy, along with your father. I transferred here in 1990. That's about the time your dad left to do his PI thing." He looked up at me. "I was at Bobby's funeral. You probably don't remember me."

I didn't. But I didn't remember much about that time other than feeling like I was trying to breathe under water. "I'm afraid not," I managed to say.

"Bobby Alvarez was a great guy. I miss him."

His 'Hail, fellow, well met' attitude threw me off. It's hard to be belligerent with someone who's being so doggoned nice, but I gave it a try. "Detective Fenner, how much longer am I going to be here? I'm trying to be cooperative but..."

"You're free to go, Miss Alvarez," he interrupted, standing up. "Sorry about the delay."

Confused, I stood up myself.

"You'll need to sign a statement, of course," he went on, "but we've kept you so long, why don't we just take care of the details tomorrow after you've had some sleep?"

I didn't need to be told twice. Grabbing my handbag, I said, "Can I please make a phone call? I was supposed to be home hours ago." If I knew Lila Alvarez, she was rounding up a pack of bloodhounds by now.

"Sure." Detective Fenner picked up his coffee cup and took a quick gulp, while crossing the small room. He held the door open for me in a very gentlemanly manner, and I passed through into the main squad room. He must have been right about the flu striking down much of the squad. I hadn't noticed it before, but over three-quarters of the desks in the room were empty. That's a lot, even in the middle of the night.

"Just pick an empty desk and make your call. Dial nine to get an outside line."

"Thanks," I tossed over my shoulder, going over to one of the corner desks. I wanted privacy for this call.

"Drop by sometime tomorrow afternoon," he said, the level of his voice rising, as I walked away. "And by the way," he added, "don't leave town for a while, okay?"

I waved my hand in acknowledgement and fell heavily into a swivel chair with a lumpy cushion in it. I knew this was going to be a tough call to make. Not only was the subject of the current surveillance dead, but he'd been the husband of one of my mother's closest friends. Taking a deep breath, I dialed Lila's cell phone. I heard her cool inflection after the first ring.

"This is Lila."

"Mom," I murmured into the phone, looking around to make sure I wasn't being overheard.

When she heard me, her mommy voice took over, "Liana, my dear, finally!"

"Mom, I've got some really bad news, so brace yourself," I whispered. "It's about Portor Wyler. I guess the only way to tell you is just to say it. He's—."

"He's dead, I know," she interrupted, sympathetically. "Such a shock. Try to remain calm, dear. Are you all right?"

"I'm fine," I stuttered, "but how did you know?"

"The police notified Yvette around ten, and she called me. I went to her house, but I was frantic that I wasn't hearing from you. Two or three hours ago, I phoned Frank. He made some calls and found out you were being held for questioning at North Beach."

"Of course, they'd notify Wyler's next of kin as soon as possible. I guess I'm so tired I'm not thinking straight."

"Why didn't you call me sooner? I would have been very concerned if Frank hadn't told me where you were and that you were all right."

"My cell phone, *se murió*, dead, dead, dead. And they've been holding me incommunicado since around seven-thirty."

"I see. Are they through with you?"

"Yes, although I've got to show up some time tomorrow and sign a statement. God, what a night," I said.

I heard muffled voices in the background and figured she'd stopped listening to me, so I shut up. I heard her talking to Tío, Dad's older and only brother, on one of those "long-term visits" after the lingering, but inevitable death last month of his wife of fifty years. Her loss, plus that of my dad two years before, left him pretty much devastated. With no children of his own, we were his only remaining family in the States. For now, he was staying with us indefinitely, and we liked it just fine.

"Mateo wants to talk to you," Lila said. "He's been very worried. You and I can discuss the details of Portor Wyler's death later on and the ramifications on the Agency," she added before passing the phone to her brother-in-law.

"*Hola, mi querida*," he said in his soft, Spanish accent.

"Tío, what are you doing up? You should be asleep. It's nearly two a.m."

"You are all right?"

"Of course, I am. You know I'm one tough cookie, Tío," I said with a lot more bravado than I was feeling.

"Not so tough, *mija*. Not so tough."

"Okay, maybe not," I admitted. "But I'm fine, and I'll be home soon. Why don't you go to bed? Please don't wait up, Tío, okay? I'm fine."

"You will drive right home, *sí*?"

"*Sí.*"

"You will lock the car doors?"

"Tío," I grumbled, "you're worse than Mom!"

"You will lock the car doors," he repeated.

"I will lock the car doors," I agreed.

"*Está bien.*"

"Now put Mom back on, and please go to bed, Tío. *Te amo.*"

"*Te amo, tambien, mi sobrina.*"

Lila came on the line again. "Maybe you should find a hotel nearby and not try to drive home, dear."

"I just had some coffee, and I feel fine, Mom," I lied. "I'll see you soon."

I left the precinct and went out into the still pounding rain. Fortunately, my car was parked out front, thank God. I unlocked the driver's door to find the entire front and floor of the car given over to the nameless kitten.

My side of the floor had the water bowl and a paper dish containing a picked over chicken burrito smelling so delicious I almost gobbled it up myself. The passenger's floor had the makeshift litter pan. On that side of the seat, the small, sleeping cat was snuggled in the blanket brought out earlier by a cat-loving cop, one which I would have to eventually wash and return along with the water bowl, me being the nice Latina girl that I am.

I climbed inside avoiding the dishes, pulled some of the unused portion of the blanket over my lap and, remembering to lock the doors, leaned the chair back just to close my eyes for a moment or two.

Five hours later, the sound of a car horn woke me up. The kitten had crawled up under my neck. I felt myself being lulled back to sleep by its soothing purr. I snapped to, realized where I was, and sat up abruptly. The kitten jumped to the seat, while I checked the time. It was nearly seven a.m. A grey light filtered through the morning rain still drumming on the car roof, but I wasn't listening to it.

I was thinking of Portor Wyler, really thinking about him for the first time. Now that the shock was gone, I was filled with an almost painful sense of guilt. Even thought he didn't know it, I had let him down. My job was not just to watch him but to watch out for him. I was so busy being bummed out and inconvenienced I never took that job seriously. And look what happened. Maybe the man wouldn't be dead if I had done my job right.

Just then, I put one foot into the water bowl and the other one into the soggy burrito. That brought me right back to the here and now. Here was a problem I could readily solve. I turned to my overnight guest.

"I've got plans for you, little guy, but they don't involve you living with me. Not that I wouldn't love to help you out and keep you myself, but I've got a busy, busy life. There is absolutely no room in it for a pet, so don't take this personally," I said, remembering my idea of unloading the little beastie on my vet friend, Ellen.

In front of me was one of those rare commodities, a payphone. I grabbed my change purse and placed a call to Vets and Pets to make sure Ellen was at her job. She was.

Getting back in the car, I turned to the kitten playing with a corner of the blanket and said, "Time to meet your new mama, kiddo, so don't waste this adorable act on me."

Chapter Three
A Four-Legged Commitment

Vets and Pets is one of these newer veterinarian clinics open twelve hours a day, seven days a week, servicing exotic animals as well as the standard dog, cat, and bird. It offers the latest in technological know-how and is run by young, energetic doctors straight out of vet school. A connected pet store carries medicine, food, litter, housing, wearing apparel, toys, collars, leashes, etc., and gives a ten percent discount to anyone using the services of the Clinic. Basically, the clients are in and out with one stop shopping. As for the vets, a share of the profits enhances their passion for their calling. Everyone's happy. I have all this insight because my good friend, Ellen, is one of the eight energetic doctors. Shortly before eight a.m., I pulled into the parking lot of the large, pale blue building off El Camino Real in Palo Alto, filled with plans to take advantage of our friendship.

I turned off the motor, leaned forward and looked up to the sky through the windshield. The storm had lessened the more I'd headed south, and in Palo Alto, it was barely sprinkling. My little passenger fell asleep beside me somewhere near Brisbane. I picked him up, and he weighed almost nothing. My heart went out to him. He was little more than skin and bones.

"Don't you worry, little guy. Ellen's going to be a real good mommy to you." I knew Ellen had about six dogs and a dozen cats living with her already. What was one more, I rationalized? I tucked him into my jacket pocket and dashed across the parking lot.

The receptionist was a large-busted, happy youth of about nineteen, and she beamed broadly despite a broken front tooth. She extended necessary forms on a plastic clipboard. Within ten minutes, the kitten and I sat inside a pristine examining room with a stainless steel table as its centerpiece. The room was filled with an antiseptic smell, and I felt almost as nervous as the little guy.

Ellen entered wearing a crisp, white smock and reading the now completed forms. She was a pretty, fair-complexioned woman about five years older than me, with shiny, light brown hair worn in soft curls all over her head. We met at Stanford when I was a student and Ellen had been a teaching assistant in a human anatomy class for extra money. That was during the lean times before she got her license to practice. "Hi, Ellen. Got any coffee?"

Ellen looked up in surprise and narrowed her hazel eyes, appraising me. "In my office. Take what you want. But what happened to you? You look like who did it and ran." I stood up for a hug but she pulled back. "Yuk! You feel like a damp sponge. And your hair! I've never seen you look so bad, and I've seen you pretty bad." Ellen, originally from the east coast, spoke a little faster than anyone else I knew and was impossible to interrupt.

"Thanks," I said after she'd finished. I glanced down at my ruined boots, baggy slacks and salt stained jacket. "Let's just say I took a swim in the Bay."

"Well, don't do it again. I take it you were in the City. I hear it's still raining cats and dogs up there. No pun intended. Flooding everywhere." The "City" was what most people who lived in the Bay Area called San Francisco. "We got lucky down here." Ellen continued, "Not much, just a light sprinkle. Is this your kitten? What a cutie. There's no name of an owner on this form. Put your name down here, will you?" She scolded me good-naturedly as she pointed to a line.

"I'm really not the owner," I put in when she took a breath. "I found him near Fisherman's Wharf. I couldn't leave him."

"I see." She became all business. "Well, let's see what we've got here," replied Ellen. She held out experienced hands for the kitten and gave over her full attention to the examination of him.

I felt anxiety run through me. *What if the little guy was sick?*

Stop it, I thought. *He didn't act sick. He's just a little skinny. Besides that, he's not your cat. You just did the right thing and brought him in from out of the rain.*

I forced myself to think of other things. My mind ran to my recent assignment and how it ended. I let out a groan.

"Lee, Lee!" Ellen brought me back to reality. "You want to stop that moaning? You're scaring the cat."

"Sorry, Ellen. Well, how is he?" I inquired anxiously.

"Pretty healthy, I'm delighted to say. He's about eight or nine weeks old. A little undernourished but no ear mites. His eyes are clear. No sign of anemia, although the chances of him having tapeworms are pretty high considering I've seen some fleas on him. He could use some fattening up plus vitamins. There's no way to tell about Feline Leukemia unless we do the test. The results would be in tomorrow. So what do you want to do? Do I start the Parvo shots? Do I do the Feline Leukemia test? What are your plans?" Ellen stared into my eyes, both of us knowing what the other was thinking.

"I thought, you know..." I began weakly, "with all the animals you have that, you know, one more..."

"I've placed three dogs and two cats in the past month," Ellen responded. "That's what I do, placement. I hold the animals, myself, until I can find a home for them. Is that what I'm doing with this one?"

We both looked soberly down at the orange and white kitten sitting small and sad on the cold, steel table. Amber-colored eyes looked from one of us to the other. He locked eyes with me and meowed silently. It was all over.

"No. You're coming home with me, aren't you, little guy?" I heard me say. I shocked myself into silence.

"Great!" answered Ellen, visibly relieved. She took the health and welfare of animals very seriously. "Then it's time to start our initial shots plus test for Feline Leukemia." She swept him up in her arms before I had time to question my sanity. "I'll weigh him and give him a quick flea bath, compliments of the house. We'll be back in about fifteen minutes. Why don't you read one of those magazines over there on the care and feeding of our feline friends?" Ellen gestured to a Lucite magazine rack hanging on the wall, which held a dozen or so different animal "how to" books and magazines. She watched as I sank into a chair. Then she looked at the kitten that had closed his eyes and begun to purr in her reassuring hands.

"Don't worry, kid," Ellen said to the little guy. "We can teach her how to do this. It may take her a little while but she's a quick study." I burst out laughing, and Ellen joined me. She grinned and closed the door, leaving me alone in the room.

What have I done, I thought? *A cat. That's all I need, an animal in my life.*

Come on, I countered, *he's awfully cute, and he's just a little guy. Cats aren't supposed to be much trouble.*

I picked up a magazine with shaking hands. "*You and Your New Kitten*," I read aloud. I felt faint.

A half an hour later, having acquired a cat carrier, litter pan, ten pounds of litter, dry and wet kitten food, vitamins, a scratching post, a myriad of instructions and receipts, and a bright green collar with a bell, I staggered out the door with my new friend and a much lighter wallet. Looking up at the sky, I noticed the rain had stopped completely, and the morning air had turned much colder. I blasted the heater in the car and headed toward the house on Chaucer Street, some fifteen minutes away. Turning onto University Avenue, I thought for the first time in a long while about food.

I looked down at the carrier on the passenger's side of the car and into the face of the kitten sticking his nose and one paw out of the wire mesh door.

"We have to make a stop, little guy," I said as I stroked his protruding paw. "You've already been fed enough to fell a horse, but I haven't had a thing since yesterday's lunch."

Turning onto Emerson Street, I pulled into a parking space in front of The Creamery, a popular establishment for locals and Stanford students alike. The Creamery has been around since the late thirties and with good reason. The comfort food is fabulous. Douglas, the manager, and I were in college together, so I often stopped in for a hamburger, beer, and some laughs at this Palo Alto mainstay, especially after my eight-year marriage fell apart.

I informed Douglas of what waited for me in the car and promised to bring in pictures of the little guy as soon as possible, in exchange for bacon, eggs, and hash browns to go. The Creamery didn't usually do take-out, but Douglas is good at making exceptions. Back in the car ten minutes later, I salivated at the smells emanating from the Styrofoam container at my side.

Trying not to think about Portor Wyler, I pulled into my driveway within five minutes and past the house I grew up in and loved, despite it being much too grand for my taste. Backlit by the morning sun, it was a rather outsized, two-story job, dominated in the front by two massive, carved columns standing on either side of the entrance stairs. My father had these columns sent from Mexico for his and my mother's fifteenth wedding anniversary, at great expense and red tape, I might add. Once your eyes get past the white columns, the rest of the house is mostly white brick with large paned windows, topped off with a Spanish tiled roof. In short, the house is homage to the Mexican-American success story, Palo Alto style, complete with glossy green shrubs, seasonally blooming foliage, hot tub, and swimming pool.

When my marriage ended, my parents offered me the garage apartment, an added inducement to my coming home. I said yes, so they completely rebuilt the upstairs, two-bedroom apartment. It had been originally constructed for a chauffeur in the heyday of the 1930s but used only for storage since I can remember. They offered to decorate the place for me, but after living with those two columns most of my life, I opted to give it my own style, whatever that is.

I followed the drive around to the back of the house to the garage and chauffeur's apartment, now my humble abode. The garage door opened electronically, and I drove inside. There are two sets of stairs going up to the apartment, one outside, one inside. The outside stairs on the right side of the building lead to the living room entrance. They are wide with a black wrought iron banister of a Mayan design, very cool. The stairs inside the garage take you to the back of the kitchen. This inside stairway, painted dove-gray, is narrow and awkward when carrying bundles. However, it was still damp and cold, and I chose to struggle rather than to freeze. Getting out of the car, I switched on the inside lights of the garage and sighed.

At one time, it had been filled with a colorful array of family cars. Richard's red MG Midget, Mom's beige Jaguar, my own turquoise bit of heaven, and Dad's green Jeep Cherokee. Now with the exception of Dad's tarp covered Jeep, empty stalls stared back at me, reminding me of how much things had changed. Secretly, I wished Mom would sell the jeep, so I didn't have to see it all the time but knew she couldn't bear to part with it.

Between these thoughts and Wyler's death, I had a hard time shaking off the depression that made it hard for me to breathe, but I gave it my best shot. The Malaysian Ministry of Culture would have been proud.

I maneuvered the carrier with the kitten and one of the bags up the inside stairway. This was the first of what I knew would be many trips. Track lighting illuminated the narrow stairs at night, but in the daytime, natural light poured in through an octagon shaped window on the landing. A hanging basket of dark green cascading leaves from some type of plant completed the look. Fortunately, the plant was on a timed-watering line or the hanging basket would have contained dark brown cascading leaves; you know how it is. I never have to lock the door at the top of the stairs because there is no way of getting into the garage without the automatic garage door opener.

I crossed through my blue and yellow tiled kitchen and into the bedroom decorated in vivid, Mexican mosaics found on one of my trips to San Miguel de Allende. The kitten began yowling at the top of his lungs. He seemed to know he was in his new home and was anxious to get acquainted with it. I "kitten proofed" the bedroom and connecting bath, according to Ellen's instructions, by checking closets, cabinets, windows, and under the bed for any hazards. Then I put his litter box, water, and food bowls temporarily in the bathroom.

When I felt the two rooms were secure, I opened the carrier door for my noisy captive. He suddenly became quiet and hesitantly put one foot outside and then, after a long pause, the other. I closed the bedroom door behind me and went back down for the breakfast cooling on the seat of the car. I decided this would be the last trip. I was tired, famished, and needed a bath, so the remaining packages would have to wait until later. Trudging up the stairs again, I realized just how exhausted I was. It had been one of the worst nights of my life, and I was trying not to think about a man's life being over, just like that. I like to think of myself as pretty tough, but this rattled me to my core.

I went back into the bedroom and looked for the little guy. He crouched in the far corner sniffing the leg of a chair. Remembering Ellen's words, I picked him up with my free hand and placed him in his litter pan.

"Now, I'm going to put you in here four or five more times tonight just to make sure you can remember where it is. This was Ellen's idea so don't get mad at me if you don't like it." He looked up at me and then studied the litter box intently. I returned to the bedroom and flopped down on the bed. I wasn't looking forward to pulling off my boots, but I couldn't ignore the feeling I had of standing in play dough one moment longer. I sat up, took a deep breath and after some struggle, I removed the damaged boots. Then I took off everything else and put on my favorite old terrycloth robe, thin with age. Disgusted, I threw my ruined things into a corner of the room, where they landed with a thump, causing the kitten to jump nearly a foot and a half in the air. I laughed and when he heard my voice, he ran to me mouthing his silent meow. It was right then and there, my heart was lost to him forever. The household had a new boss, and it sure wasn't me.

I picked him up and, after rubbing his sleek body against my face, put him on the bed beside me and opened my breakfast container. He smelled the bacon and looked wildly around for the meat, the little savage. I broke off pieces and cupped them in the palm of my hand for him to eat. The fur around his mouth, soft and clean from the recent bath, tickled my palm, and I laughed. When the telephone rang, I threw the bacon bits back into the Styrofoam container and reached across the bed for the phone.

"Hello," I said into the phone still laughing at the kitten that stood in the middle of the container voraciously eating bacon.

"You're there! Where have you been? Do you know what time it is? Don't you listen to your answering machine anymore?"

"Lila? Mom?" I responded, jerked back into the real world. I knew she was upset. Nearly every other word was emphasized. "What time is it?" I glanced at my wristwatch. "*Dios Mio*! It's nearly nine o'clock."

"I couldn't imagine where you were. I've been calling and calling for an update assuming you would go straight home."

I felt guilt growl inside me. "Oh, Mom, I'm sorry. I took a nap in the car for a few hours and then—"

"I wish you hadn't turned your cell phone off, Liana," she chastised me. "It does worry me when I can't reach you."

"I didn't turn it off," I retorted. "I told you. It keeps turning itself off. I think I need a new battery. I'll get it taken care of this afternoon." The other end of the line grew quiet. I could tell she was hurt that I hadn't called and spared her needless worrying.

"I should have called you, Mom," I admitted, "when I first woke up, and I'm sorry. I just got sidetracked. Hey! Cut that out! Listen, you..." I said in mock severity to the kitten who had made a leap for the remainder of a piece of bacon in my free hand. "You've got your own food. You can't have all of mine."

"I didn't know you had company, Liana. Possibly I'm *interrupting* something," Lila said coolly.

"Oh, that's all right." I laughed. "You're not interrupting a thing. It's not company. It's the new kitten."

"The kitten?"

"Yes. I found a kitten in the phone booth I called you from, and well, I couldn't leave him there so, I've got him." I sobered. "Mom, I am sorry about earlier, really. I should have called." I waited for a response but realized I was taking to dead air. I heard my uncle come on the line.

"What is this I hear about a kitten?" he asked. "From where comes a *gatino, mi Sobrina*?"

I laughed. I knew my uncle's love for animals. "I found him in a phone booth, Tío, and he's adorable," I added, watching the kitten that gave up on trying to extract my share of the bacon and now did battle with a hairbrush on the vanity table. "Why don't you come over and see him?" I asked on impulse. After a short discussion in which I affirmed repeatedly I was fine and would like to see him, he said he would be right over.

Now anxious to know my telephone messages, I went to the second bedroom that functioned as the office/dance studio. This is a large room, about twenty-feet square with high ceilings and a polished, light oak floor. It contains no furniture other than a computer station and desk, complete with the latest equipment, tucked away in one corner. The rest of the room was given over to the mirrored wall and workout barre. It's a rare day I don't start with my ballet barre and floor exercises.

In my soul, I am a disciplined dancer. Unfortunately, I'm not a very good one, but that doesn't stop my love or need for it. I also attend karate classes and practice three nights a week on University Place. Mom once asked why I don't practice my karate here, but I would never mix the two disciplines in my home. Karate is work; I dance for love.

The telephone machine light flickered indicating five calls, and I hoped I'd have time to listen to them all before my uncle arrived. I grabbed a pencil and pressed the play button. The first two were solicitations.

I must remember to register my phone with NoCall.com, I thought.

The third was from a man I'd met the week before at a Mondavi Wine concert. I had wondered if and when Grant would call. The fourth and fifth calls were from my mother, a little more emotional than normal. The front doorbell rang. I ran back to the bedroom, swooped the squirming kitten up in my arms, and flung open the door expecting to greet Tío.

Instead, Mom's fifty-six year old ice blue eyes sparkled at me, despite her lack of sleep. I wasn't surprised to find her accompanying my uncle Tío, even thought I could tell she was still annoyed with me. I noted that between her shoulder length, ash blond hair, year-round golden tan, white knit silk slack set, and pearl button earrings, she looked as if she'd stepped out of a fashion magazine, while I, on the other hand, looked like I had just undergone interrogation at Guantanamo Bay. There is no justice. Tío stepped from behind Mom and took the kitten from my arms.

"Listen, everybody. Why don't we go back to my bedroom?" I asked. "Ellen told me not to confuse the little guy by giving him too much space his first couple of weeks."

Dutifully, they followed me into the bedroom. Tío headed for the leather wingback chair in front of the unlit fireplace. There he sat, a silver-haired, elegant man, cooing to a kitten in Spanish. The cat batted at nimble fingers, which Mateo playfully dangled. Mom, grinning, stood at the foot of the nearby bed with her arms folded for a moment, then sobered and looked at me. She moved to a corner of the room and gestured with a tilt of her head for me to follow. I did.

"Liana, you should have found the time to call me," she said in a hushed voice. "You're an inventive person. This wasn't like you. I was up most of the night worried sick and a fifteen second phone call from you would have changed that."

"Oh, God, Mom, I'm so sorry. It just got away from me." I looked down at the floor, chagrined. "Maybe I was still a little put out about having to shadow Wyler. To be honest, I did consider it beneath me." She took a breath to speak, but I held out my hand to stop her. "I'm over that now, and I apologize for my unprofessional behavior... and other things."

Her face held surprise. "Liana, there's never been a moment I thought you were behaving unprofessionally. But if by 'other things,' you mean Portor Wyler's death, sometimes things happen beyond our control, dear. Given the look on your face, we need to talk about this Portor Wyler tragedy." She glanced over at Tío. "Later. Not now."

"Thanks, Mom. Later is good. I'm pretty wiped right now."

She smiled at me, nodded, and then changed the subject. "I wish I had known you wanted a cat," she said. "I would have prevailed upon Anne Carter to sell me one of her Persian kittens. You know she had a litter of seven about three months ago."

"I didn't know myself, Mom. It sort of just happened. I never did want a pet. I'm usually a stuffed animal person. You know, no maintenance."

"Well, are you going to keep him?" she asked, a little concerned.

"Oh, absolutely. He's mine, and I've got the vet bills to prove it. This little guy needs me. Or maybe I need him," I muttered, half ashamed of my admission.

"Well, whichever way it is, if he makes you happy, then I'm glad you have him," she said. She reached out and gave me a big hug. I hugged her back with all my heart. All was forgiven; we knew it, and we both breathed a sigh of relief. The mother/daughter pipeline was humming, as usual.

I went over to my uncle, who was having his shoelaces deftly untied by small paws. I sat on the floor by Tío's chair. He reached over and put an arm around me. Then he threw back his head and laughed heartily, the first time he had done so in months.

"What is it, Mateo?" Lila joined in the laughter, although not sure why.

"This is no *gatino*! This is a *conejito*," he said. "Look at his ears. *Mira*! When I first saw him I thought, my niece, she does not know a rabbit from a cat!" His teasing eyes twinkled, and all three of us began to laugh.

"I guess they are a little big. Maybe he'll grow into them!" I agreed. We studied the kitten fairly dancing at the attention he got.

"Liana," he continued sobering, "how can you leave this *gatino* alone all day while you go to work? You work such long hours." His soft voice caressed the kitten as tenderly as his fingers did.

"You should see all the paraphernalia I bought!" I answered with pride. "I have a self feeding dish for dry food and...." But before I could tick off the recent acquisitions on my fingers, Lila quickly crossed the room, gave me a subtle nudge on the shoulder, interrupting me.

"Your uncle's brought up a good point, Liana," Mom said. "You need someone to help take care of the kitten during the long hours you're at work."

"I do?" I asked her, mystified, my left hand frozen with one finger pointing to the ceiling.

"Yes, you do," she said with a stern face. I looked over to Tío's yearning one and got it.

"Yes, I do," I said, a little chagrined that I hadn't caught on earlier. Of course! This might be the very thing to help him get over his overwhelming sense of loss. Anyway, it was worth a try.

Recently retired, as well as widowed, my Tío was filled with nothing but sorrow these days. He sat around the house watching CNN by the hour and did little else. Tio's amazing life flashed through my mind. At twenty, he migrated from Vera Cruz to California bringing his five-year old brother, my father, with him. Both parents were dead, economic times were horrendous, but somehow he managed to get the papers and money together for the journey to "*El Norte*," his lifelong dream. That was in 1954, and the trip, mostly by foot, took nearly a month. An even harder journey was the one from the picking fields of Salinas to head chef at a prestigious restaurant in San Jose. No mean feat. But to him, his greatest success was when dad won a track scholarship to Stanford University, with a 3.9 grade average. As a child, I loved to hear Tio's stories of their struggles and would beg him to tell them to me again and again in Spanish. That's how I learned the language. Since I can remember, Mateo Alvarez has kept the Mexican side of me burning and proud.

"You know, Tio, you're right. Even though he's got enough of the essentials, I'm worried he'll need some companionship when I'm not here. Would you mind dropping by during the day to see how he's getting along? Maybe, if it's not too much trouble, you could stay with him for a couple of hours here and there? Just for the first month or two until he gets a little older and used to the place." Okay, so I'm not much of an actress, but I waited and hoped I'd managed to salvage this.

My uncle smiled broadly and continued to stroke the kitten that now rested at his feet. "Why not?" he asked, obviously delighted. "I can watch the news from here just as well. I will make sure that the little *gatino* is not lonely. *Qué es se yama?*"

"What is his name?" I echoed in surprise. "Well, I don't know, Tío. I haven't thought about it yet. We can call him anything. How about 'Cat' or 'Hey You?'" I joked.

"Every living thing needs a name, *querida*," Tío said, in a tone that was severe and reprimanding, quite unlike him. "It is a form of value and respect. You should think about it with seriousness and choose a proper name."

"Okay, I'll get right on it, promise," I demurred, and kissed him on the cheek.

Mom said, "I think we should go, Mateo, and let Liana get some rest."

"Oh, no," I protested but without much heart. Actually, I wanted to have that bath.

"Oh, *si*," said Tío firmly as he rose. "Call me the next time you are leaving, and I will come over and cat sit." He laughed heartily at his small joke, and we embraced.

After they left, I tried to relax in a bath while watching the kitten play around the bathroom. But dark thoughts flitted in and out of my mind about Portor Wyler. Sure, bad things happen to people and sometimes we can't control it. But in truth, how responsible was I for Portor Wyler's death through negligence, if nothing else?

After a forty-five minute soak, I put on flannel pajamas, and brushed my hair, noticing the small teeth marks in my best brush for the first time.

"Well," I said to the small form now curled up on the forest green towel. "You can be dangerous." I made a mental note to put away anything valuable from the teething kitten when I got up.

I put an extra blanket on the bed, feeling the chill in my bones returning, and closed the curtains to keep out the daylight. Even though I was filled with known and unknown angst, I was asleep in minutes, waking only once when I felt the kitten jump onto the bed and curled up on the pillow next to me.

Chapter Four
They Call It Murder

The phone ringing around noon startled me awake. I made a lunge for it on the first ring, and before I could croak out a greeting, Mom's voice nearly split my eardrums.

"Frank just got back to me a few minutes ago. I didn't know you had been the one to find the body! Why didn't you tell me?"

"You didn't know? What did you think I was doing at the police station?"

"I thought you were being a good citizen, and you came forward when you saw all the police cars. My God, he was shot three times in the chest, close range. That could have been you!"

"No, no. I was nowhere near him until after he was...it was all over."

"To think I sent my own daughter...Good Lord! That could have been you!" she repeated. I could tell she was working herself up into a good case of hysteria.

"Mom, calm down."

"Don't tell me to calm down," she said. Then she actually snorted.

"Okay, okay. But listen to me, I was never in any danger, I swear. You ordered me to keep my distance at all times and I did." *Except, you know, at the end*, I thought, but now was not the time to mention that.

I said aloud, "I never went near the warehouse except for when I checked on the locked door. That was long after he was dead."

"Not so long," she said, snorting again.

"I was never inside the building or anything. There was no interference, no encounter at any time. I was strictly surveillance."

I didn't add I had a gut feeling that maybe, just maybe, if I had interfered in some way, Wyler wouldn't be dead right now.

"All right. All right, Liana." I could sense Lila tried to compose herself and become professional. "Did you hear anything strange or suspicious? Maybe that could have been gunfire? Anything?"

"I was already asked that a million times before. The answer is I was too far away, plus it was a very noisy storm. I still can't believe someone killed..." My voice trailed off in shock and disbelief. "Oh, jeesh, I've got to get up to San Francisco. I have to sign that statement."

"No, you don't, Liana. Go directly to Frank's office. He's made arrangements for you to file your deposition and turn over your firearm to him for inspection instead of going up to the City."

"Oh, great," I said. I was not happy.

"Frank will fax the depo to the San Francisco Police and do a check of your revolver, as a courtesy." Lila added as an afterthought, "Where is your revolver?"

"In my safe. I have to bring it? Why? I didn't even have it with me yesterday. I never have it with me."

"You found the body. They have to officially rule you out. You know that." She paused for a moment. "Are you all right?"

"I guess I'm still a little stunned by all this. I'll be fine, Mom." I kept my overwhelming sense of guilt to myself. No point in talking about it until I got it sorted out. "Okay. I'll get over there right away, and then I'll come to the office soon as I can."

"Take the day off, Liana. I think you could use it. Just be sure you enter all the information you've recorded and anything else you can think of sometime today. We might have to turn it over to the police." Lila was referring to the computer in my second bedroom connected directly to D.I.'s mainframe.

I hung up the phone and heard the sound of crunching in the bathroom. For a moment, I was startled and then remembered my new roommate. I put on a robe and followed the noise. Then I watched the one and a half-pound feline ferociously attack a kernel of dry food. Before I left, I reminded myself, I would have to give him his teaspoon of wet food and his vitamins. I looked anxiously into the litter box.

Good, I thought with relief, *it had been used.*

Grabbing the Pooper Scooper, something I'd never heard of the day before, I took care of the deposit and considered myself a dutiful pet owner.

The kitten stopped eating, studied me for a moment, uttered one of his silent meows and ran to me. I picked him up, slid him inside my robe, and went into the kitchen. He seemed to like this carrying method and purred happily. There I started my coffee and opened a can of kitten food. I returned to the bedroom, fed the little guy, and made two calls.

The first one was to the Palo Alto Police Department to see when I had my appointment for the deposition. They told me to come in "as soon as possible." Hanging up the phone, I found my hands shaking so much I could hardly hold the cup of coffee without spilling it. I knew I had to get myself under control before I came face to face with Frank. He was tough enough when I had all my faculties about me. The second phone call was to Tío. Without going into much detail, I let him know it would probably be a long day, and any visitation with the kitten would be greatly appreciated.

This was going to be one of those rare days without my ritualistic morning exercises, which was too bad. That would have calmed me down right away, but I didn't have the time. I drank my coffee, showered, pulled my hair back into a ponytail, and went to the walk-in closet to survey the array of expensive, stylish "on-duty" clothing which hung there. Thank God I didn't have to reach for any of those.

I groped in the back for my comfy jeans and a worn turquoise wool knit turtleneck with matching blazer. I looked presentable. Not great but presentable.

By the time I was dressed and ready to leave, Tío had arrived at the door, ready to take on his new charge. I decided to take the time to run down to the car and retrieve the remaining packages, which included several expensive toys for the kitten. However, I vowed to return them as soon as I saw my uncle bring out a feather he found in the yard and tied to a string. The little guy was making hilarious leaps trying to catch the feather, and I closed the door on the sounds of Tío's chuckles. At least someone was having a good day.

Chapter Five
Frank's Lair

I arrived at the Palo Alto Police Station on Forest Avenue, shortly after lunchtime and had some difficulty finding a parking space. Palo Alto, created as a township for Stanford University, which in itself boasts residents of forty thousand plus, never expected to have the population explosion it experienced in the fifties and again in the nineties. Side streets, still containing lovely stucco houses built in the thirties, were condemned to suffer the constant movement of cars, either coming, going, or searching for parking places. I finally found one of my own after much driving in circles and cursing. Cursing is a major part of finding a spot, I've noticed.

Striding beneath a crisp, blue sky, I entered the white building serving as a combo city hall/police station. The desk sergeant on duty, a sweet man due to retire next year, waved me past. I knew exactly which office to go to, I'd been going there since forever.

Captain Frank Thompson is a black man from East Palo Alto who made good. He went to Stanford University on a scholarship, the same as my father, in the mid-seventies. The moment they met on the first day of registration, they became instant friends. Actually, they were more like brothers. It wasn't just that you had a black man and a Latino going to a very "white bread" college, as some people thought. They looked at life the same way. They liked the same things. They shared the same sense of humor. No one was surprised when they both joined the same police force, on the same day, in the early eighties. Each one not only stood up for the other at their weddings but also became godfather to each other's children. When Dad died, it almost killed Frank. He cried openly and unashamedly for weeks afterward. His wife, Abby, said that he probably would never be the same. I knew what she meant. I wouldn't be, either.

I knocked softly on the door and heard his bass voice instruct me to come in. I opened the door with dread and went in, knowing this would not be a pleasant interview. Frank always wanted me to become a doctor like his daughter and only child, Faith. She's two years my senior and a practicing pediatrician at Stanford Hospital, as Frank brags to any stranger on the street who asks him the time of day. To top it all off, she's happily married to a fellow doctor and had recently given birth to the most gorgeous little girl I've ever seen. If Faith weren't so terrific, I'd probably hate her.

When my father was alive, Frank made it clear he thought I was much too good to follow in the footsteps of a mere cop. The fact Dad had left the department and started his own detective agency complete with family in tow made little difference to Frank. I remember the time he said, "Okay, Bobby. Your wife can answer the phones if you want, and Richard can do the computer stuff, but little Liana has bigger things in store for her."

I don't know who was more insulted, Mom or me. At 5'8" since puberty, I have never been called little in my life, and Lila Hamilton Alvarez has never answered phones. She may eat them for breakfast, but she doesn't answer them. That was akin to calling Coco Chanel a seamstress. Even way back when, Mom was in charge of the major operations of the company and did most of the brainwork. Dad had the pizzazz, know-how, and connections. They were a great team.

As my godfather opened his mouth to speak, I jumped in ahead of him. "Now, Frank, I was never in any danger. I was only doing routine surveillance and that was from about half a block away. Well, maybe it was a little closer, but not much. I don't know what happened, but I'm sure it was just my bad luck to be there. Maybe it was a botched robbery. It probably didn't have anything to do with what his wife thought he was up to, which was the only reason I was there." I ran out of breath, so I stopped nattering and stood there. He leaned back in his chair and stared at me, ink black eyes boring into mine. He did not speak but gestured with his forefinger for me to sit down. I did.

"Liana, what am I going to do with you?" He leaned forward and tried to stare me down. I glared back, unblinking, and the contest was on. Finally, he said, "Is this what your father would have wanted? I know he encouraged you into this line of work but he never meant for you to start following stray husbands, I know that." He thrust that same finger at me. "If you were my daughter, and you practically are—."

"Yes, yes. I know; I know. But I'm all grown up, married, and divorced, and I'm old enough—"

Frank ignored my protests and interrupted my interruption. "Did I say you could speak? I'll let you know when you can speak. What kind of life is this, standing out in the rain spying on some strange man?" He looked at me expectantly, but I was silent, as instructed. "Now you may speak."

"It's the same kind of life you led until you got promoted to a cushy job behind a polished oak desk," I shot back.

He put the palms of both his hands out toward me as if to ward off the impending argument that inevitably followed. He changed the subject. "You brought your handgun, I take it, and the answer better be 'yes,'" he said.

"Of course." I took the holstered revolver out of my handbag and set both on his desk.

He changed the subject again and grinned at me warmly. "Faith asked about you yesterday. Wanted to know when you're going over to her house for dinner. She and Stu want you to meet a couple of their friends from the hospital."

I laughed in relief. Frank might be the occasional pain in the derriere, but I did adore him. "Faith just wants to play Cupid, Uncle Frank."

"What's wrong with that?" he demanded, smiling one of his dazzling smiles. He removed the revolver from the holster, glanced at it, and replaced it again in one swift movement, before putting his hands behind the nape of his neck and leaning back in his chair. His voice lost its warmth and his eyes narrowed. "So what happened, Lee?"

"I don't know. Nothing odd or unusual happened at any time that I could tell. Then the storm hit. I was on my way home when I doubled back and went to the warehouse. I found him dead on the back walkway. That's it." Upon Frank's insistence, I gave him a detailed report of the entire day's happenings, just as I'd done for SFPD. I left out the part of falling on my butt.

When I was finished, his black eyes bored into mine. Frank could peel the skin off an onion with those eyes.

"Okay," he said, after he'd searched my face for moment. "Let me call someone in so you can make a statement. We'll test your weapon even though the prelim says what was used on Wyler was smaller."

"Like what?"

He got up, went to the door and signaled to someone waiting outside. "Maybe a derringer. Something about a bullet they found lodged in his spinal column. We'll know more in a couple of hours."

An officer entered the room on silent feet.

"Officer Jackson, this is Liana Alvarez. You're going to take her statement."

The young man, not more than twenty-two and already balding, carried a laptop. He stoically nodded to me and sat down in a corner of the room. I followed. A half-hour later he left to print out my statement and returned several minutes later for me to read and sign it.

During this time, Frank ignored me and tackled a foot high pile of paperwork on his desk. After Officer Jackson left the room, I not so subtlety returned to our previous conversation.

"Can I see the initial report or is that breaking any rules?" I asked.

I prepared myself for more boring of eyes or lectures, but he shrugged and said, "I don't suppose there's anything in there you can't see." Swiveling his chair around, he searched through another pile of papers, this time on the file cabinet behind him. "Here it is." He glanced at it with a quick eye. "Doesn't say much, really."

It was only two pages long, mostly typed but with a few handwritten comments. I read it through, as Frank began to open the day's mail with occasional glances in my direction. The two pages contained a detailed report of where the body was found, who found it — me — and a list of the contents of his pockets and not much else. Nothing useful or important jumped out at me, unfortunately. A formal autopsy would have to be done sometime that day or the day after to determine cause of death, it noted, although in my mind it might have had something to do with the three bullet holes in his chest.

"No, it doesn't say much," I finally agreed. "But, may I have a copy of this?" I asked as I held up the papers. Frank smiled, reached across, and snatched them from my hand.

"No," he said through clenched teeth. "And if they ask me, I didn't even show it to you. You want a copy? Drive up to the City and get one from them."

"Maybe I'll just do that." I stood up. "When do I get my revolver back?"

"Tomorrow. Next day. Can't say for sure. Why? Do you think you'll need it?" he asked, fatherly concern written all over his face.

"Frank, it's been in my safe for the last eight months except for practice sessions and the occasional cleaning. I don't like those things. They're too noisy."

He visibly relaxed, got up and steered me by the arm to his office door. "Liana, save this old man a heart attack and become a doctor, please, or an airline pilot. Anything! Be a ballet dancer. Lord knows you've spent enough of your childhood leaping around on your tiptoes. You seem to love it."

"I was never good enough to do it for a living. You know that," I said. He'd hit a sore spot.

Frank put his arm around my shoulder and squeezed. "Whatever you say. I want you to be happy, that's all. I had hoped this PI thing was a passing fancy. I was so sure once Bobby was gone and Lila had been made CEO, she'd..." He stopped himself. He and Mom had never gotten along. It's not that they disliked each other. It was more that they had nothing in common other than Dad. I suspect it was never clear to Frank why Bobby picked a woman so obviously different from himself and their friends. "Never mind. Lila has to live her own life, and if she wants to run Bobby's business, I won't say a word."

I let out a hoot of laughter. "Yeah, right. That'll be the day when you never say a word. Besides, Frank, he left the business to all of us, not just Mom. Twenty-four and a half percent each to Richard and me and fifty-one percent to Lila. He wanted us to carry on as a family."

Frank brought himself up to his full six-foot two inches and looked down at me. "He wanted you to sit on the board. Make executive decisions. That's what he meant. He never meant for you to actually be involved in the day-to-day grit of it. Look at your brother. He's behind the scenes. Why can't you be more like him?"

"Don't start with my brother," I said wearily. "He's a computer geek. He likes statistics and numbers. I don't. I like people."

"So become a social director on a cruise ship." He studied the expression on my face. "Why do I bother? You are as stubborn as Bobby ever was."

"I know. That's why you love me. I remind you of Dad," I replied. Frank laughed and shook his head.

"All right. Go on. Get out of here. I've got work to do," he told me, as he opened the door. I started down the hall and he shouted after me. "And call Faith. I think she's got a live one for you!"

I exited into the clear air shielding my eyes from the bright sun. I felt a surge of depression, without knowing what exactly I was depressed about. Maybe it was Frank's fatherly concern, misplaced though it was. Maybe it was this murder I might have prevented if I had done something different. It made me feel ineffectual and inept. I didn't like it. But this oppressive feeling seemed more than that. I had a sudden revelation and looked at my watch to confirm the date.

Yup, January 24th. Today marks the third anniversary of the ending of my eight-year marriage. Today marks the acknowledgment of acts of betrayal and failure. No wonder I'm depressed.

"Don't think about Nick," I said aloud, reflecting nonetheless, on the handsome Greek American boy I'd met in high school and married after college. So much like my father, I'd thought at first, despite what anybody had said to me.

He had easily won my heart only to deceive me from the beginning with a constant flow of other women. After years of denial, I'd faced it and demanded he stop seeing them. He hit me. Twice. Once to knock me down and again to make sure I stayed there. When you're an ex-marine you know how to make sure somebody stays down. Within minutes, he'd dissolved in tears, begging my forgiveness. I forgave him but I knew better. I forgave him because I loved him. I knew better because I'd taken too many classes in spousal abuse not to know how it goes.

Shortly after that, I'd enrolled in a karate class after telling everyone I wanted to be more "self-sufficient" at my job. Becoming a black belt was not too difficult for a girl who had taken ballet all her life, and had anger and fear living inside her. Six months later when I stood up to him again about a new girlfriend, Nick took another jab at me, but I flattened him. I sued for divorce and tried not to look back. Whenever I did, though, I could never tell who I was madder at, Nick for dishing it out or me for taking it.

I forced thoughts of yesteryear out of my mind, and stopped by a Radio Shack to buy a new battery for my cell phone, praying that was the problem. That seemed to do the trick, and I speed dialed Tío. After the latest word on the "little guy" I called the office. Lila was at lunch, something I wished I were at myself, so I hung up.

With a growling stomach, I crossed the street to Togo's, a sandwich place on bustling University Avenue. Service is fast, and I love the tuna submarine sandwich. I sat on a bench under a tree and watched the world go by while I ate. Licking my fingers of the remaining tuna, I felt the sudden urge to go back to the San Francisco warehouse. Maybe if I had paid more attention, I might have prevented Wyler's death from happening. Maybe not, but that was something I would never know unless I tried to find some answers.

Forty minutes later, I arrived at the same San Francisco Street I had been on less than twenty-four hours before. However, as the song says, what a difference a day makes.
The weather was absolutely gorgeous. The parking was also a lot easier. Maybe this wasn't such a bad day, after all.

Yes, it was. A man was dead, and it might have been because of me.

Opening the car door, I stepped out into air slightly cooler than Palo Alto's and, oh, so delicious. The breeze ruffling my hair had a slightly chilled feeling to it, reminding me the bright sun was not enough to completely ward off winter. There was no evidence of the previous night's storm anywhere to be seen. The sun had dried the rain soaked streets and now shone brightly in the sky. It was close to seventy degrees but that, as I knew, could change at any moment.

I looked over to Telegraph Hill topped by Coit Tower. The tower always made me smile but not today. It was a memorial to Lily Coit, a rich and eccentric woman whose devotion to fires during the early days of San Francisco rivaled many of today's pyromaniacs. The Nob Hill widow gave money, equipment, and prestige to the fledgling firefighters of the Barbary Coast. After her death, the firemen of San Francisco built and dedicated a monument to her in the shape of a fire hose, aimed toward the sky. I'm not completely sure what was going through their minds, but it has always looked like a huge phallic symbol to me. Color me crude.

I walked briskly toward the warehouse. Everything had a slight Salvador Dali look. The slant of the winter sun caused buildings and trees to throw irregular, stark shadows, a vibrant blue sky serving as backdrop. I dug into my bag for the small, matchbook-sized video camcorder.

D.I. provides each agent with one of these camcorders, weighing less than three ounces. It sends images and sound to a receiver that lives in the trunk of each agent's car. The receiver can take in data from up to five miles away with crystal clarity, which is stored on an external flash drive. The trick is in learning how to aim one of these little things so you record what you really want. Before I got the hang of it, I meticulously recorded many a blank wall, person's foot, or bird's duff.

Agents are required to carry three 8-hour battery packs on their person at all times, each the size of a paperclip, enough for a twenty-four hour day. The battery in the receiver itself is good for twenty-four hours when it's fully charged. When we return to home or work, we enter the flash drive into the USB port of a computer, send the info off to the mainframe, and then try to remember to recharge the batteries for future use. All very ritualistic, but it sure does save from scribbling notes on the back of your checkbook, as I have done in the past.

I turned it on and began to record all the license plates of the cars in my path. I had used the camcorder right before the monsoon hit and mentally noted several cars were there for the second day. This was something the computer program we entered the data into would automatically correlate. I also made some verbal notes into the small device as I walked along. If anyone noticed me talking, they probably thought I was either on a cell phone, nuts, or possibly both.

"It's about one-thirty p.m. on January twenty-fourth. I am at Bay and Beach walking toward the warehouse," I said in barely a whisper. "If I can, I'm going inside it. One thing that really puzzles me, and I keep mulling this over, is why Watch Line was hired to patrol a dilapidated warehouse. They're more expensive than most security services. Maybe it's the cost of their cute little blue and red uniforms. Anyway, that fact should be explored. Okay, here we are."

I stopped across the street from the warehouse and noted a slim, beautiful Chinese woman, about ten years younger than me, coming out of the parking lot. She hurriedly crossed the street and opened the door of a new lime green Volkswagen Bug. She was wearing a plain black slim skirt and a long sleeve white sweater but managed to give this common outfit a lot of style. I watched her long stockinged legs swing elegantly around and into the car after she sat behind the wheel. I didn't think anybody could get into one of those small cars looking like a lady, but somehow she managed to do it. For a brief moment, she looked back toward me, shielding her eyes from the sun. That was when I got a shot of her face. Then I aimed for the license plate of her car. I wondered briefly who the woman was and if she had ever been a dancer. She certainly moved like one. My eyes followed her as she drove off, tires squealing.

I turned my attention back to the small, restricted parking lot holding one non-descript, late-model, white pickup truck covered with rust and dents. It had a recently abandoned look and one of the tires was low on air. Nobody seemed to be around, so I crossed the street and went for a closer inspection. The cab of the truck had several empty cans of Mountain Dew strewn around on the passenger's seat and floor. There was nothing else inside that I could see. I tried the doors but they were locked. A faded tarp, grimy and torn, lay crumpled in the bed up near the cab. Two cigarette butts were on the floor. Other than that, it looked recently swept clean. I continued to the back of the truck and recorded the truck's license plate.

Finished, I turned around and went to the door of the warehouse fully expecting it to be locked. To my surprise, the door was slightly ajar. Dropping the camcorder in my pocket, I pushed open the door and stepped inside, trying to adjust my eyes to the lack of light. I was struck by the moist and musty smell of a place rarely exposed to fresh air or sunshine. Brilliant shafts of light pierced through holes in the rusted roof and hit the uneven, cement floor like small spotlights. The warehouse was larger than it looked from the outside and obviously constructed many years ago. The outside structure was painted stucco, but inside it was lined in rusting, corrugated tin. Dry, wooden beams reached up to support the corroding metal of the roof. It was pretty yucko, and I could imagine things setting up housekeeping in here National Geographic might want to know about.

Beginning directly below the roofline and continuing to the floor were dozens of large, square shaped cages that lined the four walls of the warehouse. They were apparently used as temporary storage areas for merchandise taken from the ships. Three sides of each square were made of a crisscrossed heavy-duty iron, open enough for maybe a child's hand to fit through but no more. The perimeter of the warehouse completed the fourth wall. Each cage was about one hundred feet wide and had a solid door locked with various types of padlocks. Nowhere did I see yellow crime scene tape. I'd assumed the murder hadn't been committed inside the warehouse, and now I knew for sure.

All but three cages were empty. One enclosed thousands of bundles of tied steel wire, piled in neat stacks. Another cage contained hundreds of shoeboxes, strewn helter-skelter.

Next to the unloading bay, a third cage proved to be the most interesting. Inside this cage was a small room built of wood, about twenty feet square, probably used as a makeshift office. Other than that, the cage was completely empty. What caught my eye, however, was the locked door on the cage. Intrigued, I crossed the cement floor that was covered with dirt and small pebbles, making small scratching noises with my feet. My footsteps echoed in the dark, and I shivered involuntarily. It was an eerie feeling, so I tried to pretend I was both Nick and Nora Charles in an old Thin Man movie. That didn't really work, but I forgot all about my discomfort, anyway, once I got a closer look at the lock and the door.

In my job, I've learned to spot the better-made and more effective locks manufactured. This was one of them, big time. It was a Gibson, digital and state-of-the-art, with an internal, computer-generated locking code that changed within the lock several times daily. The way it's set up is, you can only access the current code with a satellite locator, tied into yet another computer in Sacramento that is only accessible after about a dozen passwords are given. This Gibson was wired to an elaborate alarm system, so elegant it brought tears to my eyes. The whole thing was about as burglarproof as you can get. Even though I didn't come across many of these in my travels, I knew the system had a price tag of several thousand dollars, not including the monthly maintenance charges.

Then, I focused on the door itself and became even more confused. It appeared to be made of solid steel, over four inches thick, with overlaid hinges. I'll bet it probably weighed in at about a ton and a half. If you were to try to open either the door or the lock by force, you'd probably have to use enough explosives to destroy whatever they were protecting. I'd certainly never seen either one on anything as ordinary as a holding place for manufactured goods. I studied the crisscrossed iron bars, so thick even a heavy duty, pneumatic wire cutter would have problems cutting through, and saw another sophisticated alarm system woven in and out, similar to one installed at a bank where we recently finished a job.

"*Qué pasa?*" I said, trying to make sense of it all. "What do they have stored in here? Diamonds? And if so, where are they?"

You didn't need to be an Einstein to know something major was wrong in this quiet, musty place. I spun around and surveyed the other cages again with a suspicious eye. Somewhat mollified, I turned back to the anomalous cage. I scrutinized the wooden room inside as best I could, as it was some forty feet back from the front of the cage. In order to get a clear look at it, I had to squint between the crisscrossing. The room also had an iron door, sort of a junior version of the behemoth one standing beside me. To the left of the door was a high, iron-barred window through which a light shone. Need I say that the iron door and window sported two more very expensive locks? I didn't think so.

I felt like I was missing a chapter of a book. You know, the one that explains what's going on. Was this or was this not an empty hold in a dilapidated, empty warehouse being protected almost as well as Fort Knox? I made up my mind I was going to find out what was in that office if I had to chew my way through the iron. I tried to shake the fencing with all my might, but it was about as responsive as the Great Wall of China. I put my toes in between the holes in the crisscrossing and climbed several feet up. This gave me a little more of a vantage point, and I could see a little bit into the window and inside the room. I strained my eyes and could see the top of a chair, a desk and the back wall of the room, although something didn't look quite right. I dropped down and walked slowly around to the side of the cage that was next to the loading bay so I could pace out the interior and exterior of the room with my size 9 running shoes.

"Okay, who are you and what are you doing?" said a gruff voice behind me.

Chapter Six
Everybody's A Suspect

As I had been concentrating on counting and math not being one of my stronger suits, I was so startled I let out a yelp and fell back against the iron cage. Then I saw the uniform of a San Francisco policeman. I was annoyed, but tried not to show it. "Whoa, officer, don't shout at someone like that. You scared me half to death," I chided him, in what I hoped was a winsome manner.

The boxy, middle-aged man was unmoved by my charms and looked more like someone who has just come across a snake in his tool shed. "I repeat, young woman, what are you doing here? Who are you?"

I did some fast thinking. "I was just looking for a warehouse to rent for my business, and I thought there just might be someone inside to talk to about it. But, my, my, what's a policeman doing here? Has something happened?" I asked, in a breathless, inquisitive voice that sounded a little like Marilyn Monroe on helium. I'd seen this approach work for Lila countless times, so I gave it a whirl. I could have saved myself the trouble. He wasn't buying any of it.

"I'm going to ask you for the last time," he rasped, staring at me in a menacing way. "What's your name and what are you doing here? This is private property. You want to rent the place? Dial the number on the sign on the outside of the building. You're trespassing. I might have to arrest you."

"That's a little over of the top, don't you think?" I replied, dropping my voice to its normal range and matching his menacing tone. "I haven't done anything other than look. What are you going to arrest me for? Trespassing seems a little thin, as the door was open, and there's no sign telling me to keep out." My change of attitude and demeanor confused him, and his body began to twitch involuntarily.

Before he could answer, another voice came from the entrance doorway. "Mitchell, go on outside. I'll take care of this." Mitchell shrugged, shrank a little in size and turned on his heel, heading past the voice, and out through the doorway.

The voice, dressed in a dark suit, sauntered towards me and became a man of about six feet tall. He was backlit so I couldn't tell much more, other than he was probably gorgeous; I have these instincts. He stopped in one of the shafts of light from the ceiling and stared at me. Nothing moved save the dust particles highlighted around his head by the makeshift spotlight.

After a moment, he spoke in a silky, calm manner unnerving me completely. "I'm Detective John Savarese. My friends call me John. You're Bob Alvarez's daughter, aren't you? What's your name, Lillian or something?"

"It's Liana. My friends call me Lee. How'd you know who I was?" I asked, trying to make out his features against the back lighting.

"I've been assigned to this case."

"So you got over the flu, huh?" I quipped.

"The flu? Oh, yes. A lot of men down. I've got a full report of D.I.'s activities, and I know you gave a depo in Palo Alto earlier today." He paused. He might have been smiling at me but, if so, it got lost in the gloom. His head moved, and I saw light blond hair, or maybe white, reflected in the narrow shaft of light. He continued speaking in the same smooth, conversational style. "That was so we could save you a trip to the City but you came, anyway. What're you doing here, Ms. Alvarez?" he asked and was quiet again.

I could feel him waiting for an answer. It would be difficult not to tell a person like this the truth, I decided, and went for it. "Look, I don't know how much you know about my part in this," I began, "but I followed Mr. Wyler here on a routine...well, not so routine, because we don't normally do this kind of thing—"

"What kind of thing is that?" he asked suddenly, his voice caressing the still air.

I felt sexual tension run through my body and tried to ignore it. "We don't normally do surveillance. I know I probably shouldn't be here, but the man died on my watch. So, I guess I needed to...know what happened." I half-laughed apologetically. "You're probably used to this. I don't really do this kind of thing, as a rule. I do..." my voice halted as I wasn't quite sure how to explain what I did.

"I know, software piracy and hi-tech fraud. I knew your father. Bob was real proud of you. A shame the way he went. Aneurysm. Sometimes no warning at all with those things. That was probably real hard on you and your family," he said softly.

Hot tears welled up in my eyes, and I hated myself for it. Damn! It had been two years now. When was I going to be able to get on with things? Richard had. He'd moved out over a year ago and got his own apartment, even a girlfriend. Mom seemed to have moved ahead, too, taking complete charge of D.I. Once more, I felt the same emotional knife that had sliced through me right after the shock of his death wore away.

"Yes," I said. Silence fell between us with a heavy thud. I changed the subject. "So where did it happen?"

"Where you found him. On the pier." He hesitated but then made some sort of decision, "Come on."

He turned and walked to the warehouse door. I followed him, glad to be going out into fresh air and daylight.

As I trailed behind, I sized him up, or at least, the back of him. I was right about the height, but he wore it even better in the sunlight. He was slender with broad shoulders that made him look good in a suit, even one off the rack. He also looked like he worked out two or three times a week unless he lifted bales of hay for a hobby. The back of his head showed him to be a natural blond, bleached a little by the sun. He had an easy walk, and I liked it. Right away he struck me as my kind of man. I made a mental note to stay clear of him. I haven't done so well with my kind of man.

We walked around the warehouse and onto a cement dock approximately ten feet wide. A decrepit metal railing festooned with bird droppings was all that stood between the green-gray waters of the Bay and us. Here I saw the yellow crime-scene tape draped from the end of the building to the railing.

"We're pretty sure he was shot out here even though the rain washed most of the blood away. Some of it got absorbed into those wooden slats at the edge of the pier. See? Over there." He pointed to a rotting wooden beam buried in the cement that had probably once supported a wooden railing before the metal one was put in place. The wooden beam had some fresh gougings in it, probably made by forensics for evidence.

I looked up and out at the Bay. The San Francisco Bay is one of the busiest waterways in the world and surely one of the most beautiful. Boats and ships glided by, some lazily, some with import and purpose. Waves lapped noisily against the pier. Seagulls called overhead. The air smelled of the sea and timelessness. Directly in front of me was Angel Island. In the distance, I could see the other islands, Alcatraz, Tiburon, and Sausalito, as well.

Detective Savarese pulled a pair of sunglasses out of his top pocket and explained apologetically before putting them on over pale blue eyes, "I've got sensitive eyes. I can't take the glare of the sun. Makes my eyes water. You don't seem to have that problem."

"Not really." I turned to face him. I wasn't interested in sunglasses, glare from the sun or even eyes that looked a lot like Paul Newman's before his salad dressing days. He was starting to get on my nerves, this John Savarese, silky voice and all.

"So Detective Savarese, do you have any idea why this happened to Portor Wyler? I mean, he seemed like such a harmless little man," I said.

"He was a rich little man whose wife says she hired you people to see if he was cheating on her. Now he's dead. Who did it? Might be her, might be the purported other woman, might be anyone. Might be you. After all, you found the body." He took a step toward me, and I saw my startled face reflected in his sunglasses. "So, you can see that when you're a rich businessman you're not as harmless as all that." He leaned on the railing and stared at me.

"His wife went to school with my mother, and I've seen Mrs. Portor every now and then throughout the years, but I didn't know him from a hole in the wall. I never saw him until my assignment three days ago. He was always working or something." We were both silent.

"Seriously, it's not me," I offered after several seconds.

"I didn't think so, Lee. You're not really a strong candidate, but for the record, you're being checked on."

He turned his attention out to the Bay. I followed his gaze, and we were both drawn for a moment to a sleek sailboat with a black lab on the deck, barking its head off at a passing pelican.

I had never been a suspect in a murder investigation before, even a gratuitous one, and I felt oddly uncomfortable. I fought the feeling and tried to stay calm.

"There's something wrong with that room back there," I stated, changing the subject. "That office room. The dimensions are off somehow," I remarked. I didn't look at the handsome detective but down at the railing. I felt his eyes burning into me.

"So you noticed that? Well, forget it." The quietness of his voice was gone. "Listen to me, Liana Alvarez. Your father did me a good turn once, a very good turn. I owe him a lot. You're fooling around with something that could be very dangerous. I want you to promise me that you'll go back to Palo Alto and forget this whole thing. The man's dead. Your job is over."

I was so startled by his speech and its intensity I had no ready response. However, I was not thrilled. This was the second man today who was telling me what to do, and I didn't like it one bit. I looked him in the eye or, rather, looked his sunglasses in the eye.

"You know, I've got to stop wearing my hair in a ponytail. People seem to think I'm a lot younger and more inexperienced than I really am. I also smelled urine."

Now it was his turn to be startled. "Excuse me?"

"Ur-ine." I broke the word up into two distinct syllables. "I smelled it from somewhere near that office. The human kind. And what's with the White House kind of security on the cage? Doesn't make sense," I added for good measure.

He smiled at me, the warmth returning to his face. "You're good. You really are. Not many people would have noticed those things. If you ever want to go into law enforcement, you let me know. Meanwhile, I'm going to ask you again not to interfere with this case and," he added, "come on, Lee. This really isn't your job. It's mine."

I gave him an initial hard look but relented, returning his smile after a moment. We both relaxed somewhat. After all, he was right, and I had a lot of work piled up on my desk. It was close to three in the afternoon, I was tired from the night before, and I really did want to go home.

"Okay," I said. I could see him let out a deep breath. I turned to leave, and he got in step with me. To my surprise, he started walking me to my car.

Is he just being a gentleman or does he want to make sure I leave, the way I said I would?

As I unlocked the door of the car, he said, "It's been nice meeting you, Ms. Lee Alvarez, but I don't want to see you back here again. Do I make myself clear?" The voice was still melodic and quiet, but there was an edge behind the words that made my mouth go dry. I got inside the car and started the motor.

"By the way, were you inside the warehouse about a half an hour ago, as well?" He nodded toward the warehouse across the street.

"No," I stammered and felt like an idiot for allowing him to intimidate me this way. I cleared my throat and looked at him defiantly. "You saw me about one minute after I arrived. Why?"

He didn't answer, but took off his sunglasses and leaned into the driver's side of the car smiling genuinely. His pale blue eyes searched mine for something. What, exactly, I didn't know.

"Give my best to your family," he said. Then he abruptly stood up, checked for traffic left and right and slapped the top of the car with his open palm, a gesture I'd seen only in the movies. "It's clear now. Pull out." He turned and strode back to the warehouse. I did as I was told and headed for 101, becoming more and more irritated by the detective's condescending behavior.

"Just who the hell does he think he is, anyway?" I asked the sun visor. "Him and his good looking suit. It's not even an Armani, for crying out loud!" I blustered, every inch the offended snob.

By the time I got home, I had worked off some of my anger. I found the kitten in the middle of the black leather sofa having a nap. He looked so adorable; I decided then and there I would surround myself with felines instead of men for the next one hundred years or so. I would be different, however. I would forgo the rocking chair.

Next to the cat were all of the toys I had bought plus several new makeshift ones. Stroking his head, I watched his little body stretch luxuriously under my touch. He never opened his eyes but purred loudly. I found a note in Spanish from Tío outlining the day's activities in such detail, you would have thought I was an anxious parent needing reassurance from the daycare worker. From what I could surmise, my uncle left only about a half an hour before I arrived after an exhausting day for both of them. I knew if things continued at this level, the kitten should begin math and philosophy lessons the following week. I picked up the phone to let Tío know I had returned, and he answered on the third ring, barely concealing a yawn.

"*Ola,* Tío," I began, "I'm home," and then repeated in Spanish, "*Estoy en casa.*"

I told him a little about my day, and then, unfortunately, he began to press me on a name for his new charge. I glanced in the direction of the "little guy," who had now arranged himself in a hilarious position. He lay on his belly with his head hanging down off the front of the sofa and his front legs stiffly pointing toward the easy chair. His back legs and tail stretched out behind him.

"*So, mi Sobrina,*" Tío Mateo questioned, "what do we call him, this 'little guy'?"

"How about Little Guy?" I offered lamely. Tío grunted his disapproval, so I added quickly, "Actually, Tío, I'm going to name him from a book written by T.S. Eliot." From where this inspiration came, I don't know, but I went with it.

"Do you know who he is?" I asked, knowing full well Tío didn't. When he confessed ignorance, I launched into a full explanation of Eliot's *Old Possum's Book of Practical Cats*, the poems therein, and the Broadway musical *Cats*.

"I'm going to read it over again tonight and pick a name from it. If you remember, Tío, I auditioned for a road tour of *Cats*. Of course, I didn't make the final cut. That was in the days when I thought I could be a dancer."

"You're a beautiful dancer." He jumped in to defend my negligible talents.

"*Gracias, Tío.*" I smiled at his protestations of my abilities despite the fact life had proven the contrary. I was, at best, a mediocre dancer and at this point of my life, an old mediocre dancer. I had learned early on that ambition may be given to many but talent to few. I also learned you need to be gracious about what you can't do and grateful for what you can do. Dad taught me a lot of survival skills and that one goes to the top of the list.

"Anyway, I want to give him a name from that book of poems. Tomorrow I'll tell you his new name. I promise."

I hung up the phone and viewed the day's recorded tapes on the laptop in the living room while I drank hot tea and stroked the kitten that slept beside me. Convinced after one cursory examination nothing could be revealed without all of the tapes being entered into the database for sorting by the program, I fed them into the network computer and sent them off to Richard with my blessings. I also sent along an email message asking him to let me know as soon as possible if he found anything of interest.

I took a cue from the kitten and fell asleep on the couch next to him while the six o'clock news blared in the background. I awoke abruptly around eight forty-five filled with anxiety and called Vets and Pets for the results of the Feline Leukemia test. They were negative, and I celebrated with the new "guy" in my life by broiling a steak and sharing half of it with him.

Chapter Seven
All In A Day's Work

The next morning was a workday. My six-thirty a.m. morning barre and floor exercises took nearly an hour. I had a quick shower, and went to my walk-in closet full of expensive, classic and trendy garments. Okay, let's get one thing very clear up front. If it were up to me, I would be wearing stuff from consignment stores instead of clothes from some big-name designer.

However, I have a trust fund left to me by my maternal grandfather; so, long ago, I came to the decision that because it was Mom's father who left me the money, I would spend every penny of it on what is important to her, chic clothes. At any given time, I have nearly three-dozen suits by the likes of Escada, Versace, Yves Saint Laurent, and Chanel in a myriad of styles and colors. There's also the assortment of dresses, shoes, handbags, and all the rest of the trappings of the well-appointed, executive woman, crammed inside this inadequate and frightened closet.

Lastly, I've got a few pieces of fine jewelry tucked away in a safe under the hallway's floorboards. I hardly ever put them on, but when I do, it's more out of obligation than anything else.

I make two weekly trips a year to New York City for the outfits I wear to the office. Anyway, that's what I've told my mother. They're actually purchased in-between sightseeing, ballet performances, and Broadway shows. Because I can wear nearly anything in either a size 6 or 8, I phone several of the shops that know me, ask one of the saleswomen to pick out what she likes in those sizes, charge it to my credit card, and have the clothes sent over to the hotel room. I keep whatever fits and return the rest. If I'm lucky, the whole shopping process takes about thirty minutes, instead of days, and no one's the wiser. Then at the end of the year, I donate most of that year's clothes to a battered women's shelter in East Palo Alto. One thing I like to see is a struggling, single mother of four wearing some of these glad rags on her way to work. It makes my day.

I glanced out the window and saw it was a dismal day, gray and humid, with "spits" of rain falling intermittently. As a native Californian, I know the look of all day precipitation and that morning I had to remind myself that Northern California needed as much winter weather as it could get. It was a rare day in summer we see even a drop.

Without the sun, the temperature had dropped into the low fifties, and I could feel a damp chill in the air. I chose a hot pink, two-piece, cashmere suit trimmed with black leather on its high-necked collar and peplum bodice. It was "bold yet classy." That's what the salesgirl told me. There are only two things I refuse to knuckle under on with Mom. One is color. Everything in my wardrobe is vibrant and bright. Not only do strong colors look best on me, they make me feel happy. No neutrals for me, much to Lila's dismay. Mom's staple colors of gray, beige, and tan will never see the inside of my closet. Color me, please.

The second thing is jewelry. Nearly anything that glitters on me comes from the silver mines of Tasco, acquired during our frequent visits to relatives in Mexico. Like many other tourists, we often make side trips to Tasco, specifically for the handmade jewelry. The artisans there are famous for making spectacular silver pieces, often designed around semiprecious or precious gems. I purchased my first one-of-a-kind piece at the tender age of eleven and never looked back.

That day, I chose swirling silver and onyx earrings, slipped on the matching bracelet, and pulled my hair off my face in a chignon at the nape of my neck. *I really need to get it cut*, I thought. It was half way down my back. I finished the outfit off with black leather, three-inch pumps and a matching handbag. I have a weakness for handbags; I must own fifty of them.

Looking at myself in the full-length mirror, I caught a glimpse of the kitten, dear Little-No-Name, staring up at me as if he had no idea who or what I was. I scooped him up and laughed, as I hugged him. He was quickly gaining weight and had adjusted to his new home remarkably well.

"Don't worry, little guy. I may look like something out of Vogue magazine, but it's just me."

He batted at the shine on one of my earrings, and I made a mental note to get up twenty minutes earlier in the mornings to play with him. Not so much for him as for me. He had a relaxing effect on me. Then I noticed all the cat hairs on the front of my suit and decided to make it twenty-five minutes earlier. I knew I'd need another five minutes for brushing all the fur off my clothes. The doorbell rang and said feline and I went to answer it. After looking through the peephole, I opened the door wide and smiled at Tío.

"*Buenos dias, Tío!*"

He shook the rain off a black umbrella, closed it, placed it under the eave outside the door, and entered stamping his feet. "Ah!" he said as he took the Furry One from me and placed him on one of his broad shoulders. Perfectly at home, the kitten balanced himself as he nuzzled the man's ear. Keeping one hand up on the kitten's body to prevent a fall, Tío strode the room looking around. "*Dónde está el libro, mi sobrina?*"

"Where's the book?" I repeated in English, puzzled. "What book? Oh, the Eliot book. Right here, Tío." I opened my handbag and took out the small, orange and black book. "Unfortunately, I fell asleep last night before I finished reading it. But I promise to at lunch, so tonight you will know his new name. I have a couple of ideas," I added mysteriously, "but I want to pick just the right one."

"*Bien,*" Tío nodded, knowing that with me a promise was as good as done. "*Mi querida.*" He changed the subject hesitantly, as he looked earnestly into my eyes. "Your mama has asked me to move in with her permanently, now that Eva is gone, and you three are all I have left."

I stared at Tío hardly believing my ears. It had never occurred to me Mom would make such a generous and thoughtful offer as this. I had wondered what he would do with the rest of his life now that his beloved wife was dead, but I never imagined —

Tio continued speaking, interrupting my whirling thoughts, "Last night your mama and me, we talk, and she said she thinks this is a good thing. The house is big —"

"And sometimes she gets lonely, Tío," I interjected.

"*Sí.*" He nodded in agreement. "We do not say this is for always. This is just to try, to see. I may miss San Jose, my friends, and the life I had there, even though your *Tía* is no longer with me. Someday I may return to Mexico, too."

"You would be nearer to Richard and me, Tío, if you stayed here. Think about that."

His dark eyes bored into me. "That is what is on my mind, *mi Sobrina.* I do not want to do anything to upset you. You have your own life. Ricardo and I, we have already talked, but you, Liana, will this be too much for you? *La verdad, por favor.*"

He knew only too well my fierce sense of privacy. Only a man as good and unselfish as he would want to know the truth even if it might hurt him or not be what he wanted to hear.

"Oh, Tío," I choked as I threw my arms around his neck, enveloping the purring kitten as well. "I think it's wonderful, just wonderful. Let's go out to dinner tonight to celebrate, all four of us." I kissed him on the cheek. "I'll call Mom and Richard. Maybe even his new girlfriend will come. My treat."

"You approve?"

"I approve!" I half-shouted. We laughed and hugged again.

"*Bien, bien*! That is good." He shook his head. "But no celebrations in restaurants when you have the greatest *cocinero de Mexico* in all of the Bay Area," he said proudly. "Besides, your *hermano* and his *novia* are busy tonight. We are thinking tomorrow night."

"Whatever you say, greatest Mexican chef in all of the Bay Area," I repeated with a laugh. "Works for me."

"I will make tamales, Vera Cruz style, and other dishes, *muy sabroso*. You, your mama, Ricardo, and Victoria will come to the big house. I cook everything. We are going to have a fiesta."

"*Qué bueno! Una fiesta!*" I felt happier than I had in a long time.

Tío took the kitten off his shoulder with a gentle hand and gazed at it in mock severity. "Except you. You cannot come. But you will be here learning your new name and playing with the many toys your new mistress has not so wisely purchased for you."

* * * *

Shortly after nine a.m., I arrived at the place in Palo Alto where I have spent much of my life, 655 Forrest Street, Palo Alto, California. The three-story building, which houses

D.I. is actually built on an angle facing the two corners of Forrest and Gilman. The exterior is of the same gold-beige sandstone that Stanford University's older buildings were constructed of before the quarry petered out, so to speak, in 1950. Between 1890 and 1950, nearly every façade in and around the campus was constructed of stones quarried on Leland Stanford's 8,000 acre farm, so I can only hope nobody was too surprised when the supply ran out one day.

The Honor Blythe Building, named for a turn-of-the-century society matron, is one of the few non-campus buildings constructed of this sandstone to remain standing. It's more than eighty-five years old, and its longevity is due largely to the bank that's been on the ground floor since 1924. Modernized internally as the years went by, it still retains the original outside facade and was declared a historical landmark in the mid nineties, mostly due to Lila's bulldogged efforts.

Green ivy covers much of the structure now. In between the sidewalk and on either side of the building, two outwardly curved, brick parapets create a crescent shape allowing for a small, cobblestone courtyard, shaded by a two hundred-year old California Native Oak. Centered in this courtyard is a round, three-tiered stone fountain. Vivid blue and green colored mosaic tiles line each basin and birds drink and bathe in the cascading waters. In the bottom, larger bowl, four small goldfish dart in and out of mossy plants. Wrought iron benches placed around the perimeter allow people to sit, rest, and whatever. It's quiet. It's peaceful. It's a small bit of calm in an otherwise busy little town.

The windows in the building are the original hand-blown, beveled glass, and the irregularity of the panes catches the sun's light on all but the gloomiest of days. Inside the lobby, two stained glass light fixtures gleam in warm sepia tones, as they stand on either side of the doorway. These, and the complementary stained glass ceiling of the lobby, were designed and executed by Tiffany and Company. Not too shabby.

Hurrying across the cobblestone, I scattered the birds fluttering about. I was anxious to talk to Richard about what he might have found on the tapes, as well as Mom about her generosity to Tío. I raced up the polished alabaster staircase, too impatient for the antiquated elevator to creak down to the ground floor.

Not that I take the elevator, anyway. For one thing, as I always tell a client when I escort him or her to the lift and then head for the stairs myself, the elevator can only hold about one and a half people comfortably. If two or more want to go to the second or third floor, they get to know each other extremely well during the trip. This always gets a laugh.

The second thing is — and it's something I don't like to talk about — I find the elevator to be so old and decrepit, no matter what Building Services says to the contrary, that the rattles of its ascent terrify me. I have this fear one day it might shudder to a stop somewhere between the second and third floors, and I might die a lingering death trapped inside. In any event, climbing stairs is good for you. Ask any doctor.

I had run up to the third floor at such a breakneck speed, I had to stop for a moment to allow my heart rate to fall. Then I walked across the burgundy-colored, plush carpet toward the double doors of D.I. with the same feelings of ownership and pride I always have. Gold leafing on black ebony doors read simply:

Discretionary Inquiries, Inc.
Data, Information and Intelligence
Room 300

I turned the ornate brass handle, and the door opened on silent hinges into a world that was more of my life than I cared to think about. Before me, the atmosphere of the open reception room, filled with workers and clients alike, conveyed its usual, quiet importance. The setting often made newcomers and employees speak in whispered tones, which I find maddening because I can never catch half of what anybody's saying. I think this odd behavior is due mostly to a combination of the thick carpeting, the heavy French furniture and the oil paintings of dead people hanging about on wood-paneled walls. To me, the place projects the feeling of a small museum or mortuary. I've felt this way ever since we moved here over a dozen years ago. That was when Silicon Valley boomed, and the business had expanded to five times its size in less than a year. Dad admitted to me the decor intimidated him, but Mom was convinced this kind of ambiance gave clients confidence. So far she has been proven right, even with the Silicon Valley crash of a few years back.

However, I believe most of our success is due to Richard — weird, but wonderful, Richard. My brother is a computer programming genius from whom all things flow. He created and designed our in-house program that is so unique in its approach to investigations it has brought D.I. light years ahead of the competition. Having stated that, however, Richard's true gift is in statistical compilation. He can link seemingly unrelated data and find answers where someone like me would just see a forest of numbers. Once he links the data, and explains it to the rest of us, everyone says: "Oh, yeah! I should have seen that," but nobody ever does before Richard.

It was around his fifteenth birthday that he broke the operations of a black market computer empire. During the previous five years, millions of computer disks were being stolen from several major Sunnyvale manufacturers, relabeled and sold to unsuspecting small businesses across the world.

Buried in layers of dummy corporations and phony addresses, the "new bad boys of high crimes" had eluded the police who seemed capable of only snaring a few errand boys on bicycles.

In desperation, three of the hardest hit companies banded together and offered a huge reward for any information that would lead to the capture of the brains behind it all. Richard was enticed. He considered that you couldn't just walk away with hundreds of pounds of software; you've got to carry it in something. He searched online records for any information about the thousands of cars, trucks, vans, motorcycles, and even helicopters that had been in those areas during the specific times of the robberies.

Block by block, he expanded the search to each succeeding outlying street, as he wrote off the preceding one. It was a mammoth undertaking, but he was determined to solve the problem. He worked on it during any spare time he had, weeks on end, checking, crosschecking, entering, and analyzing. He was relentless.

Finally he found the link: a Dodge Caravan with two unpaid parking tickets. Research found both tickets were given out about six blocks away from two of the companies that had suffered huge losses. The owner of the van was one of a three-brother team that was using "Wet, Wet, Wet and Now Dry Plumbing" as a front for a booming business in pirated software. Richard's dogged approach broke the case and earned for D.I. $1.2 million in fees, plus international recognition.

After that, Richard had been offered several lucrative jobs across the country, some asking him to name his own figure. He wasn't interested. It wasn't just that he worked in his father's business; it was a family business. Dad had trained Richard, believed in him, nurtured his talent, and turned him loose with what was then state-of-the-art equipment. Richard had carte blanche at D.I., and it was the only place he felt thoroughly comfortable. Because of Richard's talents, even Lila forgave him his eccentricities and ratty work clothes. For Lila, that's a lot.

I think I've mentioned anyone who works for D.I. adheres to the dress code or finds him or herself another job. The dress code, among other things, dictates suits for both men and women. The women can wear dresses only if they are "classic" in style, which means modest but expensive. "Ladies" can wear slacks if they are part of a slack suit, and of course, stockings and heels must be worn at all times. Ties are mandatory for men, even if they come into the office directly from the field. Anyone dropping by D.I. would swear they had gone back in time to circa 1960. Idiotic, but there you have it.

Stanley, the receptionist and a man particularly astute in fashion sense and pecking order, keeps assorted ties and jackets for the men and silk scarves, belts, and jewelry for the women on hand. You can borrow from these accessories once. The second time, you'll be hauled into Lila's office for a firm but lady-like reprimand. If it happens a third time, your services probably won't be "needed" anymore. As everyone is on a retainer contract, it's quite simple not to use the services of a particular agent when a job is over. However, D.I. pays some of the highest fees in the Bay Area, so most agents are happy to comply with this unusual policy.

Unfortunately, my close relationship to the CEO does not make me an exception to this hard and fast rule. Or any other rules, come to think of it. Richard, however, can wear his sweats, jeans, or come buck naked to work, as long as he stays out of the front offices and Lila's sight. I guess you could say I come from an eccentric family.

I smiled and waved at Stanley, who gave me two mornings' worth of mail and a friendly nod without missing a beat in the conversation he was having with a potential client. I passed him and called out the names of the two latest file clerks, Brenda and Carl. On general principles, I try to develop a good working relationship with anyone in that position, so I made a point of saying hello. When they saw me, vacant stares were dropped and smiles occurred. After that, they sighed and returned to the bottomless stacks of paper before them. My heart skipped a beat because I recognized the signs. One or both would probably give notice any day.

No matter how often one takes them out to lunch, one can't get past the fact their everyday job consists of categorizing and filing hundreds of original, work-related papers. It gives the word "tedious" new meaning. If an original isn't filed correctly, it might be lost forever in one of a thousand other files. Here's the catch-22, if a person is smart, he or she is bored silly within three days. If they're not smart, they can't learn the complex filing system and that's unacceptable. So, historically, we're either terminating them, or they're terminating us.

The Board has addressed the constant turnover repeatedly, but we haven't found a solution yet. It's a mind-numbing job, but a legally necessary one. Even paying eighteen fifty an hour with benefits hasn't kept someone in it for more than nine or ten months. Poor Stanley, who is in charge of hiring and training this sorry lot, has been given a series of bonuses and a constant supply of Advil, as a result.

I opened the door to my office and breathed deeply. Until I got into this sanctuary, I never took in or let out a full breath. My office is done in a modern Mexican look, not unlike my apartment. It is light and simple, with accents of pure colors and papier mâchè works by Sergio Bustamonte. I love it. Lila doesn't like any of the offices to be stamped with an individual personality, though. She wants each one to look pretty much the same, white and gray with touches of burgundy. You know, corporate. I argued I was the daughter, part owner, and after all, rank hath its privileges. On this issue, I was ready to create an ugly scene in front of the Board, if necessary, no idle threat to my mother.

The "Board" consists of Mom, Richard, me, plus the in-residence CPA, Ms. Packersmythe, and the family retainer, James Talbot. Ms. Packersmythe is probably one of the most foul-tempered people I've ever met in my life. She moves like a Hummer in overdrive and, for some unknown reason, thinks corduroy should be eradicated from the earth. We keep her around because she's loyal, terrific with numbers and tax loopholes, and the IRS is scared to death of her.

Mr. Talbot, surely the world's oldest practicing lawyer, is nearly deaf and refuses to wear a hearing aid. He's still as sharp as he was when he handled my grandfather's estate way back when. The best part is, he knew Mom when she was "in rompers," as he is so fond of shouting, and he is not one bit intimidated by her. It's quite a group. Needless to say, my mother backed down on going to the board about my decorating style, but to this day has never set foot in my office, an unexpected bonus.

I threw the mail down on the already littered desk, picked up the phone and dialed Richard's four digit interoffice number. Richard always checks the number of the incoming call before picking up. Most times he doesn't pick up. This morning he answered on the first ring.

"*Hola*, Lee. *Que pasa?* You okay?" he asked anxiously.

"Hi, Richard. *Esta bien.* I'm just fine," I assured my younger brother. It was the first time the firm was involved in a murder, and my kid brother tends to be very protective of me, murder notwithstanding.

I smiled into the phone. Even though I was three years older, I felt, in some ways, as if Richard had been born older. We did most of our growing up together at D.I., having become involved in our early teens, so we are very close, but in an atypical way. "Did you get the tape I transmitted last night? Sorry I couldn't send more than three hours worth."

"Working on it. Working on it," he replied.

Regarding the aforementioned tapes, the standard practice for our type of surveillance was that every other hour for at least one twelve-hour period, the agent would record the license plate numbers of all vehicles, as well as names of businesses and residents of buildings, all within a two-block square of the objective. Then you are supposed to send these tapes on to Richard. Richard's job is to compile and analyze this information with the help of the program he's created. It's tedious work for everyone except Richard, who loves it, but it often yields surprising results.

"Don't have anything for you yet, Lee. That's some gorgeous girl you got on tape yesterday. Hey, does Lila know you're still working on this job?" He changed subjects abruptly, as usual.

"I just want to tie up some loose ends, that's all. I don't know if I am still working on it, so let's not tell her about it yet."

"Yeah, right," he countered. "Like she doesn't know what's going on around here at all times. Our Lady of Investigation knows everything." Richard has a deep respect for our mother's knack for staying on top of every project D.I. is involved in at any given time.

I thought for a moment and then agreed silently with Richard. "I have to talk to her about some things today, anyway. I'll mention this to her. Meanwhile, stay on it, will you?"

"Sure. I've got some license plates in the mix as we speak. One of them is that China Doll's. She looks familiar to me," he added in a puzzled tone.

"I thought so, too," I said, glossing over the derogatory remark he'd just made about the woman. Richard makes remarks about everyone, injudiciously and without discrimination. It does no good to chastise him about it, we learned early on. I remember the time he led a discussion on the merits of his sixth grade teacher's fondness for peanut butter and sauerkraut sandwiches over the school's PA system and was expelled for two weeks. Bearing that in mind, Mom likes to keep him out of the spotlight. A loose cannon, if ever there was one.

"Whoa, gotta go, Lee. Two lines are buzzing. Catch me after lunch, okay?"

"Okay. One thirty-ish. Thanks." We hung up.

I sat for a moment, thought of the happiness on Tío's face this morning, and picked up the phone again, punching in another number I knew by heart. The voice I heard on the other end of the line was Patti, Lila's secretary. Calls were routed to her directly when Mom wasn't in the office. After a brief discussion, I found out Lila wouldn't be available until around lunchtime. Impulsively, I asked Patti to check her schedule and see if she was free for lunch. She was. Patti offered to let Mom know and make reservations at *Il Fornaio*, the up-scale Italian restaurant nearby and one of Lila's favorites.

That taken care of, I attacked a stack of unopened mail. In the pile were two letters from grateful clients. Good, I thought, making a mental note to give them to Lila for the scrapbook she drags out for prospective clients right before she tells them D.I.'s minimum fee. The rest of the mail was brochures, junk mail, and blanket invitations to openings, events, and similar happenings in Palo Alto.

I turned from mail to voicemail messages or, as I liked to think of it, That Aspen Bitch. That's the name I've given the generic cyber-female voice on the system that commands you through various levels of the program whether you want her to or not. I had eleven messages. Three were from friends, and the rest were calls that needed follow up. One odd message came from Mrs. Wyler, the recent widow, inviting me for tea at my earliest convenience. I tried to pretend I didn't get that one, something ghoulish about it, but returned the other calls.

An hour later, after getting coffee from the staff lounge, I switched on the computer and went into email. I found seventy-nine messages sent in the past two days, none of them spam. I groaned aloud and answered each one as quickly as possible. By the time I could glance at my watch, I saw it was a quarter of twelve. I got up, stretched from the two and a half-hours of sitting in one spot, and left the office.

I turned right in the hallway and toward Lila's office, the former office of my father. I didn't like to go in there much now. As I came up to Patti, a petite woman of about my age, I had to fight back an idiot grin that came to my face. The secretarial desk, dark mahogany, with hand carved legs, was deliberately opulent and impressive. It was also so large it overwhelmed this small woman. Patti, vertically challenged at about four foot ten, often looked as if she were a little kid playing grownup in the office or was here for "bring your daughter to work" day. As I approached, I could see Patti's little legs swinging in the air under the desk. I hid my smile, and she turned from her computer to face me.

"Lila said she'd meet you at the restaurant, Lee. Something about errands," Patti said, as she flashed her broad smile. It was a smile complete with about sixty-eight white-hot teeth, reminiscent of the Cheshire Cat's grin, only on steroids. I suspect that long ago someone mentioned her teeth were her best feature, and she never got over it. I think she bleaches them religiously every night.

I tried to return Patti's smile, tooth for tooth, thanked her politely, and headed out on foot for the restaurant. A light rain had settled in, and I was glad I thought to bring my umbrella. The restaurant was less than two blocks away, a very convenient lunch spot. I arrived at one minute after twelve and dashed into the outside door of the restaurant located on the bottom floor of one of Palo Alto's nicer hotels. I shook the rain off the umbrella and dropped it in the nearby umbrella stand.

The maître de, Paulo, stood behind his podium, stationed at the main entrance. He glanced up from his reservation book and smiled at me. "Good afternoon, Ms. Alvarez. Mrs. Alvarez is at the usual table. I'll just take — " he began, as the phone rang.

"Don't bother, Paulo," I hastily called to him, as I walked past. "I know my way. Thanks just the same." I wound my way in between the tables already crowded with early diners and toward the corner table directly under a large painting of a goat and a dog, dressed as people, bartering in a seventeenth century outdoor market. The table was bound in on both sides by hand painted murals of pastoral scenes. The gentle murmur of the busy restaurant had a soothing effect on me. Mom looked up, frowned, and the soothing effect nosedived.

"Do you know why TransTrek decided not to pursue their investigation?" she demanded to know.

My mind raced. *TransTrek. TransTrek. Oh, yes! The start-up company we had a meeting with several days ago. Mr. Ronald Everett, Wealthy Investor. Looking for a quick return in the computer market and had glommed onto a bright lawyer who had created a program linking every court system in the USA and Canada. Something was leaking out to a rival company, and Mr. Wealthy Investor came to Lila to see how it was done, and who did it.*

"No, no, I don't, Lila," I said, using my mother's first name, once I had figured the answer out. When it was work oriented, as it often was, the family used each other's given names. This saved a lot of explanations in the business world and, oddly enough, made everyone feel more comfortable.

The frown continued on Lila's lovely face. Her forehead crinkled in deep thought. "I want you to call them, Liana. I want you to talk personally to this Mr. Everett. See what's going on. We usually don't get dropped like this without a word," she added.

"Why me? You do those kind of phone calls," I said plaintively, my voice approaching a wail. I hate soliciting work. Lila is so much better at it than I am.

"Yes, I know but Mr. Everett seemed to take to you." The frown disappeared, and her face glowed as she looked proudly at me. She reached over and pushed back an errant lock of hair that had fought its way out of my chignon. "I want you to call him today and make an appointment to see him in person."

"But what if he won't —"

"Oh, of course, he'll see you," Lila interrupted, with a toss of her shoulder-length, straight hair. The humidity never seemed to bother her silken tresses like it did mine. If I hadn't contained my hair in this kind of weather, I would have wound up looking like a chrysanthemum.

"In any event, make him see you," Mom said and did it again, emphasized a word in the sentence. It just makes me crazy. Maybe someday I'll have the nerve to tell her.

"I'll try," I answered, as I let out a huge sigh of martyrdom and picked up a menu.

"I don't know why you bother to read the menu," My mother commented with a light laugh. "You always order the same thing."

That was true. I did and do. I like their homemade chunky tomato soup and Caesar salad with lots of breadsticks and rolls on the side. Just to be contrary, I toyed with the idea of ordering something else, but then, why should I? I continued to stare at the menu as if she hadn't spoken.

"By the way," Lila continued, "what made you go up to San Francisco yesterday? I thought you were resting."

My body gave a jerk, and I knocked over the glass of water in front of me. I grabbed the napkin from my lap and began mopping up the liquid not absorbed by the tablecloth. At just that moment the waiter appeared, much to my relief, with extra cloth napkins. He deftly covered the water stain with several, put a fresh napkin in my lap, and stood by awaiting our order. Lila ordered a pasta dish made with fresh spinach and pine nuts and a glass of Chianti. The waiter turned to me.

"The usual, Miss?" he smiled radiantly, as he took the menu from my hands.

"Oh, ah...yes," I said and returned his smile weakly. The next time I vowed to order something different. I asked for more water and looked around the room. It was a pretty room, pleasant and warm on this rainy, dark day.

"Well?" Mom asked with raised eyebrows, waiting. Fat chance Lila would lose the thread of a conversation. I searched my mother's face. There was no ill will or annoyance there, just plain curiosity.

"I just wanted to know where it happened. It was impulsive."

"You and your impulses, Liana." My mother sighed. "Well, I got a call from Detective John Savarese...."

"You did?" I interrupted. "Who is he?"

"I don't know, just the man in charge of the case, I suppose."

"But he said he knew Dad. He said Dad did him a large favor once. What was it?"

"Your father never said."

"He must have said something, Mom," I pushed.

"Roberto had a lot of friends, and some he didn't tell me about. That was ten or fifteen years ago, anyway. Don't interrupt," she ordered in a slightly louder voice, as she saw that I was about to do so again.

"Detective Savarese told me he found you inside that warehouse looking around. He further stated that this is a potentially dangerous situation, and he doesn't want to see you there again. Neither do I." Her voice softened and her smile returned. "I know how you must feel, dear, truly I do. In fact, Yvette wants to personally thank you and to apologize for endangering you in any way."

Oh, great! Lila knew about Mrs. Wyler's invitation to tea, too. Now I'll have to go. "I was only in danger of catching a bad cold," I retorted.

"I'm sorry I involved you in this in the first place."

"Well, you should be," I answered, dipping a chunk of Italian bread in the extra virgin olive oil. "You couldn't ask one of the other agents to trail a wandering husband. That's not what we're contracted to do. You took advantage of our relationship, Mom."

"That's true," Lila conceded. "Yvette was adamant about not having any outsiders know about this and begged me to "keep it in the family." You can imagine how she felt when I told her the day before yesterday about Portor and the warehouse." The waiter brought Lila's wine and she took a healthy swallow. "In any event, Liana, I feel guilty enough about involving you in his murder. Please don't compound it any more...and stop making jokes about it. Now promise me that you will stay out of this murder investigation."

I thought for a moment. "All right," I said, wording my answer carefully. "I promise to stay away from the warehouse in San Francisco."

At that moment, the waiter brought our food and fussed over us for a couple of minutes. Did we want fresh ground pepper? Did I want something else to drink? Did we need anything else? The subject of the murder and the warehouse got dropped, much to my delight. I was feeling pretty smug. After all, I only promised to avoid the warehouse. Everything else was up for grabs. As we ate the delicious food, we felt ourselves mellow and relax. It wasn't until we were halfway through the meal I remembered about Uncle Mateo.

"Oh, Mom," I began, "that's so great that you asked Tío to stay permanently with you. He seemed so happy this morning."

"Really? Good, although I hope I haven't made a mistake." Lila said, wiping her mouth with her linen napkin. "I might not have thought this through. After all, I'm used to privacy as of late."

"Privacy?" My hand froze with a spoonful of soup midway to my mouth. "Mom, the house is enormous. Even when we all lived there, it was a rare weekend we didn't have two or three friends staying over, as well." I put down the spoon. "You live in a goddamn mausoleum, for Pete's sake."

"I simply mean there might be some period of adjustment for both of us, even though he's like the older brother I never had. Take meals for example. I'm used to eating when I want and in the sunroom. I don't know that I want to continue eating again in the dining room, as we're doing now. And please watch your language," Lila added sharply, taking a sip of the wine.

"I don't see why the two of you don't eat in the sunroom right now," I said, retrieving a chunk of bread from the breadbasket and ripping it into pieces. "It's silly for two people to sit at that huge table, and the dining room has an echo if there are less than twelve people in it. I'm sure Tío's doing it because you insist."

"I was just using that as an example of how little things add up. You get used to a routine, to doing things in a certain way."

I looked down at my bowl filled with the shredded bread. "Well, if you don't want to do it, you don't want to do it. It's too bad you brought it up in the first place," I muttered more to myself than to my mother.

"I didn't say I don't want to do it, Liana. My goodness, can't I express a little concern over something as drastic as inviting another human being into my life without you getting all...?" She didn't finish the sentence and looked at me.

"Tío said this was something you both were going to try out for awhile, so I'm sure you've conveyed your doubts to him," I realized the uncertainties expressed this morning by Tío came more from my mother than from him.

I sat thinking. *I could always ask Tío to live with me in the second bedroom. I could move the office into the bedroom I occupied now and the mirror and bar into the living room.*

I forced my attention back to the sound of my mother's voice.

"I didn't convey any doubts to him at all," Mom said. "In fact, he was the one who started me thinking. He lived for fifty years with Eva. I lived for thirty-six with your father. Maybe we both can't do this," she said, draining the last of the wine. "But I want to try."

"I guess you'll see." I forced a smile. "Let me know how it goes, okay?"

"Of course I will. Do you want some dessert?" Lila asked, signaling for the waiter.

"I don't think so." I glanced at my watch. It was twelve forty-five. I had just enough time to finish reading *Old Possum* and meet Richard at one-thirty if I left now. I opened my purse and pulled out my wallet and laid a ten and a five on the table. "This should cover my share. Would you mind very much if I ran back to the office? I have some reading to do."

"Reading? Right now? Why, I guess not." She picked up the two bills from the table and handed them back to me. "This is on me. I have a stop to make before I go back, myself. I'm meeting Yvette at the mortuary to settle a few things. Will you tell Patti that I'll return around four?"

"Of course. Mom, I'm sorry I got a little sharp with you about Tío. It's really wonderful of you to offer, and I think you're to be commended for it," I added, trying to mend fences. "And thanks for lunch. I appreciate it."

"Well, you hardly ate anything," Lila replied, searching in her purse for her charge card. "Go ahead and go. I'll take care of this." She didn't look up. I hesitated for a moment, and at a loss for what more to do or say, I left. I knew I'd hurt her feelings, and was sorry about that. I retrieved my umbrella and started off toward the office. The air felt good on my flushed face, and I knew I was more upset by our conversation than I wanted to admit. I thought of going back and apologizing again but for what, exactly? I hurried through the drizzle back to the office, looking forward to the refuge of my book. Like so many books before, it would take me into another world. I needed that.

Chapter Eight
The Inner Sanctum

Shortly before one-thirty, I approached the Information Technology Wing and home of Richard's office. There were no burgundy colored rugs or any opulent furnishings. Linoleum flooring and empty walls echoed my knock. This area is at the back of the office complex and off limits to nearly everyone, certainly to the public. Here is the lifeblood of D.I. Millions of dollars worth of various computerized equipment live here, most containing highly confidential materials. There's an IT staff of eighteen, which includes Richard and his two assistants. They protect this section not only with coded doors and computers but also with their very bodies.

I once tried to get by Andy, Richard's newest assistant, on his first day of employment. Nothing I said or did would make him get out of my way. It wasn't until Richard came out, introduced us, and verbally okayed me that I was allowed to pass without winning a wrestling match. As Andy was only five foot two and I towered over him by some six inches, I was impressed with his rat terrier approach to the job. Soon after that, Richard decided to electronically lock the entrance and have a monitor, where one of his two assistants can screen people safely from inside. I waved into the camera to Andy or Erica, whichever, and heard the buzzing that allowed me to pass into the "forbidden zone," as this area has now been dubbed.

I walked down a narrow hallway until I came to Richard's unmarked door. I rapped loudly to make sure he heard me and turned the knob. There was no point in waiting for a response from inside his office. He never gave one and anybody who got this far knew they could barge right in without awaiting consent.

As I opened the door, I could hear the strains of one of his favorite mariachi songs, *"Alma, Corazon Y Vida"* playing on the stereo. A flashback of when he first learned to play it himself came into my mind. He was barely eleven years old and almost too small for the guitar he held so lovingly in his hands. But he never gave up and practiced until he and the instrument were one; until together, they were magic. To this day, I can tell what mood Richard's in by what's playing on his stereo or by his own hand on his ever-present guitar. With mariachi music playing, I knew that Richard had good news for me.

I pushed the door open, waiting for my eyes to adjust to the dark. The room was about thirty feet square with thick, curtained windows on the outside wall. In various stages of cannibalization, computers, monitors, keyboards, and little wiry things sat in piles on the floor, their importance known only to Richard.

I focused on a computer station in the center of the room where Richard sat staring into a mammoth screen. The monitor alone, called something like Blue Jean C, had cost D.I. over forty thousand dollars. I knew because the Board had a big debate about the expense. Richard usually gets anything he wants, and he had his heart set on this prototype monitor once he found out NASA had ordered three. We were lucky he only wanted one.

My brother stared intently at the screen, currently divided into six sections, with a different visual in each section. He worked his keyboard, froze several of the sections, and called out to me even though I hadn't been sure he knew I was in the room. He lowered the music and swiveled around.

"I've got her, Lee. Found her about an hour ago." He chuckled with glee.

I was confused. "Who?"

"Your China Doll. She's right here." He swiveled in his chair to face me and leaned back with satisfaction awaiting my approval.

"You're kidding!" I exclaimed and turned my attention to the screen. Sure enough, a frozen frame of the Asian woman I saw yesterday matched five others on the screen. Out of the six, two of them were grainy and one was only a side shot of her neck and ear with lots of flowing black hair. "Who is she?"

"You know, at first, Lee, I only wanted to know who she was because she's such a babe. Then, as I got into it, I had this nagging feeling I'd seen this gal before." I could tell by the way Richard talked this story was going to take awhile. I leaned on the edge of his desk and folded my arms. He noticed and began clearing off the closest of several chairs littered with parts of equipment and manuals, while never stopping his excited dissertation. "You know me, I never forget a face and what a face she has! And that body! I'm surprised you didn't know who she was right off, Lee, 'cause she's a pretty well-known Bay Area dancer!"

"A dancer!" I echoed, surprised despite my original assessment of the woman. I sat down on the edge of a now cleared chair, my body tense with excitement.

"She did the Snowflake Queen in the *Nutcracker Suite* Christmas before last at the Civic Auditorium in San Francisco. We saw it together, remember?" he teased, beaming proudly at me.

Of course! Once he told me who she was, I knew her immediately. It was one of those cases of somebody being where you didn't expect them to be, so you didn't recognize them. I'd seen her in two or three productions. She'd danced the second female lead, shining in whatever part she undertook.

"Not only that, and this is where it gets good, guess where else we've seen her?" I could tell my brother was enjoying this game immensely. He waited patiently for a response.

"Entertainment Tonight?" I queried, opening my eyes wide and feigning seriousness.

"No! Guess again." His eyes twinkled and he offered a bright smile.

"Richard," I said, "can we play Twenty Questions some other time? Just tell me who she is."

"Oh, all right," he relented, his face clouding over. "She was front page news about a year ago when she was arrested for protesting against restricting the number of Chinese immigrants coming into the States. Seems she's got nine sisters and brothers and most of them are still waiting in China to get to the States. She assaulted one of the lower city officials...what's his name..."

He got up and looked intently at some writing below one of the frozen segments on his screen. "Oh, yeah. A Leonardo Falariccia...."

"Well, who wouldn't slug somebody with that name?" I interrupted, but I did remember the incident and how it shocked the artistic community. I remember thinking at the time she had an unusual temperament for a ballet dancer, hot and fiery. More like a rock star.

"...but he decided not to press charges," Richard continued, ignoring my interruption. Richard remained standing, his slender frame stretching out the kinks that came from sitting in one position too long.

I shifted in the chair and forced my mind back to the Christmas before last. Now I knew who the woman was, I reflected on the beautiful Snowflake Queen, graceful and trim, with such perfectly precise and yet passionate movements. She hadn't worked her way up to performing the Sugar Plum Fairy but it was only a matter of time; she had the talent. I remembered the awe I'd felt as I watched her; the way I always feel when a dancer can accomplish the impossible. That ephemeral ability of a dancer to make complicated and highly rehearsed steps look natural and easy, as she glides effortlessly across the stage. It was something I had never and would never be able to do.

"What's her name?" I finally asked, coming out of my reverie.

"Grace Wong. And believe me, there are about forty of them in San Francisco alone. After I matched her face from newspaper microfilms, it took me nearly two hours to track down which Grace Wong she was. God bless the online library service. I not only have her address and phone number, I know she reads only non-fiction, just like me. She lives in San Francisco, typical single life, but there are a couple of things that are kind of odd," Richard reflected, sitting back down.

"The first thing I did was to check her DMV record and credit card charges. Now, she has the job with the San Francisco Ballet Company, which is evenings, right? But she's driving down to Princeton-by-the-Sea, hereafter known as PBS, at least two or three times a month, and always at night, which is one heck of a commute. For the past four or five months she's been gassing up at the same service station down there, almost a full tank each time. Might have a boyfriend or something, but what's strange is, I don't think she spends more than an hour there, and then she's back up to the City. Got two tickets for speeding in San Francisco around one o'clock in the morning on two of those nights. Let's see..." he said, as he closed his eyes and searched his memory. "One on Nineteenth Avenue and Noriega in the Sunset district and one on Geary."

Richard continued, "Then she got a parking ticket a couple of weeks ago in PBS shortly before midnight, even though she had a special dress rehearsal the next morning starting at eight a.m. My God, this girl gets around. Everything's on the printout." He pointed to a stack of 8 x 11½ inch paper piled on his desk. He took a stick of gum out of his shirt pocket, unwrapped it, and popped it into his mouth with a great sense of accomplishment.

I vaguely knew the area he was talking about. Some twenty or twenty-five miles south of San Francisco, Princeton-by-the-Sea, or PBS as Richard called it, is a small port town of less than four hundred people. Thousands of tourists visit each year to check out the "New England" type harbor and eat at one of the great seafood restaurants that litter the coastline, but that's pretty much it. I'd driven by it several times on Highway One, as I was heading to Half Moon Bay, Monterey, or Carmel, but never stopped.

As far as I was concerned, it was probably a pleasant enough little town but just how much charm could a harbor or a fishing boat hold in the middle of the night for a ballet dancer with a six-day a week job in San Francisco? Maybe Grace Wong did have a boyfriend in Princeton-by-the-Sea, but it somehow seemed a little off, like a lot of things lately. I decided to think about it later. At that moment, I was worried about D.I.'s involvement with the police.

"How much of this information are we giving to the police? They expect our full cooperation, Richard." This murder business was new to me, and I was a little nervous about intermingling with the San Francisco Homicide Department, especially as I was, ever so slightly, a suspect.

"We're giving them exactly what they asked for. No more, no less. I gave them dupes of everything you recorded the first three days of your surveillance. They're sending someone over this afternoon to pick up the ones you turned in last night. What they don't have is the Richard Alvarez brain," he said, nonchalantly tapping the side of his head with his forefinger.

"The rest of this stuff on China Doll is just supposition on my part, and I don't share suppositions with anybody, except maybe you. Gets you a bad rep." He wrinkled his nose as if he smelled something decaying in the room. "Besides, SFPD has resources. Let them draw their own conclusions from all of this. Like I did," he added with a wink.

"I'll try to play it the same way," I promised.

"Okay, I've got to get back to work, so here's the rest of the results," Richard said, changing the subject abruptly, as usual. "All the license plates you recorded during those four days have been accounted for. Take the rentals. Nothing there. Mr. and Mrs. Somebody or other vacationing from somewhere out of state, in for a week or two, blah, blah. Most of them parked their rentals, went sightseeing and then took the Red and White Fleet to Sausalito or Tiburon. The remainders are either locals who work in that area or out of town visitors but not out of state. Like this couple from Napa," he added pointing to a name on the list.

"Now remember, I'm only giving each person a cursory look. If everything seems normal on the surface, I leave it alone." He stressed the last part of his statement and then picked up the printout.

"Uh huh," I replied, nodding my head. "Unless they happen be as good looking as Grace Wong."

Richard went on as if I hadn't spoken. "For instance, here's a local from Oakland who was parked on that street all day and most of the night. Strange, so I checked him out. He wound up being a dentist who played hooky and took a day tour to Alcatraz. Then he gave himself a birthday party at a local bar that night. I don't think it's him, but on the other hand, if he managed to kill somebody while getting drunk with about sixty people watching, then he's too smart for me." He stopped his oration and spit his gum out in the wastepaper basket before continuing.

"The only other car that was within a two block radius that day, and was there the day before, as well..." Richard raised a forefinger in the air for emphasis. "Is Grace Wong's. I don't know what she's doing there unless she's giving longshoremen ballet lessons. Maybe that's what she's doing in PBS, too, ballet lessons." I could tell Richard was immensely pleased with himself. "This check was simple, Lee. They should all be as easy as this. Here you go."

He flung about ten sheets of paper onto my lap. All the information was printed in a painfully small font and I sighed. Richard believed in saving money, at least on paper products, so he used the smallest font possible. A couple of more years of straining my eyes like this, and I'd need a seeing-eye dog. I got up, ready to leave him to his work.

"By the way," he added with much less bravado, as he jabbed at the keyboard and made sections on the monitor disappear. "I got some news that might make you happy." He looked up at me with anxious eyes. "Nick got married a couple of weeks ago in Las Vegas."

I took in a sharp breath. How did I feel about that, I wondered instantly? Relieved. Simply relieved. Maybe an unhappy and embarrassing episode of my life might go away. I opened wide eyes at Richard, who was staring at me nervously.

"Have you been keeping tabs on him all this time?"

"It didn't take much. I just periodically checked out a few things. You know, driver's license, W2 forms, any legal papers he might have filed. That's how I found out about the nuptials. Easy as one-two-three."

"W2 forms? Why, that's illegal, Richard!" I said, more out of shock than chastisement.

"Hey, it's only illegal if you use the information for gain or profit. I don't do anything with it except, on rare occasions, let certain people know things they might be happier knowing. As far as I'm concerned, I'm happier knowing he's somebody else's problem and not my sister's."

Laughing, I leaned down and hugged Richard. "I have to admit I feel better knowing that chapter of my life is finally closed. Thanks a lot, Richard. I'm really grateful." I touched his hand with mine and looked solemnly into his lean, trusting face.

He flustered and swiveled his chair back to his computer screen. "Hey, what's a computer for?" he questioned, with a dismissive wave of his hand.

"Now, get going," my kid brother said. "I've got a lot of work to do. I take it Our Lady didn't say no on you following up on this murder thing?" he asked, as he reached for a small tower with attached cables and began hooking them up to his mainframe.

"No, she didn't say no," I uttered. I was glad the room was dark and he was concentrating on other things. I don't lie well and Richard knows me as few people do. I could never have deceived him if he had seen my face. I turned and walked across the room to the door.

"Grace Wong. What's up with this Grace Wong?" I asked aloud. I closed his door quietly and started back for my office, my mind whirling.

The woman parks her car, for no apparent reason, two days in a row near a warehouse where a man gets himself killed. There's no record of shopping, sightseeing, or dining for her on either day. She could, of course, be using cash but people rarely do these days. And why has she spent several nights a month — correction, several hours of several nights a month — in Princeton-by-the-Sea? For the past five months, she's been filling her gas tank there, too. What, if anything, does that mean? Maybe it was time to have a closer look at Grace Wong.

Chapter Nine
A Visit To The Widow

When I got back to my office, it was not quite two o'clock. I decided to return Yvette Wyler's call. I felt slightly guilty about the way I talked to Mom and thought a visit to her old high school chum might act as atonement. As I dialed, I crossed my fingers that the grieving widow wouldn't be home but luck wasn't with me. It seldom is. The housekeeper, Mrs. Malchesky, answered on the third ring and asked me to wait a moment while she went to fetch the lady of the house. As I sat with a silent phone in my hand, I hoped against hope the woman didn't feel like company. After all, she'd only lost her husband the day before yesterday. I certainly wouldn't want to talk to anybody so soon, especially the person who found his body.

Unfortunately, the housekeeper returned and said the recently widowed asked if it was convenient for me to drop by sometime today. I said a few silent curses and then one loud "yes." I was familiar with the house in Woodside and knew it was only a few minutes away from the office.

Might as well get it over with, I thought. I said I would be there in fifteen minutes.

I remembered the Mr. Everett phone call I promised to make, as well, and dialed the number after searching through my card index. I got lucky with him. He wasn't in and wasn't expected for the rest of the day. I left a message with his secretary that I had called, hung up, and felt the clear conscience of the not so young and not so innocent.

Lastly, I called Patti and asked her to relay the Wyler meeting to Lila when she came in. Might as well start mending fences as soon as possible. I grabbed my handbag and umbrella and ran out the door. After all, the sooner I got to Mrs. Wyler's, the sooner I could leave.

The Wyler Estate was a twelve-acre job directly off Woodside Avenue. Dubbed by the locals as "Flanders' Folly" years ago, the original owner, a wealthy robber baron from Ohio, had used several different architectural styles before the house was completed to his satisfaction. Captain Flanders moved his wife and seventeen children into the house and lived very happily there for over forty years. After the death of both parents within three months of one another, the surviving children sold it to Portor Wyler for a ridiculously low price just to get rid of it.

Aside from the seventy-five hundred square foot little starter-upper, there were the standard stables, tennis courts, indoor and outdoor pools, and of course, the grounds.

The house itself was a monstrous red, four-story brick job with dozens of gables, columns, chimneys and Corinthian arches that would have given Scarlett O'Hara nightmares.

Oleander bushes grew around the entire perimeter of the grounds, most over twenty feet high, in various flowering colors. I read once that oleander is poisonous and a woman was hung for giving a brewed version of it to her husband, who died a pretty painful death. Deer tend to leave it alone and people often plant a few in deer country for a spot of color in an otherwise gnawed off garden. The bush itself is pretty enough, but I think twelve acres of oleanders is a bit boring, even to keep Bambi at bay.

Once, when I was fourteen years old, I refused to go inside the house with my mother to one of Mrs. Wyler's "high teas," a ritual which gave the word 'tedious' new meaning. I decided to wait outside in the garden. Bored, I counted all of the oleanders I could find. I stopped at four hundred. When

Mrs. Wyler and Mom came out, after about an hour, looking for me, I'd turned to Mrs. Wyler and said, "*Dios mio*, get a rose bush or something, will you? Don't you have any imagination?"

Of course, I apologized like crazy afterward, but I knew I'd hurt her feelings and humiliated my mother. I grimaced when remembering the snotty kid I could be, any teenager can be. Maybe I wasn't a snotty kid anymore, but I couldn't warm up to Mrs. Wyler any better as an adult than I could as a child. I always suspected when no one was looking, she howled at the moon and chased cars for their hubcaps.

I shook my head at the shocking thoughts pinging through my brain about the recently widowed. I needed to get a handle on it. After all, I was an adult now.

As I pulled up to the ornate black, iron-gate standing sentinel in front of the infamous oleanders, a vision of Portor Wyler's unseeing eyes blurred the pastoral scene before me. Sitting in the idling car, I wondered how I could face the woman who might have lost her husband because of something I did or didn't do. I resisted the urge to turn and run, sucked it in, pressed a button on a little black box and gave my name. The gates opened wide. I passed through and down the graveled drive toward the house, wishing I'd had a splash of whiskey at lunch. Or, maybe, a shot or two.

Despite the rain, Yvette Wyler, dressed in a long sack-like black dress and holding a black umbrella, was standing in the middle of the circular drive next to the house. She gave her finest Queen Mother wave as my car pulled up to the house and halted. I, in turn, smiled my best Miss America smile and got out of the car. Mrs. Wyler embraced me awkwardly and guided me inside the house asking the standard questions about my health and state of mind. She smelled of Old Lavender, Listerine, and garlic, a charming combo. We passed our dripping umbrellas on to her housekeeper, Mrs. Malchesky, who'd been with her since before dirt.

"I asked Mrs. Malchesky to make some tea and sandwiches for us," she said as we walked into the smaller of the two main living rooms.

"*Oh, God,*" I thought, remembering tea in this room from my childhood but managed to remain calm. The room was ill lit and damp, even though a fire burned at one end inside a marble fireplace large enough for you to park an SUV in, should you run out of room in the driveway.

"Please sit down, Liana, dear," said the older woman, as she smiled and gestured to a velvet green horsehair sofa, stiff and lumpy with age. Her voice echoed in the large and sparsely furnished room that for all its supposed grandeur gave off a cold and impersonal air. I sat down and tried my best to get comfortable. Mrs. Wyler sat in a matching wing back chair directly opposite me.

A small tea table, laden with paraphernalia for afternoon tea, loitered between us. Heavily starched doilies seemed to be breeding everywhere. Stiff embroidery on the armrest and at the back of the settee stuck to all exposed parts of my skin.

"Don't bother yourself about us, Hilda, dear, I'll serve the tea this afternoon. You go ahead and pack for your trip," she said to the housekeeper, with a dismissive look. The woman gave a nod of her head and left the room. Mrs. Wyler began the ritual of serving afternoon tea, while chatting about her housekeeper's upcoming three-week tour of the Greek islands, something she hoped, herself, to do some day.

While this small dialogue was going on, I studied the woman's face, marveling once again she was only in her mid-fifties, the same age as my youthful and beautiful mother. I knew the loss of her husband contributed to her ghastly appearance, but in all honesty, she looked like death warmed over, no pun intended. Her thin brown hair, flecked with gray, was teased and coifed but still managed to droop. She wore little or no makeup, which made her yellowish eyes fade into her sallow complexion. The wrinkles on her face jumped out at me almost as much as her narrow, hooked nose. It was, however, the twitch in her right cheek I found unnerving. I found it hard not to stare or count the number of twitches per minute.

So I sat with a frozen smile on my face, a fragile teacup in my left hand, and a small plate of dreadful looking toast points covered with a brown spread that reeked of garlic and cloves in my right. As Mrs. Wyler chatted on, a frequently washed napkin threatened to slide off my lap. I could hear a distant grandfather clock ticking the painful minutes away.

I was also aware of the fire crackling at the other end of the room and wished we were closer to it. My legs were freezing, and I was sorry I hadn't worn slacks. I began to understand how the Man in the Iron Mask felt as he sat imprisoned, listening to his beard grow. I waited in agony for Mrs. Wyler to speak about the purpose of this Command Visit.

Finally, Mrs. Wyler, after taking a healthy bite out of a soggy, beige covered toast point, cleared her throat and said, "Liana, dear, I want to apologize for dragging you into this sordid affair. Little did I know when I begged your mother to send you out to help me that I might, in some way, be endangering your life."

"I don't think my life was ever en..." I began, trying to reassure her in a prim and proper manner, as befitted the occasion.

The older woman held up her hand to silence me and continued, "Please, dear, do let me say this. I don't know what was going on in my mind to send a child like you out to do something so base and contemptible as spying on my husband. I suppose, when a woman loves a man and is afraid he may no longer love her but another, younger woman, well, she can do foolish things. When I think of you standing out in the pouring rain, catching your death of cold, while my Portor was...." Mrs. Wyler stopped speaking, put down her cup of tea and brought her hand to her mouth. "I'm sorry, dear," she murmured.

I hastily set down the china plate of toast points and reached for her hand in sympathy. Unfortunately, the plate clattered on the sterling silver tray, with a sound that rang through the room like a dinner gong. She withdrew her hand from mine and touched her temple, the way you do when you feel a sudden headache coming on. I leaned back again, afraid to move.

"Please don't apologize, Mrs. Wyler," I answered, downing half the tepid tea in the cup in one gulp. "I'm just sorry that what happened...happened. You have my sincere condolences," I finished lamely.

What does this woman want of me? What am I doing here?

"I want you to allow me to pay for those new suede boots you ruined that night," she said, as if reading my thoughts.

Boots? She dragged me here for boots?

"Absolutely not. Considering all that's happened, I wouldn't dream of such a thing," I objected, with as much force as I could gather under the circumstances.

"I insist. I had a pair of my best shoes ruined the same night by the rain, and I know how heartbreaking losing a good pair of shoes can be. It was such a rainstorm! And out of the blue. Just a clap of thunder and a deluge." She clasped her breast in remembrance, something I'd only seen done in the movies.

"I've already asked your mother for the brand and size. She's such a wonderful woman, your mother, so good and kind. She's been a godsend in helping me with the funeral arrangements. The funeral is Saturday. You'll come, of course. You got them at Neiman Marcus, didn't you?" she asked, brightening up, as she reached for another wretched toast point. She munched enthusiastically as she continued, "I've already ordered a pair for you. They should be here in a week or two."

I had trouble keeping up with her thought processes but tried my best. "Of course, I'll be there. I don't know what to say about the boots, Mrs. Wyler, except you really don't have to do that!"

"Please." Mrs. Wyler held up the same hand again, but this time it contained the half-eaten toast point. "It's my way of saying thank you for trying to help."

"If it makes you feel better, then, of course, I accept. Thank you very much," I conceded.

"There! That's settled," she said, putting down her plate.

Seeing this as a sign of dismissal, I half rose, putting my teacup down on the tray between us. I looked down at the woman expecting to be allowed to go.

"I hope you weren't frightened by what happened that night and haven't had trouble sleeping or bad dreams. You are so young." Mrs. Wyler reached out a clammy hand and grasped my arm, almost throwing me off balance.

I chose to sit back down rather than fall. "Not at all, Mrs. Wyler. I'm fine, just fine," I answered, feeling about three years old and not liking it a bit. "I didn't even know something had happened until it was... too late. I didn't see or hear anything."

"Oh, dear. I was so hoping...praying...you had. That in his death throes, he managed to say something about his killer before he..." Mrs. Wyler began to sob. "The police seem so baffled. No one seems to know anything. We may never know who or why..." The woman broke off and blew her nose noisily into an already sodden handkerchief.

So that's why I was here!

My heart suddenly went out to the woman, she and her four hundred oleanders. I took a chance and reached for her hand again to squeeze it. This time she didn't pull back.

"I'm truly sorry. I wish I could help you, but I didn't see or hear anything."

"He never said anything right before he...passed over?"

"He was over by the time I got there. I mean..." I stammered and stopped talking, trying to find the right words. "I'm sorry, Mrs. Wyler, but by the time I found him, it was too late. He was gone. I would help you if I could, but I don't know anything. I'm so very sorry. I wish I could help you."

"That's all right, my dear. And I'm sorry if I've caused you any more distress," she said, blowing her nose again. She rose from the chair and straightened the creases out of her skirt. "Thank you so much for coming and be sure to give my best to your mother." Mrs. Wyler dismissed me with a small nod and, holding her head high, left the room.

I stood, picked up my handbag, and walked to the door as fast as I dared without breaking into a dead run. Once in my car, I careened down the driveway toward the imprisoning iron-gate. Fortunately, it was on an automatic eye and opened just in time, or it and I would have been one. I headed toward University Avenue and didn't actually breathe a sigh of relief until I got back to the office. Frankly, I was a mere shell of my former self.

I had several calls in my voicemail. One from the Palo Alto Police Station letting me know I could pick up my revolver at any time. Another, from Vets and Pets, instructing me the kitten was due in the following Wednesday to be altered. They included a small lecture on how good it is to fix kittens when they are between nine and twelve weeks old. I made a note on my calendar.

There won't be any more unwanted kittens in the world because of me, I vowed.

The third call was from Ronald Everett. He had returned mine and left a number in San Jose where he could be reached. I dialed the number and after going through several people was put on the line with him. He was polite but distant, and I was surprised at this change in behavior. When we initially met with him, he had seemed very eager to put an end to a problem jeopardizing his new and flourishing company. Overall, he gave me the impression of a warm and compassionate man. Now he was cold and withdrawn. The more we talked, the more suspicious I became.

After five minutes of my probing, Everett hesitated and then took a deep breath and paused. It was a pause I knew well. I figured he didn't want to pursue the matter because he now suspected or even knew who the culprit was. His behavior also indicated to me it wasn't an employee, valued or otherwise. An employee, no matter how loyal or long they are with a company, would elicit outrage and anger for their duplicity. Hang them by their toes or private parts would often be the cry.

But trusted friends, and especially family members, bring on a different reaction. The betrayal, hurt, and humiliation often make the victim feel emotionally impotent. Frequently they do nothing, hoping the problem will resolve itself or go away, and take that person with it.

"Mr. Everett, I think you want to drop this investigation because you have a suspicion as to who it is," I said.

"I don't suspect. I know," Mr. Everett uttered in a hoarse voice, after a moment's silence.

"Okay, you know. Now the next step is to think about how you want to handle it. It's not going to go away just because you now know. That's not how it happens."

"I've spoken with him. He's going to stop. He understands I'll prosecute if he doesn't." His voice had lowered and together with the hoarseness made him difficult to understand, "I have proof, irrefutable proof. He wouldn't dare continue."

"Mr. Everett, if you have proof, take it to your lawyer," I said. I didn't like the way the conversation was going and pressed on, "Let somebody else know what's going on. If you don't want to go to the police..."

"Certainly not! The scandal would kill my wife."

"I understand. Really, I do," I said. "Please remember, though, you're dealing with hundreds of thousands of dollars—"

"Try millions," he interjected.

"Exactly. Some people will do anything for that kind of money. Today someone caught pirating software at the level you've indicated is facing a jail sentence of six to ten years. Desperate people commit desperate acts. Protect yourself by giving someone else the information or the evidence."

"I don't know that I can do that."

"At least, think about it. Promise me that."

"Yes. Yes. I'll...I'll think about what you've said," he replied hurriedly, as if he couldn't wait to get off the phone. Then he let out a sigh so loud it sounded like water rushing through the phone. "Thank you, Miss Alvarez. You realize I cannot use the services of your company the way things are."

"Absolutely. I understand, and that's not the issue. You need to be careful, Mr. Everett, in whatever you decide to do," I added.

"I will. Thank you," he said again and hung up.

Listening to the dial tone, I tried to quell that awful feeling again in my solar plexus. I tried to convince myself he was the CEO and owner of a very large computer company.

He was savvy. He was smart. He was a "wheeler dealer" and could wipe up the floor with simpletons like me. He should be able to take care of himself.

I said that over and over to myself, but it didn't make me feel any better.

I hung up the phone and began reading the printout Richard had given me, more to occupy my mind than anything else. I was immersed in it within seconds. Yes, he was right about the cars. The only one unaccounted for was

Grace Wong's. That area was strictly for tourists or dockworkers. Not many other people had a reason to be there. I studied the printout of Grace's purchases of gasoline.

So nice of these businesses, I thought, *to give you this much information. Not only do they give you the date and the amount, they also give you the time of the purchase.*

Every one of Grace Wong's gas charges was made in the late evening, usually around midnight. I checked the calendar for dates going back several months and discovered another interesting fact. Her visits were always on a Thursday night at least once, if not twice, a month.

What was that all about?

I tried to reason this out. Grace Wong had to be performing on a Thursday night. The usual day off in the theatre was Monday. I grabbed a newspaper and checked the theatre section to confirm this. I was right. In addition, most performances ended around ten-thirty p.m. In order to be there shortly after midnight, in my judgment, Grace Wong must have ripped off her costume after curtain call and driven like a bat out of hell down to Princeton-by-the-Sea.

Well, tomorrow is Thursday, I mused, *and I'm going to have to visit this New England harbor on the Pacific.*

I finished the rest of the work on my desk determined to free up the following day. I left a series of voicemail and email messages for Lila and my co-workers explaining I was taking a PTO day, Personal Time Off, and I would return to work and respond to all messages on Friday. Leaving the office shortly before four-thirty, I stopped off at PAPD, where I signed several forms, retrieved my gun and managed to avoid Frank.

When I got home, I took the stairs two at a time in my excitement. Tossing my handbag on the sofa, I picked up the phone before even taking my shoes off. I called Tío with the new name for the kitten. The newly named was in his usual position on the sofa, dead to the world. He didn't even stir as I threw myself next to him.

"Tio," I said, eagerly after my uncle answered the phone. "I've got the name for the little guy. It's..."

"*Un momento, mi Sobrina*," he interrupted. "Let me call you back after my *gordas* are out of the oven. I don't want to have the *queso* to burn."

Tio hung up the phone before I could tell him that "to have the cheese to burn" was not grammatically correct. He liked to have us correct his English when called upon, and we all obliged him when necessary. However, that was the least of it. While I didn't exactly expect to hear applause because I'd finally arrived at a name for the little guy, I did expect a better reaction than what I got. I put down the receiver and leaned over the sleeping kitten, knowing I should leave him alone. He needed his sleep and would probably be conked out for hours. I watched him for a moment, as he breathed in and out. The little guy twitched his whiskers and little white paws, and I could no longer resist. I picked up his limp body, and he dangled from my hand like overdone spaghetti.

"Well, are you interested in knowing your new name, Rum Tum Tugger?" I asked and the kitten moved slightly and opened his eyes part way. "Aha! You're awake. So, what do you want to be called? Rum or Tum or Tugger?" I faced his little body toward me and cupped his rump with my other hand. His head tilted to one side. Then he gave a big yawn and closed his eyes again.

"Oh, this is great," I said and returned him to the couch where he promptly fell back to sleep. "Hassling a defenseless kitten. I should be ashamed." I went into the bathroom and drew a bath, putting in some salts for my aching feet. Dancers' feet always ache even if they don't dance for a living.

Tio returned my call before the tub filled up, and I told him the kitten's name. It was a good thing I was prepared for the letdown.

"This is a name? What kind of a name is this?"

"I told you, Tío. It comes from *Old Possum's Book of Practical Cats*. It's what cats call themselves."

"I have known a lot of *gatos en mi vida*. Not one has called himself Rummytummy, *mi Sobrina*."

"It's not Rummytummy," I replied, with exasperation. "It's Rum Tum Tugger. We can call him Rum or Tum or Rum Tum or Tugger."

"Maybe we should call him Thomas," Tío laughed and then tried to appease me when he sensed hurt feelings on the other end of the line. "I think if you want to call him Tummy you should do so. It's a fine name."

I controlled my voice and tried to remain calm. "Not Tummy. Tugger. Tugger."

"Tugger," Tío repeated.

The kitten brought his ears to an alert position and raised his head from the sofa focusing sleepy eyes on me. He gave out one of his silent meows.

"Exactly," I smiled, looking back at the kitten that looked at me contemplatively, before closing his eyes again. "His name is Tugger because he tugs at your heartstrings."

"I think I am what you call nauseous, *mi sobrina*," Tío said, with no small amount of mirth in his voice.

"Well, I still like the name, so Rum Tum Tugger it is. Good night, Tío. I'll talk to you tomorrow. Thanks for taking such good care of Tugger."

Chapter Ten
A Trip To Princeton-by-the-Sea

The next morning I got up before five o'clock. I was much too excited to sleep any later. I did my morning barre and exercises, examined the body from all angles in the full-length mirror, and decided I could have bacon for breakfast. I had my shower, while Tugger followed me around watching my every move. I picked him up and put him in the waist of my tied robe, something that had become a morning ritual for both of us. Every day he felt a little heavier, and I was delighted. After feeding both of us, and not sharing my bacon with Tugger no matter what his tricks, I dressed in dark jeans and a gray pullover sweater I'd borrowed from Richard once and forgot to return. Otherwise, I wouldn't have had something non-descript and non-attention getting. That's the downside of being 'colorful.'

By seven o'clock, I was ready to go. I had originally hoped to beat the traffic by leaving at what I thought was an early hour. That, however, was the naiveté of a person who lives several blocks from where she works and has no idea how it really goes in the Bay Area nowadays. I've since found out the fume-infested, bumper-to-bumper commute begins around six in the morning until after ten a.m. and then starts again at three in the afternoon until well past seven p.m. I guess if you really want a trouble free drive, you need to leave at three in the morning. Yes, it is a small window of opportunity, but your commute should be heaven. In any event, I joined the masses on Freeway 280, went west over the mountainous part of Route 92, and headed north on Highway One.

By the time I reached Princeton-by-the-Sea, it was nearly nine o'clock, and I was a little cranky and stiff. I'm not used to that type of aggressive driving. I needed a stretch and some coffee. Actually, I needed some Valium, but coffee was more accessible. I turned the car into the nearby parking lot of a seaside diner, all silver chrome and kitschy, that sat on the ocean side of the highway. It looked as if it had been stolen off the back lot of *"The Diner."* I half expected to see Sylvester Stallone, long before his buffed up days, bop out the door carrying one of those plastic pink flamingos the era seems to be unable to live down.

The sun started coming up about an hour earlier, but the night chill still had its grip on the day. Shivering, I walked across the parking lot toward the metallic diner gleaming in the newly risen sun. I turned around and looked back at the buildings across the highway. Most were plain houses without much style, but there was the occasional business residing in a one-story, inexpensive stucco job. I looked again at the diner, with the California coastline in the background. Princeton-by-the-Sea, or what there was of it, couldn't seem to decide if it wanted to be a working town or a tourist town. Regardless, compared to Santa Cruz, Monterey, Carmel, or even Half Moon Bay, it was tiny and unpretentious.

I might have made a mistake in coming over here. What could possibly be going on in this place? With a deep sigh, I saw a long, boring day ahead of me in a town of less than four hundred people.

After a cup of surprisingly good coffee and a killer view of the surf, I decided to start at one of the local addresses I had for Grace Wong. I went back to the car, opened the glove compartment, and pulled out a map of the area. I chose to walk and leave the car where it was, thinking the gas station might be somewhere nearby. The address wasn't given on the receipts, but I figured it shouldn't be too hard to find a Ben's Gas around here. After asking a passing local who looked like he was old enough to be one of the survivors of the Titanic, I discovered it was two or three blocks off the highway, inside the older section of town. I knew the walk would do me good, so I set out to find it.

I discovered most of the streets are named for famous universities, with Ben's Gas Station and Auto Repair located on Yale Avenue. It wound up being amidst a plethora of stored fishing boats, all aged and peeling, and stacks of ancient crab pots in a part of town tourists probably never visit. The repair part of the station had six cars, in various stages of decay, scattered here and there. They contributed nicely to the run-down look of the area. The gas pumps were unmanned, but I looked around and saw a pair of booted feet under an older, brown Toyota Celica. I went over and squatted down near the boots.

"Good morning!" I yelled to the bottom of the car in between the banging sounds coming from the underside.

"That you, Sue?" answered a young, male voice somewhere near the exhaust.

"No, it's not Sue. My name's Lee, and I wanted to ask you something. You got a minute?"

A young man of about eighteen or nineteen pushed himself out from under the car. He wore a blue uniform covered with grease, and in his dirty right hand, he clutched a wrench. The name "Ed" was embroidered in red on the left side of his chest. He glared at me first and then broke out into a friendly smile.

"Wish I did, miss, but I gotta get this car ready for Sue. She's gonna be back any minute for it."

"Sure, Ed, I understand, but I was just wondering if you've ever seen this woman." I showed him a printout picture of Grace Wong. It was amazing how clear a picture a computer can produce these days. It almost looked like a studio portrait.

"Oh, Jesus. What are you? A private detective?" He threw the wrench into a nearby toolbox and picked out another tool, ready to go back under the chassis.

I had been unprepared for this kind of reaction and forced a laugh, as I frantically searched my mind for an answer. "Of course not. Do I look like a detective?" I continued before he could answer, "I'm a dancer just like her. Her name is Grace Wong, and she dances with the San Francisco Ballet Company."

"So?" he started to go under the car, and I grabbed his shoulder.

"So, I just want to meet her. Maybe she could give me some tips. She's such a wonderful dancer. Have you ever seen her dance?" I gushed.

"Are you puttin' me on?" he answered pulling his shoulder free. "I don't have time for this."

I reached into the pocket of my jeans and pulled out a fifty-dollar bill. This, I had been prepared for. "I just want to know a little about her. Maybe meet her. She might even help get me an audition. Will you talk to me? That is, if you know anything." I thrust the bill in his face. His eyes crossed as he looked at it. He licked his lips, and I knew I had him.

He reached out with his grease-covered left hand, grabbed the bill and stuffed it into his pocket. He threw down the tool and sat up leaning against the door of the car. "Five minutes, that's all I got. And I don't know her really well, if that's what you're looking for. She seems like a nice enough girl, though, the times I seen her."

I couldn't believe my good fortune. He actually knew Grace and seemed to like her. "Just tell me anything. Anything you know."

Ed went on, obviously a little embarrassed, "I don't always work days except when Ben needs the extra help. I usually do the closing. Gotta have a strong man here for that, you know." He puffed himself up slightly with self-importance. "After eight p.m., you gotta be prepared for anything. Emergencies, robberies, weirdoes coming in wanting Lord knows what, you know?"

I nodded and made a sound, as if I really knew what it was like.

He continued, "So when she starts coming in every now and then, especially right before closing, it's something a man notices." He waggled his eyebrows at me.

"Well, what's she like?" I asked, and Ed gaped at me. "I mean, did she seem friendly? Standoffish? In a hurry? Have a lot of time on her hands? I only ask because I want to know how to approach her," I offered, still pushing the idea I only wanted to meet her for career purposes.

Ed went into some kind of deep thinking for a moment and pursed his lips. "Friendly enough, but usually in a fair hurry. Once she got gas all over her shoes. It's self-service here, you know, but I brought her a couple of wet towels to wipe them off. She was real grateful."

"Did she ever have anybody with her, or did she always come by herself?"

Ed stared at me as if I had lost my mind, but looked like he remembered the fifty dollars and went into his deep thinking routine again. "Well, once in awhile she's got her family with her, if that's what you mean. A bunch of Asians huddled in the back seat of that little car. Oh, yeah, and once she came in a beat-up pickup truck with some big oriental guy driving. She was just sitting there. Her car broke down, I think, needed a new fan belt. We always keep stuff like that on hand. I sold him one, and they went on their way. She waved at me, though. She's a nice girl. If she can, I'll bet you she gets you an audition," he added. Apparently, he believed my idiotic story. I was amazed.

He went on, "She gave me a real nice tip when I helped her clean off her shoes, but I think she's like that. Kinda sweet, you know?"

"I'm so glad. When did they come in for the fan belt? The time you said they were in the pickup truck. Do you remember?"

"I don't know, maybe a couple of weeks ago. No, more like a month. I remember now because it was Christmas Eve. I wished her a Merry Christmas. That's what made her wave to me. I don't think she knew I saw her until then. Pretty girl. Hard to miss." He waggled his eyebrows again.

I wasn't sure if I liked being one of the boys where Grace Wong was concerned, but let it pass. "When she came in by herself most of those times, did she ever say where she was coming from or going to? I mean, I might want to meet her at one of those other places rather than here."

Ed nodded, as to the wisdom of that idea, but then shook his head. "Naw, sorry, she never did. I didn't ask, either. I gotta get back to work." He glanced at the clock at the top of the garage door, picked up the previously discarded tool, and rolled himself back under the car.

"Well, thanks," I shouted to his disappearing body.

"Sure thing, and hey, good luck," he added.

I stood up to leave and had another thought. "Hey, Ed, this pickup truck. What color was it?"

"Jesus, lady," he growled in annoyance. Obviously my fifty bucks was up. "White, maybe. Some real light color, like that, but I can't say for sure. It was nighttime. It looked white to me."

I turned away and passed a woman of about forty who would be forever "cute." She was headed for either Ed or the Toyota. She was probably Sue. She looked like a Sue, I decided. All Sues were cute.

I returned to the car and sat in the front seat thinking. By now it was around ten-thirty, and the sun was taking some of the chill off the day. I took the cellphone from under the front seat, and placed a call to Richard. He didn't answer, which didn't mean he wasn't there; it only meant he didn't answer. I left a voice mail message for him to call me as soon as he could. Maybe he had some more information. I left the cell phone on and tucked it into my jeans pocket. I also decided to carry the camcorder, plus another eight-hour battery, and put those into the other pocket. This way I wouldn't have to jot down notes with a pad and pencil. Between the camera, phone, car keys and cash, it was a tight fit, especially as they were pretty tight to begin with. No more bacon for me, I decided, if I was going to be carrying half my purse in my pockets.

I had the rest of the day to explore Princeton-by-the-Sea. I figured I might as well find the place where Grace got the parking ticket. This address was easy. According to the map, it was near the harbor. Grace had been parked in front of a fire hydrant on Capistrano Street at twelve thirty-seven a.m. Even though it was late at night, some enterprising cop had given her a ticket. I guess you never know when a fire might break out.

Address in hand, I strolled back in the direction of the marina. The setting is unique. Princeton-by-the-Sea sits on the north end of a perfectly shaped crescent bay, appropriately named Half Moon Bay. At this end of the curve, a high cliff rises and drops off abruptly into deeper water. At one time, the navy maintained a tracking station on the apex of the cliff, still protected by chain fences. Huge satellite dishes tilt up to the sky beckoning to no one and nothing, save flocks of brown pelicans flying overhead. Below the cliff, an artificial breakwater made out of large rocks creates an inner harbor. There is only one entrance from the harbor to the sea, and it's on the smallish side. I assumed this is because the waters inside the harbor are too shallow to support the larger craft, so they are not invited in.

The marina itself is fairly large and looks to be the hub of the town. The surrounding sidewalk and road go up on a slight incline around the marina, about ten or fifteen feet above sea level at the highest point. Steps lead down periodically to the pier and the docks. The pier is wide, sturdy looking and well maintained. That day the surf was calm and shimmered under the sun's rays, while trim boats slowly bobbed up and down like some giant kid's plastic toys. When there was no wind, it was almost balmy, and the air smelled salty and clean. All in all, the effect was quite picturesque.

I spotted the hydrant at the end of a squared parking lot near the harbor portion of the marina.

That must be where Grace parked her ticketed car.

I looked around for a possible restaurant or bar Grace might have gone to at that hour and saw no likely candidate. Like most small towns, they probably pull in the sidewalks around eight or nine o'clock at night, possibly ten at the latest. I made a mental note to check that out.

Still, it's a pretty safe bet. Even in Palo Alto, it's a rare restaurant or bar that's open past midnight.

That brought me back to the marina and its inhabitants. I became aware of the fact there were perhaps seventy-five or eighty boats of varying types moored in numbered slips off the main pier. Several dozen larger boats were anchored outside in the deeper waters of the ocean.

Speaking of deep, I'm in it if Grace was doing something on one of those boats. If that's the case, I'll have a hell of a time finding out which one it is, although I'll bet Richard can.

My spirits picked up a little, and I made another mental note to ask him, if I didn't find anything out on my own. With all the mental notes wandering around inside my mind, I decided to take advantage of modern science and store them on the camcorder. After all, that's what it's for.

After I took care of that, I noticed an abandoned building at the other side of the marina, on a portion that was at zero sea level. Looking sad and forlorn, the building was actually half on land and half over the water. The glass of the windows and doors was covered with soap in large, swirling patterns. This was a practice some people used with closed buildings that always intrigued me.

What exactly are they trying to hide behind all that Ivory soap? Curiosity killed the cat — no offence, Tugger — and all soaping up does is make me want to break down the doors to see what's hidden behind the swirls.

I hurried down the wooden steps toward it trying to figure out what kind of a business it was in its heyday. As I closed in, the sign over one of the doors, faded and weatherworn, was finally readable. "Dew-Drop-Inn Restaurant and Bar" it stated. Not an original name, I admitted, but one with a certain, homey appeal.

"Must have been a gorgeous view while you were eating," I remarked aloud, as I strode nearer to the now defunct restaurant. "I wonder why it closed."

On the other side of the building was another paved parking lot, which served the marina, as well as the ex-restaurant patrons. There were no cars parked in it at the time. The pier off the lot appeared to be nearly deserted with the exception of a couple of men, probably fishermen, busy doing what fisherman do with their boats.

I climbed the five wooden steps at the front of the restaurant for a closer inspection. It looked like it had been built decades ago and must have been kept up until fairly recently. In some places, peeling white paint exposed bare wood and a few of the glass panes were broken. I glanced around, saw no one, and attempted to turn a door handle. Surprise, surprise, it was locked.

I trotted along a narrow walkway under an overhang, toward the side of the building and had to jump over several folding metal chairs left out in the elements and rusting nicely. I continued to the back end of the restaurant and onto a deck with a lovely view of the marina and the sea beyond. The deck joined the public pier but was separated by three-foot high pilings roped together. Several battered buckets sat near the restaurant wall, for what purpose I couldn't fathom, and were filled with water, probably from the recent rains. Leaning against a bare flagpole was a shade umbrella, broken and rusty, with the tattered remnants of red fabric flapping in the breeze.

"Wow, this looks pretty dismal. Why does this just sit here unused like this? This is a prime location."

I crossed to the back entrance consisting of two glass doors, soaped up with a vengeance. Obviously, this was where patrons would have come out to the deck from inside the restaurant. The deck was over one hundred feet long and nearly fifty feet wide, if I calculated right, so it could accommodate a pretty large crowd. An outdoor bar, disintegrating right before my eyes, was near the far end. I tried the back doors, and they, too, were locked. I leaned in, put my hand over my eyes to cut the glare of the sun and tried to peer in between soapy swirls. As I pressed my nose against the glass, I caught the smell. I pulled back, somewhat shocked, and then began sniffing at the crack of the door. As I bent down closer to the door jam, the smell was stronger. Urine.

Odd, I've been smelling that a lot lately.

Maybe vagrants had broken in and were using it periodically, but upon closer inspection, nothing actually looked broken into. The more I studied it, the more it looked as if someone had deliberately broken one or two of the windows to make the place look abandoned. I inspected the windows more carefully now and found a humdinger of an alarm system, with wiring strategically placed out of sight.

Before I got carried away, I tried to convince myself the system could have been left over from when the restaurant was open, except the wiring looked very new and well kept up. Naturally, the outside would take more of a battering from the elements than the inside, but still, I told myself, this doesn't smell right, no pun intended. How long had this restaurant been closed, anyway? I was pondering, as my phone rang. It was Richard.

There was nothing new to add to the report he gave me yesterday, he said, in an impatient tone, as brothers are wont to do when you push them too hard. Regardless, I told him the name and address of the Dew-Drop-Inn and asked him to find out anything he could. In particular, were they still paying any bills for any type of security system? Richard tried to beg off, telling me of his tight schedule, but I insisted. He finally relented and said he'd get back to me as soon as he could. I said to make it fifteen minutes or less, and as we hung up, he was swearing. Brothers.

I sat down on the deck with my back against the doors and faced the water. I pulled my knees up to my chest and rested my head against them. It was peaceful and I had gotten very little sleep. Closing my eyes, I breathed in the briny air. I listened to the cry of seagulls overhead and the soft lapping of the waves on the pilings beneath me. When I lifted my head and opened my eyes a few minutes later, one of the men from the closest slip across the water was staring at me. He was a small Asian dressed incongruously in dress slacks, black loafers and a button down blue shirt. He looked away when I caught his eye and continued to scrub down a small dinghy. I leaned my head back down again and must have drifted off because I was startled when my cellphone rang some twenty minutes later.

It was Richard, and he was in a hurry. "All hell is breaking loose here, let me tell you," and he proceeded to do so. "Our Lady is demanding all the pertinent data for the past ten years on two companies proposing a merger. However, each one thinks the other is up to no good," Richard explained. "And the CFO of both companies called today to have the other company investigated for any illegal activities before they'll go through with the merger. Before we can take this on and get caught in the middle, Lila says we have to know what each one is really up to, not what they're telling us, 'cause they could just be using us as an excuse to kill the other guy off. And if that's what it's about, we won't touch the job with a ten-foot pole, no matter how much money they're offering. Talk about doing some fast research," Richard finished with exasperation.

"Richard, stop whining, and tell me if you've found out anything for me," I said with annoyance.

"Whining?" he replied, shocked at the accusation. "I never whine. I am explaining why I'm going to be on caffeine and rock music for the next three days. Our Lady has told me to put everything else aside. Everything. And that is why, sister mine, this is my last phone call to you today if you want to see me at dinner tonight."

"Oh, Richard. I am sorry," I said, laughing. "You're being wonderful, and I couldn't possibly do anything in this world without you and your computer. Thank you, thank you, and thank you." Sensing I had somewhat appeased him, I got back to business. "Now what do you know about the Dew-Drop-Inn in the illustrious town of Princeton-by-the-Sea?"

"Not much," he answered, somewhat mollified. "The restaurant was owned by the same family, Cardozo is the name, for twenty years. Got bought out six years ago by some organization I haven't been able to run a check on called P period Y period. And don't ask me to run a check, 'cause I don't have the time," he added testily. I didn't open my mouth.

Richard went on, "Anyway, five years ago the new owners filed bankruptcy and closed. The end. Oh, yes. P period Y period pays for a monthly alarm system, and it's a pretty deluxe package. It's with Bay Area Alarms, and it's a lot more than the average person, such as me, would carry. Same deal as the warehouse, if that means anything. Does that help?"

"That helps, Richard."

"I got to go now, Lee. Andy just came in and is standing over my shoulder saying Lila is breathing fire and wanting to know where you are. We could use all the hands we can get today. Do I know where you are?"

"You do not," I answered and hung up.

Chapter Eleven
Elvis Has Left The Building

I leaned back against the double doors again and looked at my watch. It was nearly eleven-thirty, and I was famished. Cramming the phone in my jeans, I decided to return to the diner. If the food was half as good as the coffee, I'd be happy.

Crossing the threshold, I felt once again I had stepped back in time. Earlier that morning, I had vaguely noticed all the red vinyl and shiny chrome. Now Elvis Presley's "Blue Suede Shoes" blared over miniature jukeboxes at each booth, as well as strategically placed ones on the shiny, red countertop. I gazed at the panoramic view of the sparkling, sun-drenched ocean through the long row of windows at the rear of the diner. It looked as if you could reach right out and touch forever.

This was a "fun" diner, I realized, and that's why I returned. Heading for the counter, I noted business was brisk for just one waitress and a short order cook. I sat down on a stool that had the least amount of cracked red vinyl and picked up the menu.

"No use you looking at that, honey," said the large, gregarious waitress costumed in a Pepto-Bismol pink uniform, as she meandered over to me. Above her abundant right breast was a pocket holding a starched green and white embroidered hanky that flopped out in every direction. Dyed carrot red hair, somewhat contained by a beaded, jet-black hairnet, was topped with a matching pink cap. She added the final blast of ambiance to the place. She was perfect.

"Half of it we don't have," the woman continued from behind the counter. "I don't know why we keep those around," she gestured to the menu and then took it out of my hands. "It's much faster if I tell you." She leaned a calloused elbow, which was connected to a flabby upper arm, onto the counter and began her recitation.

"The meatloaf with gravy and cranberry-apple pie are the stars today. Other than that, it's sandwiches. They're okay but not great. The best is the turkey. Let me recommend the meatloaf. Nobody makes it better than Hank. And the mashed potatoes are good, too." She leaned in and dropped her voice, "Stay away from the vegetables. Hank likes to cook them six to seven hours beforehand, so they're pretty awful." Her voice went back to its normal volume. "We don't do fish. Hank doesn't like fish. You want fish, go over to Barbara's Fish Trap. She'll do ya." She smiled at me, and her whole face lit up. Her green-grey eyes twinkled when she spoke, and her face was unlined and youthful. I liked her instantly, despite the nauseatingly pink uniform.

"Whatever you say..." I leaned closer to the name embroidered on the pocket right below her maverick hanky. "...Maggie." I smiled back at her. I watched her write and throw my order onto a Lazy Susan set up half in and half out of the kitchen, in the opening of a pass through. Instantly, a meaty, red hand spun the contraption around, reached up and snatched the paper.

With nothing better to do, I studied my surroundings. I noticed everyone was eating the meatloaf and potatoes or the pie. I also noticed people got up and helped themselves to cups of coffee, utensils or whatever else they needed. It was a real family-style restaurant.

No wonder one waitress can handle such a crowd.

Two minutes later a steaming plate loaded down with food was set before me. I dug in, and it was delicious. Fat and grease will do it every time. While I was eating, I looked into the pass through and saw what had been connected to the meaty hand. A middle-aged, gum-chewing man, tattooed on nearly every part of his body except his nose, was busily slicing portions from several meatloaves and pouring gravy onto plates. He had the ruddy complexion usually associated with living on the sea or being in front of a stove all your life. This was Hank; I was sure.

"You was in here this morning, weren't you, honey?" Maggie beamed at me as she filled the sugar bowls on the counter and took cash from customers. "You visiting with us for awhile or just passing through?"

I took a sip of water, as I gave myself a moment to think and looked back at Maggie. "Well, I'm actually looking for someone. A friend of mine."

"Really?" She counted out some singles and change to a family of five anxious to pay the bill and leave. When they exited, she came over and stood across the counter from me. "Everybody's in such a rush these days," she commented on the departing family. "What's your friend's name?"

"Grace Wong. Here, I have her picture." I reached inside my pocket and drew out the photocopy, as I continued with the latest lie that had just come into my head. "You see, she was my neighbor, but she moved away last week. The day before she moved, her cat disappeared. Last night it came back, and I want to let her know I've got the cat in my apartment. She told me she was moving here to Princeton-by-the-Sea, but didn't tell me where or leave a phone number." I made a face and raised my shoulders as if to say, 'If only we had known.' I felt the story was much more believable than the one I fed Ed. I was getting better at this.

"Oh, what a shame. I like cats. Got three of them, myself," Maggie said shaking her head and taking the picture.

"Oh, what a sweet looking girl. Chinese isn't she? Such a friendly, sweet face. I'll bet her mother's proud of her. You can tell she's a good girl."

Mesmerized by the appraisal, I studied the picture Maggie set down on the counter. Grace Wong was a sweet looking girl, I observed, once you got past all the sexiness of her.

"I can tell a lot by looking in people's eyes you know," Maggie continued as she took a couple of dirty plates off the counter and threw them into black plastic bins. "Like yours. You're a nice girl, too. Just like her." She gestured with a nod in the direction of the picture, which lay on the counter between us.

"I got six kids, four of them girls. Five of my kids, good as the day is long. Sweet-natured, good to their husbands, wives, kids, me, Hank, everybody in the world. But my Darlene, I knew when I took her home from the hospital she was never going to do anybody any good in the world and she hasn't." The people nearby stopped whatever they were doing and listened intently to Maggie's assessment of her sadly lacking child.

She came over and leaned into my face. "I saw it in her eyes. The day I took her home from the hospital. It didn't matter what Hank and me did. We tried everything with her. Ran off when she was sixteen after taking all the cash from the register and my good opal earrings. Haven't heard from her since."

Maggie sighed deeply, and I felt as if everyone nearby was torn between going back to eating lunch or applauding. It occurred to me this might not be going quite the way I had intended. I tried to bring Maggie back to the subject of Grace Wong. "Well, that is too bad. I'm sure you'll hear from her someday but..."

"Good God, I hope not." Maggie interrupted and raised her eyes to heaven.

"But my friend, Grace Wong. Have you seen her?" I insisted.

Maggie wiped down the counter as old customers left and new ones came in. "No but it's odd you should show me a picture of a Chinese girl." I held my breath, unsure if Maggie might not be starting on another long, loud and nonsequitur story. Not that they weren't interesting, but I wanted to get out of this diner sometime before I applied for Social Security.

"We don't have a lot of Asian people around here," she said finally. "That's too bad because I love the food. Hank's style of cooking leaves a lot to be desired. I mean, he does a couple of things okay, but I'd love to have a good cook back there." She gestured over her shoulder to the kitchen with her thumb.

Oh, no, she's off on a tangent again.

"Anyway, it can't be your friend I've been hearing if she just moved here last week. But sometimes..." Maggie leaned in again and said in a stage whisper, "...in the middle of the night, I hear things. Our apartment's right upstairs. I'm a light sleeper. Hank's not. But I can hear a traffic light change color. Just a minute, honey," she interrupted herself, as she heard a small bell ringing in the kitchen. Maggie went to the pass through and got four more steaming plates of meatloaf and potatoes and brought them to a table in the rear. Her audience, meanwhile, once again resumed their eating or conversations. The Asian man I had seen earlier at the marina got up from one of the tables he'd been eating at alone and left the diner.

Maggie returned. "Anyway, Hank says I'm losing it, but I swear every now and then, in the middle of the night, I hear people walking underneath our window speaking Chinese or Vietnamese or one of those. I keep waiting to see a new Asian family living here, but I don't. It seems they're just passing through. Now, isn't that strange?" she asked the world at large.

"You're strange, Maggie," said an old man sitting at the counter nearby who was hunched over his plate and shoveling food in his mouth. "Didn't you see aliens once?" He challenged with his mouth full. He had a worn out plaid cap on his head that went up and down on his forehead as he chewed.

"Shut up, Mel," Maggie replied amiably. She looked down at my empty plate and beamed. "Glad you liked the meatloaf."

"Nobody likes the damn meatloaf or anything else here. There's no other place to eat something around here that ain't fish," complained Mel, shoveling in another mouthful of potatoes.

"Are you still carrying on about the Dew-Drop-Inn closing down? Mel, that was five years ago," Maggie said, and rolled her eyes toward me.

Well, in for a dime, in for a dollar, and the subject had been broached. "Are you talking about the closed restaurant on the harbor?"

"We are," Mel spat out. His mouth being full, bits of meatloaf landed on the counter. It was enough to turn you into a vegetarian. "Best damn food for miles around, too," he added belligerently, looking at Maggie who was filling salt and pepper shakers and shaking her head.

"Well, then why did it close?" I asked. "Bad management?"

Maggie cut in before Mel could answer, so he went back to chowing down. "We don't know why. They did a lot of business and had good, honest food, too. Better than ours," she added, lowering her voice again and looking in her husband's direction.

"At better prices, too," interjected Mel in a hostile tone of voice.

Maggie went on as if she had not been interrupted. "The Cardozos owned it for years. Nice people. Portuguese, you know. They sold out at a good price, I'm told, and then wham! It goes bankrupt and closes down in less than a year." Maggie shrugged her shoulders. "It's okay with Hank and me, though. We got the only other place in town with this kind of home cooking." She beamed another smile in my direction. Mel grunted.

"Thanks for the food, Maggie, and I've enjoyed talking to you," I said. I reached inside my pocket and tried to pull out my wallet. I had to take everything out, however, and Maggie noticed the camcorder as I placed it on the counter. She reached over and picked it up before I could stop her.

"Oh, what's this cute little thing?"

"Oh, nothing much," I said casually, as I seized it back. "Just a kind of a tape recorder."

"That little bitty thing? My goodness!" she exclaimed, shaking her head at the wonder of technological advancement. I took money out of my wallet, added a generous tip to the bill, handed it to Maggie and walked to the exit.

"Thanks, honey," she shouted as I was leaving. "I hope you find your friend. What was her name? Oh, yeah. Grace Wong. I'll keep my eyes peeled for her."

Sighing, I told myself it was just a matter of time before the whole town knew about my search for Grace Wong to return a non-existent, roving cat. *What a lousy detective I am.*

A glance at my watch told me it was time to get a move on and accomplish something, anything with the rest of the day.

The sun was shining brightly, but there was a cold, salty breeze in the air when you were in the shade. I shivered and wondered what the hell to do next. I really wanted to know more about that closed restaurant. Richard, the oracle from which all things flowed, was too busy to help me.

I'll have to do this the old fashioned way. I'll have to go out and search manually — or was that womanly — by myself. How gauche.

After several quick calls, I found that the county records of this small town were kept in the San Mateo County Library. It was now twelve-forty p.m. I could be there in about twenty minutes, spend the afternoon in the library and/or the hall of records, and be home by around five-thirty. Figuring that Tío was probably still with the little guy...no, Tugger...I corrected myself, I phoned my apartment.

I knew Tío would never pick up my phone, letting it roll over to the answering machine. Nevertheless, you could hear whoever was calling loud and clear when they began to leave a message. If Tío was there, I could probably persuade him to pick-up. He did so and after some confusion regarding how to turn off the machine, I informed him I would be home around five-thirty to help with any last minute things for the family fiesta. After several minutes of hearing about Tugger's latest antics, we hung up. Tío never once asked where I was or pried in any way. Another thing I loved about him.

I drove back over Highway 92, a beautiful winding drive over the mountains, and toward San Mateo. Years ago, in my youth, friends and I would often go to Half Moon Bay to swim at one of the beaches, if it was warm enough. If not, we would stroll the shore collecting shells and driftwood. It was a great life for a kid, I realized, and I had a lot of treasured memories of this area. It was funny how I had missed out on the little hamlet of a seaport all these years.

I drove to the downtown district of San Mateo and on to the county library. After a couple of starts and stops, I finally found the microfilmed records of the Princeton-by-the-Sea Bulletin, a newspaper put out twice a month and comprised mostly of ads. Going through back copies of the paper, I was sure such an event as the sale of a successful, family owned restaurant would be mentioned in one of the editions. As I searched, I learned many things about the town, such as the slow death of the fishing industry, in particular, the salmon industry. Nearly another hour went by before I found what I was looking for, a small article in the Easter edition of the paper about six years ago. It mentioned the Cardozos received several lucrative offers from the same company and decided to sell. No mention of the buyer, which was a little odd.

Replacing the microfilms, I thought aloud. "P period Y period, that's what Richard said. Where have I heard of that before?" From across the room a little girl, not much more than eleven, angrily shushed me and continued reading a Harry Potter book. I shut up and silently racked my brain. The answer was somewhere in the past, but I just couldn't get at it.

Oh, well, maybe I need a stretch.

I rose from the chair. I went outside into the daylight. The sun, as it does in the winter, had already crested and was starting its downward cycle even though it was not quite three o'clock. I walked the two blocks to City Hall and asked a nasal man, who had decided long ago he was much too good for this job, how I could find the sale records of the Dew-Drop-Inn in Princeton-by-the-Sea. He was not very helpful, and it was only after I stood in front of his desk and loudly demanded to see his supervisor that he showed me where these records might be kept. These were not on microfilm, however, and I physically pored over dozens of papers in several file drawers until I came to the one I was looking for.

Unfortunately, it was only a one-sided photocopy of the original. Incongruously enough, the law regarding photocopies of business sales allows that only the front side has to be copied, not necessarily the back. Consequently, anyone searching through these files might find only half a record. This was the case now. On the front of the document, I read the date of sale with the signature of the sellers. The back obviously had the buyers' signatures and sale price, because it wasn't here.

"You know," I told the air. "We really do need both sides of a paper if both sides are written upon." I slammed the drawer shut. I had learned absolutely nothing of any real value all day.

"Oh, to hell with it. I don't know what I'm doing," I admitted, and put my head down on my arms, which were crossed and on top of the cabinet. I was feeling very sorry for myself. "I don't want to do this any more. I want to go home." I licked my lips. "And, I want a piece of Maggie's cranberry-apple pie," I murmured into the crook of my arm.

Pie. P period Y period. PY. Then it hit me. Not exactly like a cold mackerel at the end of a wet fist, but fairly close. I slowly raised my head and smiled. "Two initials that were joined in a never-ending circle of love," I remembered her saying.

It was on a matchbook cover in their home. She had babbled on to Mom and me about how it was one her husband's new businesses, named in honor of their marriage. That was at one of those damned teas.

Portor and Yvette were P period Y period. I'll bet Portor owned that closed restaurant. For all I knew, he owned the warehouse as well. Maybe that's why we couldn't readily find the owner. Grace Wong had been seen in the vicinity of both of them, too. It was no coincidence, because I finally believed I knew why.

Did Yvette know any of this? Not likely, I thought, or she'd never have opened this can of worms and had us follow Portor to the warehouse.

I had to see that restaurant once more, I decided. Now that I knew what I was looking for, maybe I could find something similar to what I had seen at the warehouse. That would be proof enough to phone the police. I'd hate to make a fool of myself and call Detective John "I-don't-want-to-see-you-around-here-again" Savarese, if I was wrong.

I glanced at my watch. Three-fifteen. If I hurried back to Princeton-by-the-Sea I could be home by five-thirty just as I promised. Knowing Tío, he'd start worrying at five thirty-one if I wasn't there. I left the building, leapt into my car and drove off as quickly as I could. Driving over 92 was slower than I thought due to the early afternoon commute, but I arrived close for four o'clock.

It was already starting to get dark as I pulled in, once again, to the diner's parking lot. I found a space directly in front of the diner under a parking lot light, force of habit when you own a car as valuable as this one. The flashlight was still underneath the seat of the car, and I only hoped the batteries were working. It had been several months since I had replaced them, and I had meant to do so after the night of the deluge. I flipped it on and sighed, half in relief, half in annoyance. The light was not strong, but would do.

As I got out of the car, Maggie saw me through the diner's windows and waved. Waving back, I opened the door to the eatery and stood in the doorway.

"Maggie," I said before the other woman could speak. "I have a short errand to run, and then I'm coming back in about fifteen minutes for some of that pie! I hope you've got some left."

"I'll save a big piece just for you," Maggie responded with a grin. Several patrons looked toward us and laughed. I did too, and ran out.

As I hurried toward the marina, I wished I had taken the light windbreaker from the trunk of the car. Thinking of the trunk and picturing the receiver inside, I remembered to activate the camcorder again. I pushed the on button and left it running in the pocket of my jeans. Even if I couldn't visually record anything due to the lack of light, I could do a continuous narrative. I rounded the back of the restaurant directly off the water and a gust of cold wind hit me in the face. It was almost completely dark now.

"Make this fast, Lee," I murmured out loud. "It's effing freezing out here." I walked to the double doors. I located a small, unsoaped section of glass and aimed the flashlight inside the room starting from left to right. What I was looking for was a confined area large enough to hold ten to twenty people, unobtrusively. I shone the light around the large room, and I noticed the kitchen area, which was slightly to the left of center. This was the only place, I realized, that was an actual room inside the restaurant. As the building was half over water and stood on pilings, there was no basement. The restrooms were probably on the other side of the kitchen, near the entrance. It was difficult to see. The batteries were not putting out fully, and the light became diffused at about fifteen feet. On the floor near the entrance to the kitchen, a few shiny objects reflected the light. I strained my eyes and saw a couple of crushed Mountain Dew cans, just like the ones I saw in the white pickup truck. Then I noticed empty food cartons and two- or three-dozen wooden chopsticks strewn about the floor. Now I was pretty sure. All the while I kept a running narration of what I saw. I spoke softly, but loud enough for the camcorder to pick up the sound.

I pulled out my phone and called San Francisco Information for the Police Department, Homicide Division. It cost me two dollars but sometimes you gotta do what you gotta do. The night had turned cold, and while I waited for someone to answer, I leaned into the doorway facing away from the wind as much as possible. After four rings, I heard a man's voice.

"Sergeant Hernandez, Homicide."

"Yes, I would like to speak with Detective Savarese, please." I felt smug and couldn't wait to tell him what I found out.

"Say that name again, please," he said. I did. In the background, I could hear the man talking to someone else. "How do you spell that name, Miss?"

I was confused. For God's sake, how big a department was it when they didn't know each other's names? "Savarese. S.A.V.A.R.E.S.E., Detective John Savarese. Maybe he's off-duty."

"Sorry, there's no Detective John Savarese here." It sounded as if he was asking others nearby, "Any of you hear of a John Savarese?" After several seconds he came back on the line. "You're sure it was San Francisco Homicide, Miss? Maybe he's in another division. We pretty much know everybody and nobody's heard of him. Can anybody else help you?"

"No. No, thank you." Stunned, I hung up. I wracked my brain to remember exactly what happened two days before.

He told me he was with the San Francisco Homicide, didn't he? No, he never actually said those words. He just showed up. He said he was with the police, but he didn't show identification, and I didn't ask for any. I just took it for granted...If he's not with the Homicide Division, who is he?

The sound of my own thoughts kept me from hearing the footsteps behind me soon enough. I felt rather than heard them and whirled around. Midway something hard hit me on the side of my head directly above my right ear. In that split second, I felt intense pain and saw white lights behind my eyes, fragmenting my mind. I felt the force of the impact push me back into the glass of one of the doors and heard it shatter around me. I could hear and feel everything going on, but I was powerless to do anything but slide down into a world somewhere between reality and oblivion.

Before I hit the glass littered ground, I felt an arm reach out and pull me forward toward the deck and out of harm's way. In my stupor, I looked up and saw it was the small, Asian man I had seen twice that day, on the boat and in the restaurant. There was a look of anguish on his face, as he tried to keep me away from the major portion of the deadly, jagged edges.

"You kill her. You kill her, Captain Chen," I heard him say to a taller man, who had no look of anguish on his face, but one of grim determination. I looked helplessly at them, trying to move and speak but not being able to do either.

The taller man, Chinese-American and aristocratic, stared at the smaller one with contempt on his face. "Shut up, you idiot," he rasped, in a lower tone of voice looking all around him. "Get inside and turn the alarm off before the sixty seconds are up, or it will go off."

The other man, probably Cambodian, had wide cheekbones, darker skin and haunted eyes. He was a beaten down man, who had made the unfortunate choice to be born in a country war torn and devoid of opportunities. He was used to being given orders. He was used to being dealt with harshly by life. In other circumstances, he might have been a kind man. Odd that I could tell all of that, in the split second that he looked down at me, me bleeding from cuts on the head and a large gash over my right ear.

"You never say we do this kind of thing." The small man shuddered, then stood up and ran inside through the broken section of the door toward the alarm.

The leader ignored his comment and roughly turned me over, going through my pockets. He picked the cell phone off the deck and found the camcorder in my pocket. He threw them into the inky water with a grunt and pulled out the keys to my car from the back pocket. He turned on his subordinate angrily when he returned. "You didn't tell me she had a car. Where's the car?"

"Car? Car?" the other stammered. "I see no car. I follow her from here to restaurant, and then I call you. I see no car." His voice rose to a fever pitch, and his attitude was like that of a dog expecting a beating at the slightest disfavor of its owner.

"All right. All right. Keep your voice down. We don't want anybody coming over here." The man in command studied the keys and made a decision.

"To hell with it. By the time they find her car, we'll be long gone." He threw the keys into the water. "We need to get her back to the ship. Then we've got to start unloading. This trip we had to bring all of them here, so it'll take a while. We leave for China in four hours. We can't stay here any longer, or we might attract the attention of the Coast Guard," he said more to himself than the other man. "We'll throw her body overboard when we get out to sea." He looked around with sharp eyes and saw there was no one else was around. The smaller man of the two swallowed hard and nodded, willing to do what he was asked, but clearly unhappy.

"Help me get her across to the dinghy," the leader said, grunting under my dead weight as he pulled me up and over his shoulder. I tried to struggle and call out, but all that would come out was a low moan. I felt myself going in and out of consciousness and fought to stay awake.

"And then come back and get rid of the broken glass," he ordered. "Put some cardboard in that door until we can fix it. You hear me?" He snarled at the other man, "And clean up that blood."

The small man nodded again, afraid to speak and shaking with terror. His was the last face I can remember seeing.

Chapter Twelve
What's A Nice Girl Like You Doing In A Place Like This?

At first, I knew only of the intense pain in my head. I had never experienced pain like this before. It was so excruciating, I retched several times, but vomiting made my head ache even more. It was so very cold. I trembled and drew up into a fetal position trying to warm myself. My eyes wouldn't open, and I couldn't control the shaking of my body. I tried to lie very still and hoped my parents might find me.

I'm sorry I ran away from the picnic earlier, but Richard wouldn't stop teasing me.

I smiled inwardly at the memory. *No, that was long ago. Or, was it now?* I was confused and frightened. *Wasn't I lost in the woods now?* I felt muddled and wanted to think it through, but the pain prevented me. My mind drifted.

I was glad when they found me next to that big rock by Bridal Veil Falls. The waterfall was so loud it was painful to hear it, just like now. They'll find me again. I'm here in the dark, just like before.

The dark was cold. I didn't remember it being this cold the first time. I shivered uncontrollably.

Maybe they won't find me! I felt a wave of panic. *Maybe a bear will eat me.*

I tried to move, but it made the pain worse and something blocked my way. I tried to cry out, to let someone know where I was, but my throat was too dry, and the pain got worse whenever I moved.

"Por favor, mi Dios, make the pain go away," I prayed, and I must have lost consciousness.

I think some time passed. I was almost awake but drowsy, feeling very far away and disconnected. I heard voices in the distance but couldn't focus on them. The cold had changed to numbness, so I didn't mind it too much. My head still ached, but it, too, seemed far away. I didn't mind that, either. Maybe my parents would find me again. Or, maybe they would leave Yosemite without me. I could just sleep now, and everything would go away.

I thought I heard my mother's voice intermingled with other, strange voices. I wanted to yell out I was hiding under the rock, but my mouth wouldn't move. I thought it would be my father who found me, but it was Mom. I couldn't remember exactly when that was.

Was that then, or is that now?

I wanted to reassure Mom I was all right, just a little cold, but I couldn't move, and I couldn't open my eyes. I tried to squeeze her hand when it grasped mine but felt myself slipping away. I was sliding into some sort of darkness that was easy to go to, but wherever it was, I didn't want to be there.

Chapter Thirteen
A Ministering Angel

It was just light enough to focus on the blinds at the other end of the room. I squinted and tried to move, but my head throbbed when I did. I put a cautious hand up to the source of the pain and felt fabric instead of hair.

Why am I wearing a hat? Where am I?

Slowly I moved my eyes, daring not to shift my head, and saw I was in some sort of bedroom.

No, not a bedroom.

There were instruments around, and my arm was hooked up to something.

Is this a hospital room? But when we left Yosemite, they took me straight home.

No, no. I'm confused again.

My mind cleared a little, and I forced myself to remember. I recalled the pier and the flash of light and the sound of breaking glass. That forced remembrance cost me a lot. I sighed deeply and closed my eyes. My head ached still, but it was more bearable than before. I touched my head again with guarded fingers and found the cloth was really a bandage. After about five minutes of lying perfectly still, I moved my head to the right and saw a chair and two doors. I turned it to the left and saw my mother slumped in a chair, eyes closed, head lolled to the side breathing evenly. She was covered with a cotton blanket. I was so stunned to see my mother sitting there that I called out to her.

"Mom!" My voice sounded hoarse, but was deafening compared to the utter silence.

Lila jerked her head upright, looked at me and ran to my bedside. "Oh, thank God," She cried.

"Where am I? What happened?" I struggled to form the words. My mouth had never felt so dry. "Water. Can I have some water?"

"You're going to be fine, just fine," Mom said, as she reached by the bedside and poured water from a pitcher into a cup. She inserted a straw into it, talking all the while, her voice shaking almost as much as her hands. "The doctors said if you woke up within seventy-two hours, it meant you would be just fine." She smiled at me.

"Doctors? What happened? Oh, my head." I murmured with difficulty. I closed my eyes and tried to stay very still. "Is this a hospital? How did I get here? How badly am I...?"

"I've got to ring some people, and let them know," Lila interrupted me, as she pressed the call button by my right side. "They told me it could be up to seventy-two hours before we knew, and here it is, just a little more than twenty-four. This is wonderful news, my darling." She kissed me very gently on the forehead.

"I know this is serious if you're calling me your darling and kissing my forehead, Mom. You haven't done that since I fell off the horse at camp and broke my leg," I managed to say. I tried to move my legs and arms one at a time to see if they still worked. They did, but the effort cost me. My head was starting to pound.

The door to the room swung open and a nurse entered. She was a small, thin woman, originally from Pakistan I was to find out later, and spoke with a soft accent. "I see our little patient has awakened. This is excellent." She looked at an incongruously large, silver watch on her minuscule wrist. "Five forty-five a.m. The doctor will be in around eight o'clock, and he will be pleased to know this." She crossed over to the bed and looked at the I.V. and other indicators of my health. "Look at this; her pulse and temperature are almost normal. I am so relieved." She smiled at me and turned to my mother. She crossed her arms in front of her bird-like chest and scowled.

"And you, my friend, must go home now," she said. Lila began to protest, and the nurse, used to strong personalities, spoke over the protestations. "Or, at the very least, you must go to the visitors' room down the hall and lie down on the sofa. You have been up too many hours. You will get sick." She shook a slender finger in Mom's face. "You will be of no use to anyone if you become ill yourself."

Lila smiled and looked at me. "I'm not tired. My daughter needs me. You want me to stay, Liana, don't you?"

"No, I don't, Mom," I contradicted her, closing my eyes. "I want you to go get some sleep. How long have you been sitting here, anyway?" My head throbbed, but I forced my eyes opened and looked at my mother with concern.

"Too long," answered the nurse before Lila could speak. "Now, you both must rest." She forcefully escorted Mom to the door. "You know where the visitors' rest center is. Your family has been there most of the time."

"Yes, but first I must call Richard and tell Mateo." Lila furrowed her brow and began to fret as the nurse pushed her out the door. "Richard will want to..."

"Do not call your son yet," the nurse's firm voice overrode Lila's, much to my surprise. "He needs his sleep, too. There is time enough in the morning. His friend, Victoria, telephoned about an hour ago and told me to tell you he had finally fallen asleep. Your brother-in-law? He is waiting for you in the visitors' lounge. He is a light sleeper. He will wake when you go in, and you can tell him all is well, Mrs. Alvarez. Now please rest. Everything is taken care of. We are all starting to worry about you. Go get some rest!" she scolded, as she shut the door in Lila's face.

The ministering angel, who had just delightfully humbled the mighty, paused and hurried back to me. She fixed the bed linens and looked at me fondly. The woman was a born caregiver. "You are doing much better than we thought. This is good. Now go to sleep."

"But I," I protested weakly, finding my mind starting to wander. Bizarre thoughts flitted in and out, such as the colors of scented day lilies, Wayne Newton's best song, and Chelsea Clinton's marital status. My eyes opened suddenly. "Tugger. Has anybody been feeding Tugger?"

The nurse bent over and said into my right ear, "If Tugger is your cat, then we know your uncle has been taking care of him whenever he has not been with you in the hospital."

"But...but..." I said groggily hardly able to form the words. "How much weight has he gained? Is he growing into his ears?"

"Shhh. Time for questions in the morning." The answer came just as I fell into a deep sleep.

Chapter Fourteen
Alice At The Tea Party

I felt myself jerk awake with an abruptness that startled me, but I wasn't half as startled as the three anxious faces leaning in, studying my every move. Lila let out a gasp, Tío said something like "*ay carrumba*," and Richard dropped his can of soda, which after hitting the floor with a "clunk," made hissing noises, carbonated soda spilling out under the bed. Then all three of them started talking at once. Finally, I waved my arms in the air, hoping they would shut up. They did and stared at me, grinning. I opened my mouth and tried to form words, but I was a little the worse for wear. Nothing much came out, save a dry, reedy gurgling sound.

"Shhhh!" Tío said to my mother and brother. "Liana is trying to speak, but her voice is soft. Let us listen well." They all leaned in, and I felt a little like a heroine in the third act of a bad melodrama. The part right after the villain was caught but before she went to spa for a makeover.

Mom thrust a glass of water with a straw in it into my hand. I slurped noisily, as my family hugged and kissed me, careful to avoid the area around the top of my head and the water glass. It was nice, the water and the attention. I felt amazingly well, considering the fact I knew something serious had happened to me. Besides, hugging and kissing always makes one feel better. It's a scientific fact.

When I finally felt sufficiently lubricated for speech, I asked, "What time is it?"

Tio looked from my mother to Richard. "This is the first question? 'What time is it?' What kind of a question is that, *mi sobrina*? Not what happened? Not how am I? Not am I going to be all right?"

"Of course, she's going to be all right," Mom interjected and turned to me. "This has been very trying on your uncle, on all of us, so try to ask a question worthy of the situation, Liana."

"I'm sorry," I stuttered and thought for a moment. "So do you think the U.S. HMO model has international application for improving cost utilization outcomes?" They stared at me. "Never mind. Just kidding." I handed the glass back to Lila and made an effort to sit up. Richard, meanwhile, found a towel and mopped up the spilled soda on the floor.

"Lay back, Liana. Don't try to sit up yet," Mom ordered. "And stop making jokes."

"Listen," I said, "I just want to get a handle on how long I've been here." I did take Mom's advice, though, and stopped struggling. Aside from a tightness over my right ear and the feeling I was wearing about sixty-pounds of plaster of Paris on my head, I felt pretty good. There was no point in pushing it, however, so I lay my head back on the pillow.

"Is anybody going to tell me what time it is?" I asked again. "And what day it is?"

"It's five minutes after three on Saturday afternoon, to answer your question, you ninny," my brother said, laughing. "I see there's been no major damage. It's the same old Liana Alvarez."

"Not so old," he and I said in unison and laughed.

He grasped my hand and squeezed it hard before going on, "You were brought in late Thursday night, stayed in a coma for a little more that twenty-four hours, and you've been sleeping ever since. As for what happened before that, it's an awesome story, Lee, totally awesome," Richard added.

I made a face at him, or I tried to. It was hard to move my features with so much constriction on top of my head.

"I know you hate it when I use that Valley Girl vocabulary, but the word "awesome" is the *palabra sympatico*. Our mother was awesome, Lee."

"Now, stop taunting your sister, Richard," Lila said, nonetheless preening a little.

"I just did what any other mother in that situation would have done."

I held my breath. I didn't like the sound of this. "What did you do?"

She walked to the other side of the bed and gently sat down on it. She took my free hand. "How much do you remember, Liana?" Mom asked.

"*Nada*," I said.

"Do you remember anything about the Coast Guard or your mama rescuing you?" asked Tio, stepping in front of Richard and caressing my shoulder.

For the first time in my life, I was speechless. "Mom," I finally sputtered. "You rescued me? How did you do it? How did you know where I was? Actually, where was I?"

"You had been kidnapped and were being held aboard the *Feng Shen*. Mom rented a boat with the ten thousand dollars she keeps in the trunk of her car." Richard fairly hollered with pride.

I stared at him with eyes, as they say, as big as saucers.

"I don't like that talked about, Richard," Mom reprimanded him. "Even among ourselves. You know better."

"Sorry, Mom," Richard said but winked at me. "I won't mention it again."

"Well, certainly don't shout it out again," Lila said in a softer tone, as she turned to me. "It's just your father and I have always kept money in the trunk of our cars for just such an emergency, but I don't want it broadcast."

"Ten thousand dollars?" I mouthed, stupefied.

"Anyway," Richard went on, "after Tío broke into your car with a tire iron, and we listened to everything that happened to you on the receiver..."

"We had to do the break in, *mi sobrina*," Tío interrupted. "There was no other way."

"No other way, Lee," Richard agreed and continued. "So, after we learned where you were, Mom chased down Captain Chen's boat — he's the guy who kidnapped you — by hiring a charter boat. When we finally caught up with Chen, Mom kicked off her shoes and shinnied up the side of that boat in the middle of the ocean, in the middle of the night, and got you back," he finished with a flourish.

I gaped. No other way to say it. Color me stunned.

Richard went on, oblivious to my reaction. "You should have heard Fred Anderson." A "whoop" went up from all three upon hearing this name.

I did more of my gaping routine. The crowd ignored me.

"Oh, yes, Captain Anderson. A rare person," Mom said, rolling her eyes.

"*Sí*," agreed *Tio*. "*Un hombre unico*."

"He was really impressed with you, Mom," Richard teased and turned back to me.

"Captain Anderson owns the *Molly Belle* and took us out to the Coast Guard cutter after Mom paid him the money. I heard him say 'I'd like to have her nerve in my teeth' as he watched Mom go right up the side of that boat!" Richard laughed at the recollection. "What a cool guy he is."

Mom rolled her eyes again. I managed to glean the verdict wasn't in yet as to whether or not this Anderson was really a cool guy.

"It was a ship, Ricardo," Tío said firmly, as if this was an everyday conversation.

At a loss, I clutched my face with my hands.

Tio went on, emphasizing his words, "We were on a boat called the *Molly Belle,* chasing a ship, the *Feng Shen,* which was being pursued by the Coast Guard, yet another ship. Remember? Capitan Anderson was very definite about his craft being a boat and the Coast Guard cutter and the *Feng Shen* both being ships, *mi sobrino.*"

"Oh, right," Richard said. "I have to do some research to see what the difference is between a boat and a ship. I don't think it's just the footage."

I looked up at my mother and managed to ask in a faltering voice, "You shimmied up a Coast Guard cutter named the *Feng Shen*?"

"No, no, no, not the ship from the Coast Guard," said Tío impatiently, before Mom could reply. "She went up the other ship — the *Feng Shen.*" He looked at my mother and my brother with uncertainty in his eyes. "Did it have a name, this cutter ship?"

"I think it had numbers on the side, not a name, Mateo," Lila answered.

"She didn't shimmy. She shinnied. There's a difference, Lee," Richard corrected me.

I would have laughed, but I could see everyone was serious. I re-clutched my face.

"I didn't shimmy or shinny up the side of anything," Lila said primly. "I used the rope ladder Lieutenant Commander Carter so very kindly provided. You know, Liana, he's Lincoln Carter's son. That's why he even let me come aboard. Lincoln was a great friend of your father's, but that's another story. I'll tell you that one when you're feeling a little better."

She smiled benevolently at me. I looked at Richard and Tío and they, too, were smiling benevolently at me. I was just deciding I was in a world gone mad when Richard's girlfriend, Victoria, walked in wearing — I swear — a Mad

Hatter's hat in blue velvet with a yellow band. I froze with fear.

To top it all off, my mother, the woman who snorted just the other day — "What does Richard see in that child? Victoria hasn't even finished college. Victoria's skirts are too short. Victoria wears horrifying hats in horrifying colors," and so on and so on — this woman stood up and embraced the aforesaid miscreant! I found that the most unbelievable thing I had witnessed so far.

That's when I knew. It was the concussion. I had read about delusions stemming from a bump on the head. I was hallucinating. That was it. No one was really there. This drivel I thought my family was saying wasn't really being said at all. No. Ha ha. They weren't even there!

Of course, it could also be dehydration. I remembered in the movie, *Gunga Din*, a whole squad of legionnaires became delusional during a desert drill from a lack of water, too much heat and excessive camel dung. I slurped more water, thinking.

Maybe I'm on too many drugs. Yes, I'm drugged. It must be a very strong hallucinogenic, though, because this whole thing feels very real. Yet, if this is real, that means I'm Alice in Wonderland at the tea party, and my entire family has been invited along by the Mad Hatter, who seems to be Victoria. Hell, maybe they're all Mad Hatters.

"I take mine with lemon," I said, as I closed my eyes and rolled over, covering my face with a blanket.

****

That evening I was sitting up in bed eating what the hospital loosely called dinner. Everyone except Mom had left hours ago. Lila sat in a chair, reading work-related papers and answering my questions as they came to mind. Right then, I was deciding what to eat first. Should it be tepid chicken broth, red Jell-O, or watered down tea? Decisions, decisions. I chose the Jell-O and wished I'd had some Haagen Dazs ice cream to drown it in.

"But Mom," I asked, as I munched on a gelatin cube, "how did you know I was missing so fast? You found me after only a few hours."

She put her work aside. "When you didn't show up at five-thirty, Mateo was in a panic. He knew from the beginning something was wrong. You are very reliable about showing up when you say you will."

"Especially when food's involved," I acknowledged.

"Then Richard and Victoria came, and Richard said he thought you might still be in Princeton-by-the-Sea. Just when I was in a quandary as to how to find you there, Victoria offered a solution."

"She did?"

"Yes. She said she has a cousin, Bryan Brown, who is with the Half Moon Bay Police Department. She called Officer Brown, and within minutes, he located your car in the parking lot of the diner. We drove there immediately, leaving Victoria to stay by the phone at home, in case someone called with more information about you."

"Wow! No wonder you suddenly like her."

"I have never not liked Victoria," Lila sniffed. "It's just that due to this experience, I've had an opportunity to see her true character. She is a loving and thoughtful young woman."

"Weird hats, though," I remarked, drinking some lukewarm tea.

Lila took a breath and closed her eyes. "Putting her hats aside…"

"If only one could."

"Liana!" My mother sharply rebuked me.

I started and spilled tea down the front of my hospital gown. I found a paper napkin and dried myself off as best I could.

"Let's stick to the germane issues, shall we?" Mom asked.

"Okay, Mom. Go on. So you located the car."

"Yes. I met Maggie…"

"Is she great or what?" I interrupted.

"She was very helpful. You seem to have made a favorable impression on her, too. She likes you very much. She told me about seeing your camcorder on the counter. That's when I knew we had to get into the trunk of your car to listen to everything that had taken place. You're always so good about recording everything." She allowed herself to smile at me.

"Hey, I've been trained by the best," I said.

"Once we located the receiver, we knew right away what had happened and where you were. I notified the various police agencies, including the Coast Guard, and asked Officer Brown if he knew anyone with a speedboat or the like, so I could help find you myself."

"And, that's where Captain Fred Anderson and the *Molly Belle* comes into the story."

"Yes, once he agreed to let us use his charter boat, which has been altered into something of a speedboat, we caught up with the two ships. By that time, the Coast Guard had boarded and done its initial search of the *Feng Shen*. They didn't find you the first go-round." Mom's voice caught suddenly, and I looked up from my Jell-O.

"The only reason the Commander let me come aboard was because of your father, but once there, I was able to implore the crew to let me know where you were. I don't think anyone else could have gotten through to them. Even with an interpreter, I could tell they were a hardened lot, surly and unyielding. All except this one small man, the man who had helped to bring you onboard and hide you…" She stopped talking and put her hand to her throat.

My eyes filled and the Jell-O felt hot in my throat. "You don't have to go on, Mom. Really," I whispered.

She brushed at her eyes quickly, got up, and came to me. "Of course, I'll go on. You have a right to know. When I begged the men to help me, he was the only one who said he would, despite his fear of that horrid man, Captain Chen. Then he took us — some officers, a medic and me — down below to the engine room. It was a squalid, filthy place, and there you were, hidden under the floorboards, all drawn up in a fetal position. So pale and still..." she broke off speaking.

I grabbed her arm. "Mom, it's okay. You found me, and I'm okay. It's all over now."

"Yes, it is. It is." She embraced me, and I clung to her like never before.

Then Lila Hamilton Alvarez started to cry, and I started to cry, and we both were having a good one, when all of a sudden my head began to throb. I must have moaned a little because she released me and scrutinized my face.

"You look terrible. All puffy and red."

"Well, some of us don't cry like you," I retorted. You just glisten when you cry. I get all puffy and red. Besides, I'm getting a headache."

Within seconds, Lila grabbed a towel from the bathroom, took some ice out of the water carafe, wrapped the ice in the towel, and applied it to my forehead.

"Ahhh! That feels so good," I said, as I closed my eyes.

"You lie still and get some rest," she said, as she kissed my cheek. "I'll be back in the morning."

"Thanks, Mom," I muttered. "Thanks for making me feel like your little girl again."

"You'll always be my little girl," I heard her say, as she wafted out of the room.

Chapter Fifteen
UnGeneral Hospital

Two days later, I lay in my bed staring at the white smock of my doctor and the clipboard he held directly in front of his face. This was not the first time the doc had been in on his rounds, but I didn't think he would actually know who I was if he fell over me. Interns, nurses and orderlies chatted with me throughout the day, but whenever the man who saved my life dropped by, he spent his time reading my chart or talking to everybody else. I couldn't remember him actually saying one direct word to me, and I was feeling a tad left out because of it.

Dr. Vernon Parsley was well named, as he did have a slight greenish hue. He was a tall, ageless man with faded, thin blond hair and a weak chin but supposedly a dynamo in the operating room. He was quite methodical in his movements and seemed to enjoy saying "hmmmmmmm" a lot.

"Hmmmmmmm, Miss Alvarez," he said now into the chart, so his words were slightly masked. "I see here that you are making excellent progress."

During the past two days, I had begun to feel more myself. The headaches had subsided, and I took short walks around the room. My family was visiting so often and watching my every move so intently I began to understand what it must be like to be a celebrity haunted by the paparazzi. That afternoon was going to be the first time I was allowed regular visitors.

What would that be like? I mean, what does a star say after she's survived an exotic disease? Does she say to the masses 'I'm feeling much better, thanks? Let's move on?' Or do you give a blow-by-blow description of each excruciating minute because inquiring minds want to know?

Whoops. I was having one of those mental wanderings again. I needed to work on that. I focused my attention on the doctor again or, rather, the back of his clipboard.

"Have I made excellent progress?" I repeated politely. "How so?"

"Oh, yes," he replied, dropping the chart for a nano-second before covering his face with it again. "I was quite alarmed when they brought you in several days ago." Doctor Parsley reflected for a moment. "This has been an interesting case. I originally thought, at the very least, we might have to put a shunt in your head to drain the fluid from the swelling of your brain. Possibly for the rest of your life, but no."

He sighed. I wasn't sure if he was disappointed or not. He then proceeded to give me a very detailed rundown on his initial findings and the appropriate measures that followed, all of which were said in unfathomable medical terms. I felt my eyes glaze over. At the end of the lecture, I was more than relieved when he began to write on his chart again. He carefully read back to himself what he wrote, before speaking again.

"To put this in layman's terms…"

"Oh, thank you. I have no idea what you said before."

"No?" His tone of voice indicated he thought I probably had the mental processes of a blade of grass. "Well, plainly put, we were fortunate you were placed in an inch or so of cold water because that helped to keep your brain from swelling more than it did. The low temperature of the water retarded your entire circulatory system, which was quite a good thing. I was pleased about that."

He dropped the chart for the moment and, for the first time, I saw he had hazel eyes. He stared out in reverie. "I have never before encountered that specific situation, although it has been written up in journals. Most gratifying." He didn't exactly break into a jig over this, but I could tell he was very close to it.

"Of course," he continued, frowning somewhat, "the hypothermia was not good for the rest of your body, sent it into shock, but we didn't care about that. We managed to get it under control after awhile. It's the brain that interests us, is it not? What did you say?" He queried, finally looking at me, as I made slight sucking sounds with my mouth.

"I'm sorry," I said. "I didn't mean to interrupt you, Dr. Parsley. Got the hiccups." I smiled my Miss America smile and only wished I'd had my chart to throw at him.

"Right," he responded. "In any event, we sewed up all the cuts once we removed the glass slivers from your scalp. I believe there were seventeen of them. Cuts, not slivers," he clarified. "There were hundreds of those," he remembered, with an odd fondness. "And, of course, the wound from the blunt instrument was amazingly long. It required nearly forty-five stitches." He chuckled and then sobered for a moment. "Sorry about your hair. We had to get it off as quickly as possible, and I'm afraid it's a little short. Actually, it's very short."

"My hair?" I echoed, biting my lower lip. I had been afraid to ask about it but knew the bandage was not as bulky as it would have been if it had been added to a full head of hair.

"Yes, your mother was upset at how much we had to remove, but after all, we're not a beauty salon, are we?"

"No, indeedie," I managed to say.

"Anyway," he added sagely, "it will grow back, and the important thing was to get those wounds sewed up as quickly as possible." I had little response to this logic and merely touched the top of my bandaged head with my hand.

"Day after tomorrow, we'll remove the bandages permanently," he continued. "I think you'll see there will be a minimum of scarring, and your hair, which I remember as quite thick, will hide any remaining scars. What a mess you were when they first brought you in." He returned the chart to the foot of my bed and stared at me. "I didn't know if you would ever come out of the coma. If there had been any further delay in getting you in here..." He stopped speaking and shook his head, once again, in fond remembrance. "But there's no brain damage, no seizures, not even a grand mal. The MRIs have confirmed that. We are very lucky because it could have been so much worse. As I said, I've never quite encountered this particular situation before, but aren't we glad it turned out the way it did?"

"You betcha!" I responded with true enthusiasm.

"The way things are going, you'll be able to go home in a couple of days." He returned the pen to the lapel pocket of his crisp, white smock. "See you tomorrow." He grinned as he left the room in a whirl, possibly eager to visit his next chart.

I took a moment to compose myself, focusing on my private room. It was light and airy, painted a pale blue with white trim. The walls held copies of seascape paintings, unfortunately. One I found particularly nauseating was a palate work of a harbor with small, white boats basking in the sun. I never wanted to see a boat, a harbor, or a body of water again in my life. In fact, I wasn't even sure if I could face a bathtub full of H2O.

Flowers and get-well cards filled the table and the sill of the window, which faced a parking lot but let in a great deal of sun. A large vase of flowers, complete with an enormous, handmade card, came from Maggie and Hank. This was my favorite even though it was filled with names I didn't recognize. It would be so like Maggie to make everyone leaving the diner sign the card, whether they knew me or not. I felt ashamed of myself for thinking of Princeton-by-the-Sea as a "backwater" town.

It was really a charming place filled with warm, caring people. I waxed sentimental.

I glanced at the abundant arrangement. I suspected the flowers came from someone's winter garden, maybe a few gardens, and that made them all the more touching. Even Ed, the repairman from the gas station, had towed my car free of charge to a body shop in San Mateo, so the trunk could be repaired. As soon as I could, I would have to drop by and thank him, maybe even slip him another fifty. I might even look up this Captain Fred Anderson. Anyone who made Lila roll her eyes and Richard finds "cool," I had to meet.

The door opened and Mom came sailing into the room. She was dressed for work and looked spectacular, as usual, in a moss green, double-breasted suit with matching overcoat. Her eyes sparkled even though her mouth was set in a grim line.

"Liana, I can't stay long because there are a million things to do at work. I just wanted to bring you some things." With that, she dumped the contents of a large Nordstrom's shopping bag at the foot of the bed.

"Oh, thanks, Mom," I said a little taken aback at the fast pace and energy exuding from the woman. I had to constantly remind myself the world still went on as I lay in bed recuperating.

"It's freezing outside," commented Lila, shivering a little and removing her coat. Underneath the jacket, she wore her favorite long-sleeved, white chiffon blouse. The usual pearl pin decorated the neckline. She looked fabulous, and it wasn't even seven-thirty in the morning.

"Now, I've made arrangements for Enrico to come and style your hair the day after tomorrow at around eight in the morning."

"Oh, that's great because..." I began with a smile.

"I hope you're prepared for how short it is. I ran into the doctor outside, and he told me he told you," said Lila, interrupting me as she arranged the contents of the shopping bag on the bed. "Never mind though, because I have a feeling you will look quite gamine with short, wispy hair."

"Gamine?"

"By the way," Mom went on. "Now that visitors can drop by to see you, I've brought some choices in bed jackets and short robes for you. I like this one," she stated, holding up a royal blue chenille bed jacket decorated at the neck with green and pink flowers. "It suits your coloring. I also brought your make-up kit and several scarves, in case you want to put one over the hideous bandage on your head."

I had been reaching out for the bed jacket, but as her last words struck me, I put my hands to my head. I was beginning to feel overwhelmed.

What do I have, a mother or a whirling dervish?

"Mom! Can we slow down? I can't keep up with you this morning."

"Oh, I'd love to, darling, but I can't," she responded as she glanced at her wristwatch. "It took me forever to get here — I left at six-thirty — and I have to rush back for a nine a.m. appointment with *Ms. Davidson.*" Lila stressed the woman's name, especially the 'Ms.' and I felt the tightness start in my stomach. "You remember the *merger*? It's all going to take place in three months time, providing a couple of allegations can be cleared up. We've got two agents on it, plus Richard. It's been chaotic."

"Well, don't let me keep you from your merger," I said peevishly, kicking at the scarves and bed jackets at the bottom of the bed. I lay back and crossed my arms over my chest. Mom looked at me in surprise.

"You know, I'm short one valuable agent, so I have a lot of extra work to do," she said, touching one of my feet with her hand lightly. "That's in *addition* to having my daughter in here."

"Oh, I'm sorry, Mom," I said in a frustrated tone. "But I feel the world rushing by, and I'm here stuck in this bed." I smiled or, rather, tried to. My mother leaned forward, and I smelled Bal a Versailles as she brushed a kiss on my cheek and sat down on the side of the bed. She studied my face and reached some sort of decision.

"Liana, I know that this is a difficult time for you, but let me tell you, it has not been easy for your family, either. Mateo is not a young man. Aside from the obvious stress of what happened on that *horrible night*, the poor man had to have several stitches in his right hand from forcing the trunk of your car open so we could get at the receiver. He has also been taking care of that stupid cat of yours as if it were the Virgin Mary."

"Mom, I..."

"Let me finish," Lila said, obviously just warming up. "Your brother has been functioning on three or four hours sleep a night. He comes here each evening, while carrying a sixteen to eighteen hour workday. This is after having been up for over twenty-four hours at your bedside in the first place. I don't think he's ever made up that lost sleep."

"I know, Mom. I..."

"I don't need to tell you what it's done to me or do I?" Lila went on as if I had not spoken. "If you hadn't gone off like that, risking your very life, none of this would have happened in the first place, and you wouldn't be in here behaving like a *spoiled brat!*" she added, as the grand finale to her speech.

"Mom, everything you say is true," I admitted meekly. "I can be a spoiled brat sometimes. I'm really sorry, and you're right. All of this is my fault," I added.

"Well see that it doesn't happen again. I lost one of my best pairs of shoes when I climbed up the side of the *Feng*

Shen, not to mention having a brand new blouse completely ruined!" she said seriously, but then winked at me and burst out laughing.

"Your face, Liana, your beautiful face, so serious, so contrite. My impetuous, exasperating, beautiful daughter, what am I going to do with you? But how can I ever stay mad at you when I love you so much?" She bent down and hugged me hard. I held onto her gratefully.

"I was only trying to do what I felt was right. He died on my watch, Mom. Mr. Wyler died, and maybe it was because I didn't do enough. I'll never know," I whispered into her soft hair. I broke free, glanced into her eyes, and then looked away, ashamed of the admission.

"We all feel that way sometimes, Liana, as we try to get through life. 'Should I have done that? Should I have done this? Did I do enough? What would I do differently if I had it to do over again?' It comes under the heading of 'what might have been.' It can tear you apart or you live with it, and you go on. But you don't do stupid things to *compound* it, understand?"

I nodded and lay back suddenly feeling a lot older but not very much wiser.

"I have to go, sweetheart, but I'll be back later on this afternoon. By the way, just so you know, I'm finding I enjoy having someone else around the house. It's less lonely. I think Mateo and I are going to do just *fine*." Mom retrieved her coat from the bed and started for the door.

"Mom," I called to her. Lila stopped in the doorway and turned back to me. "If I haven't said it before, thanks for saving my life." She blew me a kiss and closed the door.

After lunch, I decided to wear the blue bed jacket my mother selected, admitting to myself it was pretty and did make me look healthier. I eschewed wrapping the scarf over the bandage. After trying it out and viewing the results in a mirror, all I needed was some fruit on top for a nifty imitation of Carmen Miranda. Even though I'll watch her every time *That Night in Rio* is on — a great film classic — I don't particularly want to look like her. I put on a touch of lipstick and leaned back, ready for visitors, should anyone come. Most everyone I knew had already called or sent cards. I reviewed the recent phone calls in my mind, smiling. There's nothing like feeling loved.

Aside from the usual friends and loved ones, there had also been the young man, Grant, from the concert of several weeks ago. The newspaper listed the name of the hospital I was in, and he called to wish me well. Naturally, there had been Frank, who managed to stave off his "I told you so" speech for at least five minutes into the call. As Captain of the PAPD, he wanted to use his pull to have me transferred to Stanford General, so I could be taken care of by the 'best doctor in the world,' his daughter, Faith. Putting aside she is a pediatrician, I wanted to stay right where I was, the Pacific Coast Hospital. Tío usually called or came around nine a.m., starting with an account of the kitten, but always anxious to know how I had done the night before. Richard generally called when he could and dropped by every evening.

Mom was right, I reflected. *My family has spent a lot of time here. And, they're yawning a lot, too. I need to think more about them and less about me. I am a spoiled brat.*

Victoria came first, dropping by for a chat about everything and nothing. She's an auburn-haired sweetie, mid- to late-twenties, with intelligent green eyes and a slight overbite.

"Hello there, you," she said brightly, as she strutted into the room carrying a stack of magazines and a small vase of flowers. Victoria struts very well. She has a distinctive fashion style, in that she likes flowing shawls, short skirts over colored, textured stockings, and the highest platform shoes or spike heels known to man. I have never seen her without some sort of hat, and that day, she topped off her look with a red felt beret encrusted with small, colored glass replicas of different types of dinosaurs.

"Hello, yourself," I answered. "How about a hug?" She rushed over, put down the flowers and kissed me on the cheek with gusto. All the while, I studied the assortment of terrible lizards on her cranium. "Wow, what a hat!"

"Oh, you like?" she asked, as she shook her head and about one hundred tiny dinosaurs noisily came to life. "I designed this myself," she actually admitted.

Victoria owns a millinery shop, a thriving establishment called "The Obsessive Chapeau," where similar lids sell for something slightly less than the national deficit. I've said it before, and I'll say it again, it's amazing what people will pay good money for.

"I can order you one, wholesale," she offered, and I managed not to shiver in repulsion.

"You know, Victoria," I said, as sincerely as I could. "I'm really not a hat person, but thank you so much, anyway."

"Aw," she said with disappointment. "Well, not everyone is. It's a question of pizzazz."

"I think it is."

"If you ever change your mind, just let me know."

"I'll do that." I smiled.

"Look what I've brought you, Lee," she said, as she thrust the magazines in my hand. "I just bought every magazine they had in the gift shop. I wasn't sure what you'd like."

"I like that you came to visit me," I said, throwing the magazines to the foot of the bed. "Sit down and tell me everything in your life that's new and different."

She did and for over a half an hour we laughed, told secrets, and I marveled once again at what a perfect match she was for my brother. Both were weird but wonderful.

After she left, I had just settled down with an article on money management in one of the magazines when John Savarese walked in, bold as brass, and said hello. I was shocked. He was wearing solid black and looked good enough to eat, but I was on a diet. I stared at him with what I hoped passed for mild disdain, when all the while I couldn't wait to let him have it. Maybe I would even call the police and have him arrested for something, anything, after I told him off.

"What are you doing here?" I asked in as civil a tone as I could muster.

He was surprised by my tone of voice and raised an eyebrow. "Well, I thought I would drive down and see how you're doing. How are you doing?"

"Listen, you," I blurted out. "Just who the hell are you? You're not a policeman because I called Homicide, and you've got a lot of nerve passing yourself off as one. I've got a good mind to report you. It's against the law to impersonate a police officer!" With that I threw my Time magazine at him. So much for mild disdain.

"What?" he stared at me, baffled, then the realization hit him right after the magazine did. "Ow! Oh, that!"

"'Oh, that?' That's all you have to say, 'Oh, that?'"

He came to edge of the bed and smiled at me. "Look, I really am a policeman."

"Oh, yeah? Where's your ID, Bub?"

"Here's my identification." He reached inside his pocket and pulled out his wallet. Attached to it was a badge. He flipped the wallet open and pointed to the ID. "I'm with the Department of Immigration and Naturalization." I snatched the wallet out of his hand and scrutinized the official document, as he continued speaking.

"If you remember, I never actually said I was with Homicide. You jumped to that conclusion at the warehouse, and I let you think it. I figured it would carry more weight if you thought I was investigating Wyler's murder instead of his illegal activities. Besides, I didn't want to tip my hand. At that time, we didn't want anyone to know we were dealing with a ring of illegal immigration. I'm sorry I had to deceive you."

"So am I," I said, calming down a bit. "For a while there, I thought you were one of the bad guys."

"Well, I'm not. I'm a good guy."

He stared at me with his intense blue eyes, and I suddenly felt uncomfortable. I started babbling, as I am wont to do when I'm embarrassed.

"So Wyler was smuggling illegal immigrants into the country! All this time, we thought he made his money in real estate. How long had he been doing it? How did Grace Wong get involved with him? What has she got to do with it?" I asked.

"Wait. I'll tell you everything from the beginning." He smiled. "Since you helped break the case and found one of the drop off points, I owe you that much." He went over to a chair and settled himself comfortably.

"Several months ago, we heard a rumor of a fairly sophisticated operation of illegal immigration in the Bay Area." He looked at me questioningly and asked, "How much do you know about this problem?"

"*Nada*," I answered quickly, anxious for him to get on with it.

"Well, to sum it up, the United States has a quota saying no one country can send more than seven percent of the total worldwide immigration each year, translating to roughly twenty-five thousand allotments per country, per year. You can see this system puts large countries at a disadvantage; the quota is the same for India and China with a billion people each, as it is for some place like Nauru, with approximately ten thousand people. Unfortunately, hundreds of thousands apply every year from Mainland China and many of the surrounding islands. Most will wait a lifetime and never make it."

"That's terrible," I remarked. "I had no idea."

"Many are willing to pay upwards of twenty thousand dollars to get into the country any way they can, legally or illegally. Do you have any idea how long it takes some of these people to save that kind of money?"

I shook my head numbly.

"An entire village of people will work, steal, sell whatever they possess, for years so just one member of the community can get to the States. Once a person is here, he or she works and saves money, sending it back home for the next person to come over. Then those two work and save for the next person and so on until everyone is here."

His voice took on a harder edge. "That's their plan, anyway. But once they're able to scrape together the required money, then they're at the mercy of coyotes like Portor Wyler or his partner, David Chen. They herd people into ships that travel from one remote village to another drumming up business. When they get enough, sometimes as many as sixty or seventy on a vessel meant to hold only ten or twelve passengers, they cross the Pacific, forcing these people to endure hideous living conditions, for ten days to two weeks. A few don't even live through the ordeal."

"That's the most horrendous thing I've ever...wait a minute," I interrupted myself. "At twenty thousand dollars a pop, that's..." Pausing to get a pencil, I added up all the zeros on the back of the magazine. "That's over a million dollars a crossing!"

"At least."

"And you say it was done twice a month for years?"

"Illegal immigration can be a very lucrative business, if you have the stomach for it."

"I don't know many people who do," I said quietly. I lay there for a minute, hardly able to wrap my mind around it all. "But once they were here, how did Wyler and Chen get them into the states?"

"The San Francisco warehouse, which was owned by those two jointly, was the first stop. Ready-made women's clothing was unloaded and stored in the warehouse for one or two days until it could be shipped by land to a small chain of low-end department stores. That part was completely above board. What Chen and Wyler would do, however, was disguise the illegals, one by one, as workers already 'green carded' and on the payroll. At the right time, the substitute would carry a bundle of clothing from the ship to the warehouse. When instructed, he or she would hide in the concealed room in back of the office, waiting until the dead of night when the pier was deserted. Then they would be trucked off to wherever."

"Unbelievable! This was going on under everyone's noses?"

"Yes. By the way, Watch Line played a part in this, too. That was one of Wyler's other businesses, we just found out. He paid a couple of the guards to look the other way or even help out from time to time."

"How many people were in on this?"

"About a dozen or so, but they were only paid chump change. Once they got to the states, Wyler needed people to drive the 'new arrivals' to other drop sites via cars or trucks. Some drivers were no more than indentured slaves to Wyler and Chen and did as they were told, like Grace Wong."

"As we now know, San Francisco was only phase one," John said, grimly. "After dark, the ship would begin its journey back to China hugging the coastline and pausing, for lack of a better word, for an hour or so in the waters off Princeton-by-the-Sea. Remember, the *Feng Shen* had no legitimate reason for being there. If the Coast Guard stumbled on them, Chen could say they were having engine trouble or some such. They had compartments in the floorboards, where they could hide people in such an event," he added.

"That's where they kept me, I'm told." I involuntarily shuddered.

"I know," he said, leaning forward and touching my cheek with his hand. He went on, "They would drop off the second group and shuttle them by dinghy to that abandoned restaurant."

"Wyler owned that, too, didn't he?" I broke in.

"He and Chen, yes. They thought by breaking this up into two separate operations, they would increase their chances of going undetected, which it did for years."

"But Chen had to unload everyone in Princeton last time, didn't he?"

"The entire group, all fifty-four of them. Chen was afraid to go near the warehouse because of Wyler's murder. The extra time it took to unload everybody is probably what saved your life. That, plus he felt he needed to get far enough out to sea to feel safe enough to throw you overboard, so your body wouldn't be found right away, if ever. We think he was within minutes of doing just that when the Coast Guard got to him."

"I guess I was pretty lucky."

"You were damned lucky," John said. "After having the warehouse in San Francisco become off-limits, he would really have been out of business if you had blown it wide open for him down the coast. He was a desperate man."

"Is the man who helped find me going to go to jail?" I asked, suddenly thinking of the small, unhappy man.

"Yes, but by turning State's evidence, it will probably be for much less time. Why, are you interested in being his character witness?" He asked wryly.

"I don't know about that, but I can't help feeling sorry for him. What happens to the other people who were on Chen's ship?"

"Most of them have already been flown back to China, courtesy of the United States government. No charges have been brought against them."

"Grace Wong," I murmured. "How was she involved in this, and why did you refer to her as one of the indentured slaves?"

"Grace Wong has a lot of family still in China."

"That's right!" I burst in, slapping the bed with my hand for emphasis. "She has six brothers still in China," I said, remembering Richard's report.

"And that's not counting her sisters, her cousins, and her aunts, as Gilbert and Sullivan would say. Anyway, you ask about Miss Wong's affiliation with this. Wyler was forcing her to have sex with him in exchange for bringing members of her family over to the states."

I was stunned. Of all the answers I anticipated hearing, this was not one of them. "What?"

"You may look shocked, but the kind of scum that's into this business certainly wouldn't stop at blackmailing a woman into sleeping with him."

I thought for a moment. "But she was a successful dancer. I don't understand."

"Even for well paid dancers, twenty-thousand dollars per person is a lot of money. We believe she's brought two of her brothers illegally into the country just this year. We checked with our sources in China, and they're having trouble locating those two. They're probably here."

"Poor Grace Wong," I said, shaking my head. What would I be willing to do for Richard, given the same situation?

"I'd save my sympathy, if I were you. She's been arrested for killing Portor Wyler."

I was so taken aback I could not utter a word. Finally, after several seconds, I found speech and sputtered, "I don't believe it. Why do they think it was she? What possible reason could she have? He was helping to bring her family into the country. Why kill him?" I demanded.

"Whoa," he said. "I don't know any of the details on the murder, and it's not any of my business. I only know we've got Captain Chen, his men, and the *Feng Shen*. Their smuggling days are over, largely due to your efforts. You know, we hadn't connected Grace Wong with any of this." He looked at me for a moment. "May I ask you a question?"

"*Naturalmente,*" I said with panache, greatly pleased he acknowledged the work I had done.

"What made you focus on her? What singled her out?"

"Well," I began reluctantly, not wanting to drag Richard into it. "I just got lucky. Remember the day you asked me if I had been in the warehouse a half an hour earlier? Well, I hadn't, but I got Grace on tape getting into her car just beforehand. I had a hunch it was she who had been inside the warehouse, so I went with it." I smiled.

When he saw I would say no more, he stood up, ready to leave. "Whatever you say, Lee. I'm glad you're going to be all right. You had us all worried there for a time." He looked down at his feet and then back up at me, a little flushed. "Maybe I can call you sometime, and we can get together. You know, have a cup of coffee."

"I'd like that," I said, forgetting about my vow to stay as far away from him as possible. After all, he did have those Paul Newman eyes. "You're not married, are you?" I asked.

"No, I'm not, but I do have a dog, so I'm somewhat committed. What about you?"

"I have a cat, so I'm somewhat committed, too."

"Well, then I'll see you."

"Right. You'll see me."

"I'll see you soon."

"You'll see me soon," I answered, laughing.

As he walked out of the room, I was very glad I had worn the blue bed jacket with the bright flowers, although I'd never admit it to Mom. I sunk into a kind of depression within minutes of his departure, though. Grace Wong arrested for Portor Wyler's murder! I had no idea what was going on in the world and was going to remedy that.

Phoning the hospital gift store, I asked for the two major Bay Area newspapers, and any back issues, to be sent up. I also asked a passing candy striper to have the television turned on in the room, realizing I would have known all of these things days ago if I had been watching TV like most of the other patients.

The San Francisco Chronicle still headlined the arrest of Grace Wong for the murder of Portor Wyler, I discovered. The San Jose Mercury gave a very sordid description of the beautiful dancer, the older man, and the illegal immigration ring on pages two and three. My name was sprinkled about, as well as D.I.'s. Both papers gave little in the way of real information but offered a great deal of juicy speculation. Yellow journalism at its best. I felt a pang of sadness for Yvette Wyler. What a way to find out about your husband's secret life! I wondered if she'd regretted asking D.I. to investigate her husband's indiscretions. It had become a real Pandora's Box.

An hour later Richard called, and after our usual banter, I asked if he knew about the circumstances of Grace Wong's arrest. Richard seemed eager to talk about it and needed little prompting.

"Oddly enough," he offered, "it was our tapes of the license plates that made the arrest possible; at least that's what the cops said. It didn't help she called in sick to the theatre on the night Wyler was killed. She can't or won't say where she was, Lee. She's completely mum. Can you believe it? Anyway, they say she had the motive and opportunity."

"But what motive, Richard?" I wanted to know. "He was the source for bringing her family into the country."

"Except..." Richard began grandly. "It seems he refused to bring in any more of her relatives. He felt he had done too much already, bringing in two brothers in one year and her grandmother the year before. After all, she was just another lay," Richard added and then coughed self-consciously.

"Good God!" I exclaimed. "Where did you learn all of that?"

"Well, mostly on the internet. Two of those seamen, who spoke English, said Wyler argued with her, telling her he was finished bringing in her family. Boy, they talked their heads off to the authorities once they got behind bars. Then, the Captain of the ship swore it had to be Grace Wong who shot Wyler, because he heard her voice when he was talking to Wyler on the phone that night. Chen was out at sea at the time, but he swears he heard her. It's been on in the news and on television for days. Haven't you been watching?"

"No, I just read today's papers, and I'm appalled."

"Bad grammar or what? Why are you appalled?"

"It's not any newspaper's bad grammar," I replied. "It's the idea of the killer being Grace Wong."

"I know. Can you believe it? She struck me like basically a sweet girl, if you know what I mean, unpredictable, but sweet. At least, that's the impression I got when I did her dossier for you," he added.

Strange, I thought. This was one more person calling Grace Wong a sweet girl. Ed, Maggie, and now Richard. Not only did she appear to be a 'sweet girl,' but also she had done a great deal to help her family, albeit illegally, come into this country. So she slept with a man to make that possible. Did that automatically make her a murderer?

"Do they have a smoking gun? None of the papers say," I asked.

"Gun?" Richard said, as if I had asked him if the police had a polar bear on water skis.

"Literarily, Richard. The murder weapon," I said pointedly. "Did they find the revolver? Frank told me it was some type of derringer."

"No, they didn't or, at least, they're not saying," he said. "But they have three more witnesses who say about a month ago she threatened to kill Wyler after he refused to help her any more. I got that online from the CNN Breaking News." He paused; I paused, and I guess there was too much still air on his end of the telephone.

"Lee? You still there?"

"Yes, Richard. I'm here."

"What's the matter? Don't you think she did it?"

"No, I don't, Richard, but I base this on practically nothing. Don't pay any attention to me."

"Now that I think about it, I don't think she did it, either."

We sat in mutual silence on the phone for the better part of a minute breathing into each other's ear. Richard broke the silence. "Sister mine, I think I'll find out exactly what the prosecution has got and let you know."

"Can you do that?" I asked, aghast. "I mean, facts, Richard. Not rumors, not innuendos, but hard facts. Can you do that?"

"Yes, I can, but it isn't easy, and if anybody asks you, I can't. Understand? Now what exactly do we want to know?"

I felt my heartbeat quicken. "Wait a minute, Richard. Mom says you're on overload now. I don't want to add to what you already have."

"Don't worry about it. This strikes me as about two or three hours worth of work, max. Besides, if she's innocent..." He stopped talking and the thought hung out there over the telephone lines.

"That's how I feel. Let's see what we can do, Richard, to help her. Get a pencil and write this down, okay?"

"Okay."

"Ready?" I heard him grunt an assent and began organizing my mind. I closed my eyes to help myself concentrate. "Okay. Do they have a murder weapon? If so, to whom is it registered?"

"Oh, how proper we are," Richard interjected. "I would have just asked 'Who's it registered to?'"

"Shush! Don't interrupt me. Where was I? Oh, yes. If they've got the weapon, whose fingerprints are on it? Has Grace Wong actually admitted shooting him? I mean, maybe we're both wrong, and she did do it. What are the exact charges, anyway? Does she have an attorney? If so, who is it? And lastly, Richard, and this is important, is there any way I can see her?"

"You?" Richard choked on the other side of the phone. "See her? What do you want to see her for? Or should I have said, 'for what do you want to see her?' Did it ever occur to you, Liana, that she might feel you are responsible for her downfall? *Estas loca!*"

"I'm not crazy, and I don't think she blames me." I thought for a moment. "But can you find out?"

"Listen, Lee, unless she's said that to someone, or it's written it down somewhere, I can't find out if she blames you. I don't do magic, I just do computer."

"I've seen you pull magic tricks out of your computer hat all the time. Just the other day..."

"Besides," he interrupted, paying no attention to my oily words, "you've got to take it easy when you come out of the hospital for a couple of weeks. You know that," Richard said, with an edge to his voice. "You're not going to jeopardize your health again."

"No, I'm not going to do anything to jeopardize my health or anything else. However..."

"Uh oh. Here's the 'however,'" he replied.

"However, it might not be necessary to meet her in person," I reflected. "How about if you see if it's an option? I promise not to do anything without you knowing about it. How's that? I promise," I said again, trying to appease him.

"All right," Richard said after a pause. "I'll do what I can today or tomorrow in between trying to get this stupid merger finished for Our Lady."

"Thanks, Richard. I appreciate it." I was silent for a moment, suddenly filled with a myriad of emotions. "Richard?"

"Still here, Lee, although I've got to go in a minute."

"I love you, Richard." After saying that, I felt suddenly idiotic. "I wanted to say it, because I hardly ever do," I added.

"I love you, too, Banana Breath."

We both burst out laughing at the memory of the childhood nickname he'd given me when I ate five bananas on a dare and burped into the night.

"Gotta go, Lee. Our Lady wants some stats by five o'clock tonight. I'll get back to you as soon as I can. I promise."

The next day came, and I got a short phone call in the morning from Richard telling me he hadn't had time to get on "that" information.

In the afternoon Tío showed up with snapshots of Tugger taken the day before. I was surprised to see how big he had gotten in less than a week. Rather selfishly, I wondered if the kitten was bonding more with my uncle than me.

It would only be natural if the cat does. In fact, maybe I should let my uncle have Tugger. He's becoming more and more attached to the little guy. Maybe Tío needs him even more than I do.

I felt my throat tighten, as the thought went through my mind that I probably should make the offer. It was the least I could do. The day after tomorrow I would go home and see if Tugger really belonged with Tío or with me. That night I asked for a sleeping pill for the first time since I had been in the hospital.

Chapter Sixteen
By A Hair's Breadth

I awoke before seven a.m. anticipating a big day. Hospital routine being what it was, I had heard movements in the hallway and knew the hospital had been long awake. I was a little excited but nervous, because Doctor Parsley would tell me whether or not I could go home the following day. He would also be removing the bandages. I was glad for a variety of reasons, not the least of which was my scalp itched where the stitches were, and the idea of washing my hair sounded like nirvana.

I had never met Mom's hairdresser, Enrico, and wondered what he would be like. I didn't have long to wonder. He came bouncing in shortly after breakfast carrying a small suitcase. A short, slender young man, he wore an unstructured, black linen suit, beneath that, a black silk shirt with mother-of-pearl buttons and matching cufflinks. He wore his own black hair elegantly styled in short, spiked tufts, artfully arranged around his oval face. In one ear, a diamond stud sparkled brightly. I knew immediately why Lila liked him. He was very put together for seven-thirty in the morning. Now, if only he could cut hair.

Enrico was exceedingly friendly. As he set his case down and began extracting equipment, he chatted nonstop. He "was dying to see what these butchers had done," so he had just "zipped over at the crack of dawn," because he couldn't wait any longer. Fortunately, he stopped talking long enough for me to tell him the doctor wasn't scheduled to remove the bandages until eight a.m.

I sent Enrico down to the coffee shop to wait and hoped the doctor would show up on time. He did and removed the bandages with absolutely no pomp and circumstance. Doctor Parsley examined each wound saying "Hmmmmm" with each one. I thought better than to ask him any questions, and he probably wouldn't have heard me, anyway.

"Coming along very nicely, Ms. Alvarez, especially the jagged one in the back. Excellent!" I murmured something insignificant, as he picked up the chart lovingly and began scribbling. "I don't see why you can't leave tomorrow morning, right? No more headaches, correct? No fever, right? No infections, no, no." He was, of course, asking the chart and not me, but I felt obliged to shake or nod my head, whatever seemed appropriate.

"Well, off I go, Ms. Alvarez," he said to the chart. "The nurse will make an appointment for you to see me next week in my office to remove those stitches. Meanwhile, no alcohol, and if you get a mild headache, take an aspirin. If you should get a severe one, give us a call. Oh, and about your scalp," he added, "there's a special shampoo you have to use. The nurse will bring it in to you. Be very careful washing around the stitches. We don't want them opening up and you bleeding on us again!" He smiled, finally looking into my face. I grinned back at him like an idiot. He left the room in a flurry, clutching several files to his bosom.

I got out of bed and examined my hair closely in the mirror over the sink in the bathroom. Well, Enrico had called it. "Butchered" just about summed it up. What was still three or four inches long had been pushed flat on my scalp by the bandage. A few clumps of about a half an inch long stuck out near each one of the sutured areas the doctor examined. A nurse entered the bathroom and together we managed to wash my hair in the shower with a maximum of fuss and bother.

It surprised me how much this wore me out. I was glad to get back into bed afterward with a towel wrapped around my head. Enrico, finishing up a cheese Danish, returned from the coffee shop a short time later. After several minutes of examining my hair from every angle, he held his hand over his heart and aimed his eyes heavenward.

"What I do for the scintillating Lila Alvarez," he muttered and began his task.

After an hour, just as I thought he would never be done, he stood back and sighed contentedly. "Well, my clients tell me I'm a genius, and now I know they're right. Voila!" he exclaimed and put a hand mirror in front of my face. I took it hesitantly and braved a look in the mirror. What had begun as something looking like it came straight out of a medieval lunatic asylum, now resembled a stylish do. I had to admit, even though I had worn my hair long all my life, this short style looked good. Sort of Audrey Hepburn in *Roman Holiday*. I thanked Enrico, tipped him profusely, and took a long nap when he left.

The afternoon was less busy. Remembering the fatigue of the morning, I took several walks in the hallway trying to build up my stamina. Other than phone calls from Mom and Tío, I spent the rest of the time thinking and napping. Richard didn't call, and I assumed it meant he didn't have any information yet. In the evening, I packed the few things I had and fell asleep right after *Jeopardy*.

At six a.m., the phone rang waking me from a light slumber. I answered feeling better than I had in days. It was Richard. "Morning, Glory. *Qué tal*? Sorry if I woke you," he said anxiously.

"Richard, what a surprise! No, I was just getting up. Where are you?"

"I'm at the office. I've been here since about two," he said, his voice a little scratchy.

"Two? Two o'clock in the morning? You're kidding!" I exclaimed.

"No, I'm not. It's the best time to access certain things," he added with an enigmatic air.

"How does Victoria feel about you leaving at that hour?" Victoria had moved in with Richard about six months ago.

"She's used to it." I could sense him shrug over the phone. "I have to work weird hours. She knows that."

I could hold back no longer in expressing my opinion on the young woman currently in my brother's life. "Richard, grab this gal. She's a gem."

He laughed lightly. "Don't worry, I will. Now do you want to know what I have or not?" He heard my sharp intake of breath and went on. "I've made notes. Ready?"

"Ready." I found a pencil and waited silently. I heard the rustle of papers on his end of the line.

Richard read from his notes. "Grace Wong has not been officially charged with anything, as of yet, because they are trying to build a good case against her first. Apparently the fact that she, number one, had a nasty fight in front of witnesses with Wyler a month before he died and, number two, will not say where she was the night of the murder, has the State of California convinced it's her. The scuttlebutt is she will probably be arraigned sometime next week on charges of Murder One. They do not have the smoking gun. Repeat, no smoking gun. The prosecution is saying she probably threw it in the Bay and is making half-hearted attempts at recovery. However, they don't expect to find it, the currents are very strong, it could be out to sea or buried under tons of silt and blah, blah, woof, woof. My sources say they're going to try to build a case on circumstantial evidence, and so far what they have is pretty strong. The prosecuting attorney is Warren Thacker. Heard of him?"

"No."

"Well, you will. Out to make a name for himself with this case and pushing hard. The police are questioning everyone, and the most damning evidence against Gracie, ironically, is the Captain of the *Feng Shen*. He's trying to cut a deal. He's cooperating on the murder of Wyler hoping he can plead to lesser charges for what he did to you. The word out is it won't get him very far, but he is talking to anyone who will listen. He swears he heard her voice over the phone that night when he was talking to Wyler ship-to-shore. Meanwhile, her lawyer, Jake Feinstein, who has a so-so reputation, is trying to get her released into her own recognizance."

"How does that look?"

"The judge hasn't made a ruling yet, but she probably won't get it, because she won't defend herself. Also, there isn't anybody else the defense can come up with who could have committed the murder other than 'person or persons unknown.' Mrs. Wyler was home all night, her housekeeper swears to that. Captain Chen was in the middle of the Pacific Ocean."

"So those two are out," I said.

"Yeah, and I had wondered about Mrs. Wyler. You know what they say, '*cherchez la femme.*'"

"Who says that?" I demanded.

"Nobody in particular says it. It's just a French saying. It means 'look for the woman.'"

"Not in this case. She's been cleared."

"I know that, Lee," Richard said testily. "I was just…"

"Showing off your French?" I finished for him.

"Never mind my French. Should I go on?"

"Please do but let's stick to English or Spanish, okay?"

"Boy, are you obnoxious when you're bored."

"I'm listening, Richard."

"Okay, to continue, even Ernie Butler..."

"Who's Ernie Butler?" I interrupted.

"Are you ever going to let me get a complete sentence out?" he asked, through what sounded like gritted teeth.

"Sorry," I said contritely. "I'll shut up."

"Ernie Butler is or was his legit partner. He attended a tailgate party for the Stanford-Cal game that night with about twenty other people. Wyler didn't have any friends or girlfriends besides Grace Wong — if you can call her a girlfriend — or even a private life from what they can find. Too busy making money. I mean, Lee, they got nobody, no how, but her. Did you know Butler inherits the real estate business, lock, stock and barrel? A right of survivorship will they both signed last year."

"So it could be this Butler guy, too," I mused. Just to make sure I had the cast of characters, I said, "Tell me again about Ernie Butler."

"The other half of the real estate development thing Wyler had going in Palo Alto for the past twenty, thirty years. This illegal immigration business with Chen was his real moneymaker, though. Here's the kicker, Lee, they've found over thirty million dollars in a bank account in the Cayman Islands. Wyler's wife practically fainted when she found out about that. I understand she's been on tranqs for days now. Of course, what can the INS do about that money? They'd have to prove it's illegally gotten, and from what I understand, Wyler laundered it pretty well. I don't even think they can bring it back into the country to tax it. It's just sitting there on an island in the middle of the Caribbean."

"You amaze me, Richard. You really do. Did you find out all of this last night?" I asked in an awed tone of voice.

"Well, most of it," he answered humbly. "Hey, it's what I do, Lee."

"This is all for real? I mean, you're sure of it?"

"Yeah, I'm sure. And forget going to see her. The prosecution isn't letting anyone near Grace Wong, not even her father and mother. Boy, is her lawyer going to have to do some dancing, no pun intended. She is totally uncooperative. From what I understand, she just sits and stares at the cops every time they question her. The police are starting not to like our China Doll, and I don't like that."

"I don't like that, either," I said, chewing on my lower lip. "Richard, don't call her China Doll any more. It's demeaning."

"It is?" Richard asked in an astonished voice.

"Yes."

"Okay, whatever you say."

"Richard, none of this sounds right," I said. "I don't know what; I can't place it, but something's definitely wrong. I need to think about this."

"Okay. I gotta go." He expelled a deep sigh. "I'm going to lie down on one of the sofas for a couple of hours before my real day starts. When do you go home?"

I glanced up at the wall clock. "In about an hour. Richard, thank you so very, very much. Get some sleep."

"You're so very, very welcome," he replied, mocking my tone. "Call me later if you think of anything. We're partners in this, you know."

"You bet we are!" I responded.

* * * *

An hour later, Mom arrived with Tío. Necessary paperwork was signed, and they drove me home. All the way back, Tío spoke enthusiastically about Tugger and his antics. I was heartsick to admit it, but I knew it was the right thing to give the cat to my uncle. The thought of parting with Tugger filled me with more emptiness than I would have believed possible. I credited it to maternal hormones acting up. I'd just have to get over it, that's all, I told myself. Maybe they had some pills for this kind of thing. I'd ask the doctor on my next visit. After all, a cat was just a cat…unless it was Tugger.

They fussed over me on the trip back to the apartment, until I thought I would scream. I turned the key in the lock, called out, and saw an orange and white ball of fluff run from the kitchen towards us. I half expected Tugger to run to Tío's feet, but he didn't. He stopped at mine, giving me his small, silent meow. He remembers me, I thought inanely. I bent down closer to him. He, meanwhile, rubbed my ankles and purred loudly.

"Look!" I turned to Tío and Mom in utter happiness, "He remembers me. He likes me!"

"Of course, he remembers you, Liana," Mom said matter-of-factly. "My goodness, it's only been five days," she added, as she went into the kitchen.

"He was lonely, *mi sobrina*," Tío confirmed. "He would roam around looking for you. I spent last night on the sofa with him."

"Oh, Tío," I murmured. "You didn't have to do that. Or, at least, you could have slept in my bed." I held the purring animal in my arms and looked down at his contented, half-closed eyes. "I missed you, you little scamp. I'm so glad you missed me."

"I've never gotten a greeting like this from Liana. Have you, Mateo? I think she likes that stupid cat more than she likes us," Lila said, as she came to the kitchen door and looked at both of us, laughter in her eyes. "I'm brewing some green tea," she added, walking towards the hall closet and taking out bed linens. "I read an article yesterday that says it's one of nature's cure-alls. Then we're going to leave *you* to rest." She looked directly at me.

I set the cat down and went to my mother, who was unfolding a blanket. I reached out and hugged her. "Mom, thank you for all you've done. You, too, Tío." I crossed over to him and walked into his bear-like hug. "I'm so lucky."

"Don't go maudlin on us, Liana, or I'll think there's more to your head injury than the doctors say there is." Mom smiled as she made up the sofa. "Besides, it's unnecessary. Now lie down," she ordered. "The sweat suit you're wearing can double as your pajamas for now."

"Liana is never maudlin, if it means what I think it means," Mateo countered good-naturedly. "It means boring, right?"

"Not exactly, Mateo. It means overly sentimental," Mom answered.

"She is emotional, our Liana. She is vibrant! She is a Latina!" he said with gusto. All three of us laughed, as I wrapped myself in a blanket on the sofa. Mom served the tea.

Lila was right, though. I had become maudlin, insipid, and overly sentimental. I guess that's what a life and death experience can do to you. Maybe I would snap out of it in a day or two. If not, I would rent a few Andy Hardy movies. They were enough to snap anybody out of anything. The kitten ran over and curled up in my lap. I felt another pang of guilt about depriving my uncle of Tugger's company.

"*Mi Sobrina*," Tío said abruptly, as if reading my thoughts, "now that you are home and able to care for Tagger..."

"Tugger, Tío," I said.

"*Si*, Tugger," he repeated carefully. "I will be going to the animal shelter every day to help take care of some of the less fortunate ones there."

"What?" I gasped, nearly spilling tea on Tugger.

His eyes sparkled with pride. "Yes, I have gone to the shelter and volunteered my time for the last week or so when I was not here or at the hospital. I find I enjoy taking care of animals, and there is so great a need," he finished solemnly. "Your mother has even suggested I build a few cages in the backyard for the recuperating ones until we can find each of them a good home."

"You do realize, Mateo," interjected Lila, "that Palo Alto has a very strict ordinance regarding the number of animals allowed in a private residence at one time." She poured herself more tea, content in the realization she had taken the side of the right and the just. Mothers.

"Oh, *si*, and we will never go over that amount," he answered. "We must not break any laws…but bending them occasionally, I do not mind," he added with a twinkle. Mom and I could see his mind drifting back in time and instinctively waited for him to speak.

"I always wanted a dog, but your *Tía* was allergic, so it was not possible. Besides, with my long days and nights at the restaurant, my life was too busy."

"Now I will take care of many, many dogs that need me. And cats, too, and rabbits and whatever else is in need. It is a good thing to do, and I am pleased with myself." He put down his teacup for emphasis.

I leaned forward and kissed him on the cheek. "I'm so happy for you, Tío. Thanks again for taking such good care of Tugger."

"*De nada, mi sobrina*. What is family for, if not such things? Now I will go and let your mama quiet you down. You need your rest." He kissed me on the forehead and left.

We watched him go, and as the door closed, Mom took my hands in hers. "I have some disturbing news to tell you, sweetheart, and I hope you won't be too upset."

Of course, I panicked. People always do when they're told someone hopes they won't be too upset. "What's wrong? What's happened?"

"Shh. Calm down and listen to me. Captain Chen's lawyer has managed to make a case for bail. It was set at one million, five hundred thousand, and well, somehow Chen found the money. They released him this morning."

Frankly, I was relieved that's all it was. Although I didn't like the idea of my would-be assassin walking the streets, it could have been a lot worse; something could have been wrong with one of the family. You get your priorities straight when you have a near-death experience.

"That's okay, Mom, really. I'm sure the law will do its stuff later on. He's got money and it talks, but only so much."

"There's more, Liana. We found out he lives right here in Palo Alto."

"What?" My heart did a somersault and thudded against my back teeth.

"Yes. Richard found that out when Chen put his house up for collateral. He lives right off University Street."

"*Hijo de perra!*" I exclaimed without thinking and then waited for Mom to tell me to watch my language. When she didn't, I knew she was distressed.

"Even though the judge issued a restraining order keeping him away from you and the rest of us, I am worried, Liana. We don't know how many months it will be until he comes to trial…"

I interrupted her. "Mom, we've lived in Palo Alto all our lives, and we've never run into him. Why should it happen now, especially with the restraining order?"

"I don't know, Liana," Mom whispered and shook her head. Lila's face was drained of color, and I could see the strain of the last few weeks on it.

"It'll be fine, just fine. You'll see, Mom." I hugged her and didn't let go. My mother's arms enveloped me, and I smelled the perfume I had known all my life. Instantly, I felt warm and safe and at the same time, protective. No one was going to hurt my family or me like that ever again. Or intimidate us, either.

"Mom, we can't let lowlife like that get us down. Besides, Chen would never be stupid enough to do anything else to me. He's in enough trouble. Palo Alto is Frank's territory, too. Do you think he would let Chen get away with anything?"

"You should have heard Frank when he found out." Mom actually let out a soft chuckle. "Frank said he was going to put a twenty-four hour surveillance on him, just to make sure Chen didn't break any more laws."

I released my mother and looked into her eyes. "Well, there. You see? It's all going to be fine, Mom, really." I felt my head begin to throb and was suddenly overcome with fatigue. I leaned back and closed my eyes. Mom adjusted the covers, and then I felt her stroke my forehead.

"I think you're right," she said in a matter-of-fact tone. "The worst is over. I'm going to go now. I'll be at work all day if you need me, so don't hesitate to call. You get some rest, Liana. I mean it. Don't try to go out today."

"I won't, Mom, I promise. All I want to do is just lie around, play with Tugger and get well." I had a sudden thought. "How's Mrs. Wyler been taking all of this? You must have talked to her recently." I opened my eyes and looked at Mom.

"Not well at all. Every time I see her, her nerves seem to be more and more shot. Poor Yvette. I'm going to try to make her forget about all of this for a while. Here's something that should interest you, knowing your newfound love of cats. The day after tomorrow she and I are going to the San Francisco Zoo. It's the official one-year birthday party for the two Siberian tiger cubs were born there last year. My goodness, I seem to be surrounded by animals these days! What is happening to my life?" she asked dramatically and laughed. So did I.

"Guadalupe will bring your lunch around eleven-thirty today. Look for her. And call her if you need anything else," Lila said. She picked up her purse and headed for the door. "I'll look in on you tonight. Now get some rest. *Dormiendos dulces, mi hija,"* she added softly, as she closed the door and double locked it.

I slept on and off throughout the day to the sounds of drizzling rain. I woke up periodically with a nagging feeling I had forgotten something really important; but no matter how hard I tried, I couldn't remember what it was. I gave up trying around six o'clock and sent out for pizza with everything on it. I'd been lusting for one the last two days at the hospital. Between the kitten and me, we ate the entire thing by midnight.

Chapter Seventeen
It's Been A Hard Day's Night

That night I had one of the weirdest dreams of my life. I was running through the woods wearing a chiffon evening gown that kept changing colors on me. I had a scarf tied around my neck about a hundred yards long. As it trailed behind me, it kept getting caught in all the trees and bushes. My baby pink toe shoes kept coming untied, and I couldn't do any pirouettes. Gene Kelly showed up in a clearing. He tried to teach me a buck and wing, but I had lost the toe shoes by then and was barefoot. Mr. Kelly was very annoyed because my feet weren't making any tapping sounds. Suddenly I was Dorothy in *The Wizard of Oz* clicking those stupid red sequin shoes together and saying "there's no place like home" over and over. I woke up all tangled up in the bed covers with a wide-eyed kitten staring at me from the safety of the night table. I tell you, you've got to watch out for those midnight snacks.

It took me a few seconds to figure out where I was, and by then, Guadalupe was knocking on my door with a breakfast tray laden with a carafe of coffee, Canadian bacon, and steel-cut oatmeal topped with brown sugar and raisins. Life doesn't get much better.

After feeding the kitten and myself and doing a modified barre, I was at loose ends. It was around nine-thirty and one of the most gorgeous mornings I'd ever seen. Standing in the doorway of the back deck, I looked out. The sun shone brightly, it was about sixty-eight degrees, and a soft breeze caressed my skin. I went outside with a second cup of coffee, followed by Tugger. One of the many things Tío did was put up temporary screening against the wooden slats of the railing so the kitten couldn't slip through. Hanging from the guardrail are window boxes filled with various flowering plants. Like all the rest of the plant kingdom dependent on me, they're on a self-watering timer.

Maybe when Tugger gets older, he'll figure out a way to jump into those boxes, but I'll deal with it then, I thought.

Said companion plopped himself down in the sun, rolled around a bit and wound up with his belly in the air watching me intently through tawny eyes. I sat down on the floor of the deck and played with him. What with one thing and another, a full hour went by. He was ready for a nap, and I was ready to pull what was left of my hair out. I was antsy, bored and tired of squashing down a niggling feeling, so I decided to take a walk.

I took a shower and got out a clean sweat suit from the back of the closet. It was a faded hot pink number with stains and rips, but one I couldn't bear to part with. To keep a modicum of self-respect, I added my old black leather jacket, since the one I wore to the warehouse was currently being boiled in oil, reconstituted and prayed over by Leatherworks. The outlook wasn't good. I grabbed a baseball cap to protect my recovering scalp from the rays of the sun, and headed out.

The main drag of Palo Alto is a street called University running east to west. It's chockfull of shops, upscale restaurants, fast-food places, hotels, and shade trees, all the things to make a charming little town charming. From where we live, it's only about five blocks, and I knew the walk would do me good. I took my time and wound up in front of Borders bookstore in about fifteen or twenty minutes.

I was weighing the pros and cons of going inside when I saw a man out of the corner of my eye, who looked suspiciously like Captain Chen. Not believing it to be so, I stared right at him and saw it was he, indeed. He was talking on a payphone — one of the few remaining in Palo Alto — and in such a deep conversation that when a bird pooped on his shoulder, he didn't even notice. I lowered the brim of my cap and circled around to the back of him. I couldn't quite hear what he said, but I could tell from his body language he was angry, hostile and firm. After expelling an evil little laugh, he hung up the phone, picked up a folded newspaper and walked west.

I'm going to be completely honest here. For somebody who was bored and antsy, with a nagging niggle, this was like manna from heaven.

Who was he talking to on the phone? What was up with the evil, Boris Karloff laugh? Where is the dastardly Chen going now?

It amazed me I was more intrigued by these questions than frightened by my former assailant, but that's me. Nothing could have stopped me from following him, from a safe distance, of course. He walked another block on University. I darted in and out of doorways just like I'd seen in every B movie of the forties, trying to keep from knocking pedestrians over in the process. Then he turned left onto a side street called Dorcus.

Like most of Palo Alto's streets, both sides of Dorcus are lined with large, old trees. You know the kind I mean, the ones where the roots have upturned most of the sidewalks and created natural speed bumps in the road. If you want to keep your rear axle, you have to drive less than fifteen miles an hour, a boon to a neighborhood filled with children. I found myself hiding behind the thick trunks, as I followed him. Chen finally stopped at the third house from the end. He opened the white picket gate, went up the steps and checked the mailbox.

I hugged the far side of a tree, elated at my vantage point, when I heard a commotion at my feet. Not daring to move, I glanced down and saw one of those small dogs on an expandable leash of about thirty feet long. It was attached to an elderly man on the other end. The octogenarian plodded behind, muttering, "Brutus, come," "No, Brutus," and so forth.

The dog, reminiscent of a fox that had been shrunk in the rain, ignored his owner. He was too enthralled with whatever scent presented itself to him at the base of my tree. Wouldn't you know, an overhead squirrel spied the dog and began making those chattering noises squirrels make. Now, I like dogs and this Brutus was small, cute and fuzzy, but he was a yapper. With Brutus yapping his head off below, the chattering rodent started to circle the upper trunk as if its tail was on fire.

Not to be outdone, the yapper tried to keep up with the squirrel and the race was on. Brutus tore around the base of the tree several times pulling along his owner who looked like a man who had a whale on the end of a fishing line. During all of this, I didn't move. I just knew Captain Chen was following this drama from the steps of his house, like everyone else on the block. I stayed quiet and allowed myself to be trussed up on the far side of the tree. For about five minutes, the dog yapped, the squirrel chattered, and the old man fussed. I just stood there like Joan of Arc before the lighting of the bonfire.

Eventually, the senior citizen unwrapped me, apologized profusely and, carrying a still yapping Brutus, went on his way. The squirrel, now silent, watched me sink to the ground and had the nerve to come down the side of the tree headfirst and stop about five inches from my face, where it stared deeply into my eyes. By this time, I had had it, so I took off my cap, and swatted at the furry rodent.

"Go find your own damn tree," I growled. Startled, it leapt onto the ground, ran across the street and straight up another tree. There's nothing more rewarding than a well-trained animal.

I sat there for about fifteen minutes wondering what I had done in a past life to deserve this, when I became aware of more impending doom. A small child stared at me from a yard across the street. With my luck, the child's mother had already called the police, who were on their way to arrest me for vagrancy. I got up, pulled the cap down to my nose and tried to saunter casually away, hoping no one other than the kid was still watching me. I immediately went to a nearby Starbucks and ordered a double mocha latte with whipped cream on top. There had never been a greater need.

After that, I returned home and tried to put a positive spin on my latest adventure. Not being able to do so, I took a nap. The rest of the day passed uneventfully except for the delicious meals delivered by the wondrous Guadalupe. Mom and Tío dropped by in the early evening, and I went to bed around eight p.m. sleeping until nine-thirty the next morning. I had turned off the ringer of the phone in my bedroom and was in such a deep sleep, I hadn't heard Mom, Tío or Guadalupe knock on the door. Worried, Lila let herself in with her key and finding me dead to the world with a sleeping kitten perched upon my chest, left a note and my breakfast on the kitchen table.

I was dressed in another pair of ratty sweats — more faded than purple — and in the middle of reheating the omelet, when I heard a pounding on the front door. I opened it to find Frank standing there and in a rare mood, even for Frank. He had a look in his eyes that could peel paint off a wall.

"And just where were you last night, young lady?" he demanded in a voice so loud Tugger darted under a chair. With that, Frank pushed past me to the center of the room where he wheeled around to continue his paint-peeling look. I stared at him uncomprehendingly.

"Well? Where were you?"

"I...I was here, Frank," I stuttered. "I never left the place."

"That's not true," he bellowed. "Yesterday you were seen in downtown Palo Alto by one of my men. One of my men, Liana! How do you think this makes me look?"

"But that was yesterday morning. You asked me about last night," I answered him, mystified by his behavior. I had never seen this side of Frank in my life, and I've seen a lot of sides. Watching him try to restrain himself, I wondered what this was all about. I was afraid to say anything until he got himself under control. He paced the room for a few seconds and then turned on me, blurting out,

"Chen is dead. Dead! Shot three times in the chest, just like Wyler." I stared at him and felt my legs go rubbery. I sank into a nearby chair.

"A PG&E employee sent out to read the gas meter found him early this morning. The back door was wide open. Chen was lying in the middle of the kitchen floor covered in blood."

"*Dios mio!*" I exclaimed, too shocked to say much more.

"You'd better ask the good *Dios* for help, because you're in serious trouble, and I might not be able to get you out of it."

"Why am I in trouble? I don't understand."

He leaned down and got so close to me our noses almost touched. My eyes crossed as he spoke slowly and quietly. "Because this is the second murder you have been involved in, and they are suspiciously alike. It has the same MO. It has the same everything. And you were there. Both times. You even found the first body. This doesn't look good for you. Not one bit. So I'm asking you again, where were you last night?"

I pulled back a little, uncrossed my eyes, feeling a little huffy. "You can't seriously believe I killed him! Why on earth would I do that?"

"Right off the top of my head, I might say it's because he tried to kill you. That's what a prosecuting attorney would say. But I don't deal in motives. I'm just a cop. I deal in means and opportunity, of which you had plenty."

"But Portor Wyler was shot with a derringer. You said so yourself. I don't own one of those things." I was trying not to panic.

He straightened up and began pacing the room again. "You're a PI. You could have picked one up in your travels. You could have bought one on the Internet. Hell, I don't know. The preliminary tests show Chen was shot with a similar weapon as Wyler, if not the same one." Frank threw himself into the chair across from me, the one under which Tugger was wisely keeping out of sight. He covered his face with both hands and shook his head. Then he took a deep breath and looked at me, waiting.

Tears sprang to my eyes. I didn't know whether I was more shocked Captain Chen had been murdered or more hurt Frank thought I might have done it. "I didn't kill him, Frank. I swear to you. I didn't kill him." With all the anger drained from him, I could see his fatigue and worry.

"Oh, I know that, Liana, I do. I'm just scared for you. Don't you see? You were the last known person to see Wyler alive, and you have no alibi for his death. Then you were kidnapped by his partner, Captain Chen, and almost killed. Now Chen shows up dead in the house you followed him to earlier in the day. It's in one of my own reports written by one of my men, assigned to keep an eye on him." He became exasperated again. "You idiotic child! How could you follow him like that? Don't you realize what kind of compromising position you've put yourself in?"

"Wait a minute!" I saw a glimmer of hope. "If you had someone watching Chen's house, then he knows I didn't come back after I left in the morning, doesn't he?"

Frank leaned back, completely deflated. When he spoke, his tone was low and expressionless. "Not really. We had a five-car pileup, with two fatalities, shortly before midnight. I had to pull Leo off the job for about two hours late last night." He continued speaking, his voice filled with guilt. "We're hurting, Liana. I didn't have the budget to keep someone around the clock on Chen exclusively. I could only do it when, and if, nothing else was happening, but I didn't want to tell your mother that. I knew she was worried enough. There's a two hour window where I can't prove you didn't go back and shoot him."

I was more than a little scared. "What should I do, Frank? Tell me and I'll do it."

"Well, first of all, answer me. Where you were between ten-thirty p.m. and twelve-thirty a.m. last night?"

"I was here, asleep."

"Please tell me Lila was with you or your uncle. Someone. Anyone."

I shook my head slowly. "I'm sorry, Frank. There's nobody. I was alone, and I was asleep."

He sighed deeply. "You'd better hope we find the killer and fast, or it's going to be you in jail instead of that Wong woman. It's not going to take San Francisco long to find out you are a common denominator. I only have this little time now because the killings took place in two different counties. They're going to piece them together, and when they do, you become the number one suspect. I'll do all I can, but you may want to get yourself a lawyer."

"A lawyer? But I…"

He interrupted me sternly. "Yes, a lawyer, Liana, or we might be continuing this conversation from a jail cell. Now I mean it. If you don't know a good criminal lawyer, I do. I won't have Bobby's baby girl in jail. I won't have it."

We were on the same page with that thought.

Frank left shortly after that, with a promise he would keep me up to the minute on everything. I also promised to stay put. I had several cups of chamomile tea to settle my jangled nerves and just sat there. I wasn't sure what to do, so as Dad always said, when you don't know what to do, do nothing. That was me, the Queen of Nothing.

It was eleven-thirty a.m. when the doorbell rang. I assumed it would be Guadalupe with lunch and opened the door to find a deliveryman holding a package from Neiman Marcus. Surprised, I signed for it, tipped him generously and sent him on his way. When I ripped open the box, I saw a pair of black, suede boots exactly like the pair I'd worn at the warehouse.

"That was the night that started everything," I mused aloud. "Poor Portor Wyler. Even though he turned out to be a real scumbag," I added. I put the boots back in the box and set it down on the coffee table.

Tugger felt compelled to investigate the new item coming into "his" house and jumped onto the table for a closer look. The smell of new suede, an irresistible item for any cat, attracted his full attention. Several seconds later, I noticed he was standing on top of one of the boots in the box, gnawing on a leather tie.

"No. No. Bad boy!" I shouted, shooing him away. "What do you want to do? Ruin my new boots before I even put them on?" I asked him crossly. I stopped and looked down at the kitten that studied me with marked curiosity. I had never yelled at him before, and he didn't quite understand what I was doing. He was curious but certainly not fearful. Laughing, I picked him up in one hand and the chewed boot in the other. Then I froze. A new, and formerly inconceivable, thought came into my mind. I had heard the phrase "bolt out of the blue" but had never experienced one before this moment. Color me bolted.

"Ruined shoes," I said slowly. I dropped the boot as if it were on fire and ran to the phone, absentmindedly still carrying a lolling Tugger. I hit the autodial on the phone, waited a minute while it rang repeatedly then rolled over to the secretary's desk.

"Patti!" I said urgently, not allowing her to finish her usual telephone greeting. "This is Lee. Is Lila there?" After learning Lila wasn't, I remembered Mom had left me a note reminding me this was the day she was going to the zoo with Mrs. Wyler.

Fighting back the mounting fear, I asked her to transfer me to Richard and, instead, got his assistant, Erica. Richard, too, had taken the day off and had departed for parts unknown. He was going to call in later on in the day. Could Erica relay a message to him when he did?

You're damned straight you can, I thought, but kept my tone professional.

"Yes, ask him to call me, as soon as he can," I replied, gripping the receiver tightly. "Tell him it's urgent. Tell him I know it wasn't Grace Wong. Tell him that exactly." I then had another thought.

"Erica, is there any way you can give me the weather report for January twenty-second on the Peninsula? Maybe it's online somewhere. Thanks, I'll hold." I was pretty sure what I was going to hear, but listened intently to Erica's reply, anyway, and hung up. I started to dial Tío, but remembered he was working at the animal shelter today.

"Wait a minute!" I chided myself. The cell phones! Why didn't I think of that in the first place? I finally dropped the now squirming cat on the sofa and quickly dialed Lila's cell phone number. Of course it wasn't on. They never are when you need them to be. Then I called Richard's cell phone. It was on but call forwarded to the office. When I heard Erica's voice again, I hung up. Alarmed at not being able to reach anyone, I went to the floor safe to get my revolver. I checked to see if it was loaded and took an extra round of shells.

I threw on my leather jacket and almost ran out the door when I remembered I didn't have a car. It was still in the shop and wouldn't be delivered until next week. The battery was out of Dad's car and stored somewhere in the garage. I had no idea how to put one in a car, even if I could find it. I sat down on the sofa to think, and forced myself not to listen to the pounding of my heart.

"Douglas!" The name came to me, and I abruptly stood up. Douglas was only about four blocks away and had a car. I called The Creamery, and as luck would have it, he happened to pick up the phone. Overriding his demand for information about my current health, I asked to borrow his car for the afternoon on urgent business, promising to explain at a later time. Renting a car would take too much time was all I said and time was of the essence. His car was less than five months old, but Douglas finally acquiesced. He's that kind of guy. "Just try to get it back in one piece. Ha, ha," he added. I was more concerned about getting me back in one piece. Ha, ha.

Chapter Eighteen
A Trip To The Zoo

My destination was the San Francisco Zoo. I took Route 280, Skyline Boulevard, and then the Great Highway, which runs along the ocean. Gripping the wheel with white knuckled hands, I often pushed the car to eighty miles per hour. It was still close to one p.m. by the time I arrived at the Zoo. Parking is difficult at the best of times in that area, and I didn't want to spend precious time looking for a space. I parked in the first spot I came to, a fire hydrant, and didn't give a tinker's dam if the car got towed. Douglas would understand...eventually.

Just as I opened the car door to get out, the cell phone rang. It was Richard. I was so relieved I had to control my voice to keep it from shaking. "Richard! Where have you been?"

"Never mind that. Erica said you know it isn't Grace Wong. Do you mean you know who killed Portor Wyler?"

"Yes," I replied eagerly. "Not only that..."

"Well, sit tight on it, would you? We're in Las Vegas. Victoria and I flew here last night. Where are you? Home?" he asked anxiously.

"Not exactly. I'm at the San Francisco Zoo."

"What! Why?"

"Richard, listen to me. Mrs. Wyler killed her husband; I don't care what her housekeeper says. I've got proof. And I'm pretty sure she also killed David Chen last night."

"Chen is dead? What happened? My God, what's going on?"

"I'll tell you everything later. Right now Mom's with Mrs. Wyler at the Zoo, and I'm here to grab our mother and take her home."

"If you think the wife did it, call the police, Liana. Let them take care of it. You can't just march in there with both guns blazing like John Wayne! You didn't bring your gun, did you? You know how I hate those things," he exclaimed, with panic ringing in his voice.

"Yes, I did, but I promise to keep my six-shooter in its holster. I just want to go and quietly get Mom out of there."

"Jesus Christ, Lee, you're crazy! Please, don't do anything stupid. You said she's already with Mrs. Wyler, didn't you? What are you going to say to them? Don't you think they're going to wonder what you're doing there?"

I kept my voice calm. "I'll tell Lila something urgent has come up, and she's needed at the office. Once I separate them, then..."

"Don't you dare go in there. That's all I need is both of you getting hurt! Go find a policeman! God, Lee, you almost died a couple of days ago! This has got to be brain fever or something."

Victoria's anxious voice sounded in the background, as Richard's tone became higher pitched and louder. I could tell my brother was beginning to work himself into a frenzy.

"Wait. Wait. Slow down, Richard. Take a couple of deep breaths, will you?" I deliberately took a deep breath myself and began talking very slowly and clearly. "Richard, if I had thought this through, I would have probably just waited for Mom to come home later on today. Maybe I went off the deep end."

"Maybe?" Richard commented, but he was calming down somewhat.

"I'm sure I'm worrying about nothing," I added. "They're here for some kind of birthday party for Siberian tiger cubs. There was no reason for me to drive up here like a bat out of hell like I did, but as long as I did..."

"Oh, God, she's off," my brother interjected.

"Richard, I might as well go get her. Yvette Wyler doesn't suspect anything. Why should she?" I added, stressing the last sentence. "Just let me go in and get Mom, okay, partner? Both you and I will feel better if I separate the two of them. Right? We can deal with who killed Portor Wyler later."

Richard's voice sounded somewhat reluctant as he answered, "Okay, but you'd better know what you're talking about and not scaring the bejesus out of me for nothing."

"Okay! I'll call you when we get home," I answered and started to break the connection.

"Oh, no, you don't," he countered. "Lee, leave your phone on. I want to hear what's happening. Don't do anything stupid, Liana, or I'll call the police from here right now. I swear it. And don't hang up on me, either."

"What do you mean, don't hang up? I can't leave this phone on. Everything's going to be just fine, Richard. You can trust me."

"I never trust anybody who tells me I can trust them," Richard stated flatly. "Now, leave the phone on, go get Mom, and take her home."

"Oh, all right. Can you hear me?" I asked anxiously, as I stuck the phone in the pocket of my sweatpants.

"Okay, yes, yes. I hear you. Don't do anything stupid, Lee!" he shouted.

"Stop saying that."

"Can you hear me, Lee?" Richard shouted even louder.

"Of course, I can hear you and so can the rest of the Bay Area. Keep your voice down. Don't say anything. It looks strange to have my pants talking," I said as I stepped out of the car. I felt much calmer now than I did before. Just having Richard overwrought on the other end of the line sort of had a soothing affect on me. Brothers and sisters can be like that.

I told myself to concentrate on my goal. The primary thing was to find our mother and take her home, I repeated again and again. The fact the woman she was with murdered two people would have to become a secondary issue.

However, precautions should be taken. I opened my handbag and checked the revolver regretting it was too large for the shallow pockets of my jacket and too heavy for the sweats. I held the handbag tightly to my side and started across the street to the entrance of the Zoo. Every now and then Richard would ask what was going on, and I had to threaten to turn the phone off to silence him.

Paying the entrance fee, I walked inside and headed for the large cat area. I fought the urge to run, which would only attract attention and probably start my head pounding. As it was, I was feeling a little delicate and precariously close to getting a headache. I wondered if I had any aspirin with me, as I approached the door of the stucco building.

I heard the growls and movements of large animals plus the sounds of an excited crowd. There was also a smell, but we won't go into that. I worked my way through the throng and came upon the one-year old feline celebrities in their glass enclosed pen sound asleep, oblivious to the pink and blue balloons, gawking spectators and photographers. Okay, I found the cubs but where was the party?

I looked around and saw a young woman dressed in a faded brown uniform standing by a door marked "staff only" and went to her. I asked about the location of the party and was told the birthday cake had just been cut. Pieces of the five-tiered, eighty-five pound cake were now being handed out only to a "select crowd, members who had donated a certain amount of money," the attendant added, contemptuously. Knowing Lila was always part of the "select crowd," with or without contempt, I asked where that was.

"Unless you've got a gold membership card from the Zoo, you can't get in. Do you have one?" the young woman asked in a tone of voice daring me to produce one, given how I was dressed.

"Yes, I've got one," I replied, as I searched my handbag for my wallet. We donated to the zoo under the family plan, so each of us had a card. Flashing it, I smiled as sincerely as I could and pushed past her.

"Outside in the enclosed green," the attendant finally said curtly, pointing with a dirty, stubby finger to a door on the far side of the room. "Show the security man at the entrance gate the card."

"Thanks, and I'll bring you back a piece of cake, if I can," I said over my shoulder.

The attendant, in surprise, gave me a "thumbs up" sign.

Buildings surrounded the outside patio on all sides. This was an area usually reserved for private parties. In the center of the grassy knoll, all four sides of a large white tent flapped uneasily in the winter winds. Stakes strained against periodic gusts in water-saturated ground. The whole thing looked like it might blow down any minute. I wondered why on earth they didn't simply have the party inside a building during this type of weather, or better yet, hold it in May. I walked the two or three yards to the entrance.

Once inside, overhead heat lamps beamed down on over two hundred people crammed in an area that normally should accommodate seventy-five or eighty. It was oppressively hot. Balloons bobbed up and down on strings tied to support poles as "The March of the Baby Elephants" blared from overhead speakers. Frankly, I would have rather been in the cage with the sleeping cubs. I weaved in and out of the crowd feeling my head begin to throb. With some difficulty, I found an empty corner where I could search my bag for aspirin, hoping I had brought the bottle along. Fortunately, I found it and swallowed three aspirin without any water, one of my least favorite things to do. I grimaced from the acrid, sharp taste in my mouth. I heard my mother's voice.

"Liana! My God! I thought it was you! I saw you from over there," Lila gestured to a group of several dozen people talking animatedly to one another some ten feet away. I gagged on the residue of the aspirins and tried speaking, as Mom continued excitedly, "What are you doing here? And what are you wearing?" Lila added derisively as she looked down at my battered sweatpants and beat up running shoes. I coughed in a very unlady-like manner, sort of like Tugger bringing up a hairball, while I reached for my mother's arm.

"Yvette," she called over to her friend who was chatting nearby. "Look who's here. Liana."

I managed to swallow enough of the grainy medicine to find part of my voice. "M... Mom, I came to get you. You've got to come home with me right..." I had another coughing fit and Mrs. Wyler joined us, wearing a thin smile. I returned her smile and continued brokenly,

"So, Mother, really, you turned off your cell phone and now nobody at the office can reach you. So I came."

Lila ignored me as she touched my forehead with her hand. "You shouldn't be out of bed, dear. What's so important they have to track me down at the San Francisco Zoo?" Lila looked at her friend and both women turned to stare at me while I choked a little more quietly. I had the undivided attention of both of them, unfortunately.

I felt my throat become even drier and the coughing started again. I noticed a plastic glass of liquid in my mother's hand. I grabbed it and drank the green-colored glop down. It was nauseatingly sweet, but at least it was wet, and it washed the aspirin residue down.

I made a face as I asked, "What was that? Melted lollipops?"

"Never mind that," Lila retorted. "What are you doing here when you should be in bed recuperating?"

I tried to smile winningly at my mother. "I think it's too complicated to go into right now, Mother. I'm sure Patti can explain it to you better. Why don't we just go? We..."

I could see anger swell in her breast, and she interrupted indignantly, "Of all the nerve! Sending my daughter from her sick bed to come and get me." She pulled her cell phone out of her handbag. "I'm going to give that Patti a piece of my mind. I've never in all my life..."

I reached out and took the phone from my mother's hand, seeing this was not going as I'd planned.

If only I can get her away from Mrs. Wyler for five minutes to explain.

"No, no, Mom. Don't bother calling. Let's just go. Come on." I put my arm around my mother's shoulder and tugged at her. "I'll explain to you in the car." I turned to Mrs. Wyler and said brightly, "You don't mind if I take Mother away, do you?"

"Liana, give that back to me," Lila ordered as she took the phone from me and shook her shoulders free. "Now, what's going on here? You're acting very strangely."

Mrs. Wyler, who had been watching the two of us intently, finally spoke up. "Why don't we all go, Lila? We've been here for several hours, and Liana looks as if she really wants you to leave with her," she said as she looked directly into my eyes. Her smile was tight, and her eyes were cold. She took hold of Mom's arm and began pulling her towards the exit. Lila, too much of a lady to protest, tried valiantly to keep up with her friend as Yvette moved through the crowd like the prow of a ship, with her in tow. Lila reached back and grasped my hand. I followed as closely as possible, while Mrs. Wyler pushed her way through the mob.

Lila was the first to speak as they returned to the relative open space of the large cat room. "I don't know what's happening," she began as she turned over her shoulder and spoke to me, "but I'm going to take you home and put you to bed, young lady." Then she turned back to her friend who was still pulling her across the lion house and toward the exit. I struggled to keep up.

"Yvette, you don't have to leave. Why don't you stay here and listen to the lecture on The Loss of Habitats across the World? It should be fascinating."

We were near the exit of the Zoo, and Mrs. Wyler wheeled around and stopped. She looked past Lila at me and said in almost a whisper, "You know, don't you?"

I was so stunned by her words, I took a step backward, then tried to regain my composure. The falter had been slight, but it probably didn't make any difference. Mrs. Wyler seemed to know the answer to the question before she asked it.

"Know? What does she know? For pity's sake, why are you two acting so oddly?" Lila demanded, in an irritated tone. By now, Mom had followed Mrs. Wyler out of the Zoo and stood on the sidewalk buttoning her powder pink coat against the sharp gusts coming off the ocean. She looked from one to the other.

Mrs. Wyler glanced around her, reached out and pulled Lila closer to her with one free hand. The other was inside her jacket, which had kangaroo style pockets.

"Stop yanking me around, Yvette," Lila said, losing her temper. She tried to pull free, but Mrs. Wyler held her in a vise-like grip.

The woman is much stronger than she looks, I thought.

"Quit squirming, Lila," she ordered. "Tell your mother, Liana. Tell her what you know," she said with a harsh smile.

"I'm leaving," said Lila finally pulling free. "This is a highly unorthodox way to behave, Yvette, I must say. I think you've lost your…"

"Shut up," snarled Mrs. Wyler as she grabbed Mom's arm again and turned back to me. My mother's mouth dropped open, and she stared at her friend, who seemed to be going mad before her eyes.

Mrs. Wyler glared at me and said, "They never found the gun. That's because I've got it right here. Daddy's antique derringer." She moved the pocket of her jacket, revealing the vague outline of the pistol inside. "If you don't want me to use it right now, start walking in the direction of the parking lot."

Lila gasped and reached out to me. I moved toward her protectively. "Derringer? What are you...?" Lila stuttered, trying to comprehend what was happening.

"Move!" Mrs. Wyler demanded. "Don't make me shoot you right here." She started pushing us with her free hand. We crossed the street and headed for the parking lot, about two hundred yards away.

"Yvette! What do you mean, shoot us? You can't mean that. Why, we've been friends..." Lila broke off and tried to laugh but stopped when Mrs. Wyler did not reply. "What's going on, Liana?" Mom asked, as she drew me to her.

I thought of the phone in my pocket and hoped Richard was still listening. Maybe he would call the police, as he threatened before.

Please, oh, please, call the police, Richard, I prayed silently. I said aloud, "Mrs. Wyler killed her husband, Mom. It wasn't Grace Wong."

"Yvette, you...killed Portor?" Lila asked.

"Just keep moving," was the harsh reply from the woman holding us captive.

"It's true, Mom. I'm sorry." I looked back over my shoulder. "How much did you pay your housekeeper to lie for you? I thought it rather telling she went on a very expensive vacation immediately after the death of your husband."

"You! You don't know anything." Mrs. Wyler's response was bitter. "Money wasn't the issue, although I have rewarded her with a considerable sum. She believes in me. She's on my side. She understands why I had to do what I did," Yvette told us in a trembling voice. "You have no idea what I've been through." We arrived at her four-door sedan and both of us looked expectantly at Mrs. Wyler, afraid to make a wrong move.

"Liana, you drive, and keep both hands where I can see them. You get in the front seat with her," she told Lila.

I looked around and saw there was no one else either in the parking lot or on the sidewalk. At this time of year, there wasn't the influx of crowds coming and going you would have in the summer. The party for the Siberian cubs was still in full swing, and no one would be leaving for quite a while. It was windy, cold, and lonely. Except for the cars whizzing by on the highway nearly a block away, it was just the three of us.

I opened the car door, got in and placed my purse by my side. At the first opportunity, I would try to retrieve my revolver. I should have had it more accessible, I rebuked myself. However, a "shoot out" with Mrs. Wyler was almost as repugnant a thought as being kidnapped, I realized. I started the car and pulled out of the parking lot. We came to the intersection of the Great Highway and stopped for a red light. I watched several cars driving through the intersection at fairly high speeds. Directly across the highway were the sand dunes, which led down to a three-mile long stretch of beach. Mother and I sat in the front seat with Mrs. Wyler directly behind, waiting for the light to change.

Yvette Wyler rubbed her forehead with the tips of her fingers and said harshly, "Don't wait for the light. Turn right. Turn right. I remember where we're going now."

She pulled the pistol out of her pocket, leaned forward between us and gestured with it. Actually seeing the pistol for the first time drove home the seriousness of this to us. I saw small beads of perspiration form on Lila's top lip.

I turned the car right, trying to stay cool-headed, but my heart pounded.

Have I brought all this on Mom and me by coming down here? Have I sent Mrs. Wyler over the edge? It's obvious to me the woman is becoming more unglued by the minute. We have to try to keep her as calm as possible. If we do, maybe nobody will get hurt.

My mother said in as natural a voice as she could manage, "I don't understand any of this, Yvette. If you killed Portor, I'm sure you had a very good reason. I know you loved him. You can talk to me. We're friends." Lila turned a sympathetic face toward her friend.

"Turn around and face the front, Lila," Mrs. Wyler said coldly. "Don't make me shoot you right now. I will, you know. If you're so interested, I'll tell you all you need to know when we get to where we're going. There will be plenty of time to talk then."

"Where are we going, Mrs. Wyler?" I asked, trying to keep the fear out of my voice.

"We're going to the Dutch Windmill up the road. You know, the one that's nearly completed, with the vanes. You're going to park on the side of the road where I tell you. Now drive."

I drove slowly toward the two windmills sitting about three-quarters of a mile apart and taller than anything else on this stretch of the Great Highway. I had been reading a lot of newspaper reports recently about the north and the south windmills, named The Dutch and Murphy windmills, both considered an important part of San Francisco's history.

Four to five stories high, they had originally been constructed in 1902 to pump water for Golden Gate Park's irrigation system by using the wind from the ocean. About ten years later, unfortunately for them, electricity came along.

With the windmills no longer performing a primary function, their maintenance was neglected, and they eventually ceased to operate.

The Dutch Windmill had been renovated twice and looked pretty good from the outside. It had no innards, from what I understood, but the Restoration Committee of Golden

Gate Park moved on to the south windmill, which had never had any work at all, to bring it up to a similar state. Both windmills would be worked on internally at the same time within the next few years. These thoughts raced through my mind, as we did the short drive to our destination. Was one of these Dutch behemoths going to be the last place on earth my mother and I saw?

I dropped my right hand from the wheel, feeling the time was right to get my revolver. I opened the handbag and reached inside, trying to be as unobtrusive as possible.

"Give me that!" screamed Mrs. Wyler as she snatched my purse from over the top of the backrest. I've watched you clutching that bag to you. You've got a gun in there, don't you?"

"No, I don't. I was going to get some more aspirin. My head is aching," I answered quietly.

My mother's old friend sounded out of control. Her hands shook so much I feared the pistol might go off accidentally. If she was having a nervous breakdown right in front of us, I didn't want anybody to get shot because of it. Lila looked at me. I tried to smile reassuringly, but nothing much gets by Mom. She knows a bad situation when she sees one.

"Never mind the aspirin," Mrs. Wyler retorted as she rolled down her window and threw my bag into a shrub nearby.

"Hey! What's the matter with you? You didn't have to throw my handbag away. It's a Kate Spade. I'm going to go back and get it!" It was a long shot, but she was so nutty, I thought she might let me.

I felt the barrel pressed against the side of my head. "Just drive the car, can't you?"

"Leave her alone, Yvette," my mother said. "She's not well. Don't hurt her. She'll behave."

"Both of you just shut up. Stop talking. I mean it. Pull off the road here," she demanded, gesturing to a spot a little north of the turnoff to the street that actually went by the windmill.

As I pulled over, I had a terrifying thought that maybe my cell phone might not be working, like before. I started to pray to the Energizer Bunny, hoping it was one of his batteries I was using.

"We're going to take that path leading to the windmill. See it? It's more private. Now get out of the car, both of you." Mrs. Wyler pointed to a narrow dirt path barely wide enough for one person. It cut through the small brush and sparsely limbed trees that fought the constant wind and salt air for survival.

We moved toward the path as Mrs. Wyler began talking. "Portor and I used to come here when we were young and in love. Portor lived nearby with his parents. That was before he took over my father's business. You remember those days, Lila. It was our freshman year at Stanford. Sometimes he and I would make love inside the windmill before they sealed it off. If only my mother had known what we were doing," she said, her voice softening momentarily by the memory.

It took on the hard edge again. "Keep walking on this path and hurry up. There's a door on the other side of the windmill. As one of the trustees, I have a key to it. Nobody will think to look for you there, at least, not until after all the work gets done on the south windmill. That won't be for two years."

As if answering my thoughts about whether or not I brought this on by my rushing up to the zoo, she continued, "I wanted you to come with me today, Lila, because I thought you suspected me."

"Suspected you? I never…" Lila began.

"I couldn't tell anymore," Mrs. Wyler interrupted. "I didn't know if I was becoming paranoid or….It's just that I can't sleep. I haven't slept since it happened. I...I can't think anymore, either."

"I never thought it was you for an instant," Lila answered in a tight voice, as she tripped over a root on the footpath. "Why would I?"

Mrs. Wyler's tone became more matter-of-fact. "Well, I couldn't live with the idea one day you might. Or you either, Liana. I'll have to get out of the country sooner than I thought," she said, more to herself than to us. "Thirty million dollars goes a long way in a third-world country. At least I've got that."

I almost said thirty million goes a long way in our country, Toots, but I thought better of it. Both Mom and I remained silent and exchanged glances.

"Why did I shoot him, you asked?" Mrs. Wyler's voice broke into our morbid thoughts. "You know he was cheating on me. I found that out after I asked you to have Liana follow him. I couldn't bear the thought of losing him. I loved him so much." Her voice choked up, and she stopped speaking for a moment.

We came to a clearing. A light rain had started, blown sideways by the harsh and persistent wind. The weather was ghastly. I could see why there were no other living beings around, except for a couple of wet birds hunkered down in a tree.

Ahead of us, possibly a hundred yards more, stood the three- to four-story high windmill, shingled in brown-stained wooden slats. Midway up, a circular deck wrapped itself around the structure. Jutting out above the deck and facing toward the sea, were the skeleton vanes, beautiful and useless, made of latticed strips of timber. No longer covered with the canvas that acted as sails against the wind, they were a silent testimony to the benign indifference of progress.

I had forgotten how grand and imposing this windmill was, as we began to trudge around to the other side. I noted that windows, large and small, had been mortared in with brick to prevent anyone from getting in — or maybe in our case — from getting out. When we got to the front of the windmill, iron double doors still looked functional, even thought they were covered with a thin coat of rust. A large padlock secured them, and Mrs. Wyler drew out a matching key from her pocket. My heart began to pound. I was scared to death. Not just for me, but for my mother. I had to think of something.

We can't just die like this, I thought. *We can't.*

Mrs. Wyler began talking again in a faraway voice. "After Lila gave me the report about the warehouse in San Francisco, I had to go see it for myself. I mean, I thought I knew everything about our lives. Portor and I were one, united, two parts of a team, PY."

"What was he doing there, I kept asking myself? And what else didn't I know about him? When he called and gave me some cock and bull story about a meeting after work, I knew he was going to the warehouse. I drove as fast as I could and beat him there by about fifteen minutes. I took my father's pearl handled pistol with me. I wasn't sure what I would do with it. Maybe I wanted to scare him. Maybe I wanted to show him how serious I was." She stopped walking and so did we. Mother and daughter turned around to face the woman, as she continued speaking in a monotonous, cracked voice, a far away look in her eye.

"I hid in one of the cages, the one with the boxes of shoes, waiting for him to come. When he showed up, he went into the small office. I followed him and stayed outside near the window hoping I could hear something. Well, I heard something, all right. He called this woman, this Grace Wong, on the phone. I didn't even have to be close by. His voice echoed in that awful building. He was so needy, so loud, so vulgar! I couldn't hear her side of the conversation, but I heard enough. I learned about the illegal immigrants and how he was forcing her to have...to have...sex with him in exchange for her family's freedom. He practically begged her to sleep with him one more time. He didn't care she loathed him; he said as much. He said he'd think about bringing over another one of her brothers, if she would."

Mrs. Wyler's face became distorted and tears ran down her cheeks. "I thought to myself, 'Who is this man? Who is this horrible person who would do all these awful things to people and then come home to me and crawl in my bed?' I was mortified."

Lila opened her mouth to speak. but Mrs. Wyler's ranting went on. "After he hung up, I stepped inside the office and waited for him to see me. I thought he would be ashamed or guilty." Her eyes took on a frightened look.

"Yvette," said Lila, "you were out of your mind with horror and grief. No one can blame you for..."

"Shut up, can't you?" Mrs. Wyler screamed, aiming the quivering pistol at my mother's chest. "Can't you see I'm trying to explain this to you? Why I had to do it? Don't interrupt me," Mrs. Wyler blubbered a little more and waved the derringer back and forth between the two of us.

"He was angry at me. Can you believe it? He was angry at *me* for following him." Mrs. Wyler's entire body trembled as she said this. "He told me he was glad I knew, and if I didn't like it, I could clear out! I took the gun out and showed it to him. He laughed. He laughed at me and started coming toward me, daring me to shoot him. I didn't know what to do, so I turned and ran out of the warehouse. I didn't know where I was going. I couldn't see anything; it was raining so hard. I couldn't stay inside with him. I just couldn't. I was disgusted."

During this diatribe, I tried to put more distance between Mom and me, as surreptitiously as possible. Unfortunately, the less coherent Mrs. Wyler became, the closer Lila was instinctively drawn to my side.

"He followed me, trying to make me listen to him. I could barely see him for the downpour, but I could hear him. Then he grabbed me and slapped me across the face." Her hand went to her cheek in remembrance. "That's when I shot him. Three times. I would have fired more, but it ran out of shells or something. Anyway, it stopped going off, and then he fell down. He had the most surprised look on his face." Yvette laughed softly and began to sob again.

"I tried to get back into the warehouse, but the door was locked. I ran and ran in the rain until I couldn't run any more. Somehow, later that night, I found my car and drove home." Her eyes were clouded over with grief and tears, but she still managed to keep both of us in her sight.

"Why don't you tell us about Captain Chen, Mrs. Wyler? Tell us why you killed him," I said. Mom stared at me with horror written all over her face. I looked at her and nodded. "She shot him last night, Mom."

"Oh, my God," Lila said in a hoarse voice. "You killed someone else?"

"I had to, Lila. Don't you see?' Yvette looked pleadingly at her old friend. "He called Portor from the ship that night. Portor told him he couldn't talk because I was there. Chen figured everything out. He was blackmailing me for the money in the Cayman Islands. That's all I had. He wanted everything, everything!"

She covered her eyes with her free hand for a moment and during that time, I reached out and pushed my mother away. Lila threw me a stunned glance. Mrs. Wyler stopped sobbing and focused on me. She tightened her grip on the pistol, aiming it at my face.

"What are you doing?" she said between clenched teeth.

"Nothing, Mrs. Wyler. Nothing," I said, as innocently as I could, given the circumstances. "I was just trying to get my mother away from some poison oak, that's all.

"I don't trust you. What are you up to? I've never liked you, Liana, never. That's why it didn't bother me knowing you might be there that night. I thought, 'well, if she shows up and sees me, I'll just shoot her, too,'" she added in a half cocky, half-crazed tone.

I could see a mixture of shock and outrage come over my mother's face. "Why, you bitch," Mom shouted in a very unladylike fashion. Practically spewing fire, Lila lunged at her.

With a look of astonishment, Mrs. Wyler turned her attention to the oncoming woman. It was the split second I needed. I stepped forward between them and twisted my body to put the bulk of my weight onto my left leg. My right leg flew up in the air with the force and height needed to knock the pistol from the woman's hand. I was a little out of condition, and I heard a snap, crackle, and pop as I executed the move, but I did it perfectly, if I must say so myself.

The derringer soared over Mrs. Wyler's head and into nearby brush. Now I shifted my weight from my left leg to the right, as my body returned to the ground and centered. Turning slightly, I kicked my left foot into the woman's stomach with all my body weight behind it. It felt so good. With a loud grunt, Mrs. Wyler involuntarily doubled over in pain. She hit the ground almost in a fetal position, rolled over several times, and lay very still. I automatically went into my third defense position, until I realized Mrs. Wyler would not be getting up any time soon.

For a moment, Lila stared at me and then at the woman lying on the ground. "Oh, thank God, Liana." She ran to my side. "Are you all right? I can't believe it. She was going to kill us! What's that noise?" Lila's last remark referred to the muffled sounds coming from my pants. I reached inside my sweats and retrieved the phone.

"Richard, are you still there? No, we're fine. We're fine. Ow!" I pulled the phone away from my ear, as Richard began yelling full throttle. I handed it over to our mother. Let her deal with him.

I wanted to concentrate on the woman on the ground, who was beginning to moan. There was no telling what Mrs. Wyler would do once she came around, and I didn't want to take any chances. I reached over and tugged at the long, off-white, cashmere scarf Mom wore around the collar of her coat. She was so busy trying to soothe Richard, she didn't even notice I'd taken it off her. I pushed the barely conscious Mrs. Wyler over on her stomach and tied her hands behind her back with the scarf. Then I went to retrieve the pistol. The derringer had landed under some leaves, and it took me a moment to locate it. I made one of my mental notes to go get my bag containing my own revolver, as soon as I stopped shaking. When I returned, Lila was sitting primly on Mrs. Wyler's back, no longer talking on the phone.

"My God, what a day. Be careful with that thing, Liana," Lila said looking at the small pistol in my hand. "Well, everything's going to be fine. Richard had Victoria call the police on the hotel phone about ten minutes ago, so they should be here any second. He also taped the entire confession over the phone. Isn't he a bright boy with all his equipment and everything?" she asked proudly.

"Yes, he is, Mom," I answered. I stared down at the two women, one face down in the dirt with a designer scarf around her wrists and the other sitting lady-like, ankles crossed, on top of her. I felt a little weak in the knees and wished there was a soft chair close at hand. I compromised by crouching down and rocking back and forth on my heels. My head and back were grateful.

Lila continued with her own thoughts, "And my goodness, Liana. Is that the sort of thing they teach you in the self-defense class?" My mother looked at me with open awe. "I am very impressed. You must teach me to do that sometime. How's your head? Is that aspirin working yet, dear?"

I burst out laughing. My mother's unruffled nature, which sometimes drives me mad, comes in handy most of the time. Lila is a survivor; there is no doubt about that. Maybe someday I'd learn to be one myself.

"Mom, do you think you can handle Mrs. Wyler for a few minutes?" I stood and shook my legs out. "I would really like to walk back and get my handbag. It has my revolver in it, and I don't want that falling into someone else's hands. There's no telling what they would do with it."

"Are you sure you're up to it, Liana? Maybe you should go sit in the car and rest," my mother asked anxiously.

"It's only a block or two back and, besides, Kate Spade handbags do not grow on trees. I'm fine," I reassured her as she gave me a worried look. "I'm concerned about Mrs. Wyler, though. Do you want this derringer to hold on her in case she tries anything?"

Lila brandished a club shaped tree limb, which had been languishing in her right hand and gone unnoticed by me. "Not to worry, dear. The only sport I was good at in high school was softball. I've hit many home runs in my time." She looked down at Mrs. Wyler who lay motionless and softly sobbing into the ground. "I don't think there will be a problem, but if there is, I can handle it."

Chapter Nineteen
All's Well That Ends Well

Nearly two weeks later, the family finally had the "fiesta" we were promised on the night I was abducted. The party included Frank and Abby Johnson, our sweet Victoria, and John Savarese, as he and I had recently become something of an item, I'm pleased to say.

Tío had spent days preparing the feast, plus decorating the dining room, which none of us had been allowed to go into, not even for a peek. Behind the doors, gleaming under decades of polish and care, I could envision the Sheridan dining table and twelve chairs, plus matching hutch and credenza that had been in my mother's family for generations.

Mom liked to tell the story of how the set came around Cape Horn before the Panama Canal was put in. Anything that was too delicate or valuable often came to the Bay Area by ship rather than overland. It was an onerous trip; one that took many months and sometimes met with nautical disaster, such as my great, great grandmother's Steinway. Built in New York City, the piano had traveled several thousand miles around the Horn only to sink in the treacherous waters near Big Sur in 1848, the ship and its crew going down with it. But the dining room set I loved so much had made it the year before, without a scratch.

Finally, as the dining room doors opened wide, the kaleidoscope of colors amazed us. Dozens of small piñatas filled with coins and candy bobbed from the ceiling on multi-colored silk ribbons. Hand painted pottery and folk art sat atop furniture, artfully displayed next to sparkling cut crystal. Candles of varying heights flickered brightly in the center of the table and throughout the room, while the scent of fresh cut flowers filled the air. Red, yellow, blue and green crepe paper festooned the Austrian crystal chandelier, while underneath an enormous burrito piñata smiled down benignly on the table below.

The *piece de resistance,* however, were the small, papier-mâché Mexican dolls sitting behind each place setting, complete with name card. About eleven inches high and dressed in traditional costumes, some had been crafted in a family member's likeness and were unbelievably detailed, down to things like Mom's pearl stud earrings.

For the others, Tío had hand tooled traditional, peasant dolls in different types of poses, each one unique and beautifully crafted. Abby, who ran a small boutique, later offered to sell as many dolls as Mateo could make. It looked as if Tío would have trouble keeping up with all the projects in his new life. So different from a month before!

We were already sipping French champagne as we entered the room, served in honor of this special celebration. With our food, we would have the best of Mexican wines from several regions. From as far back as I can remember, only *los vinos de Mexico* has accompanied meals in our home. Many compare quite favorably to California wines. For instance, *L.A. Cetto's Reserva Privada* 1993, an excellent Merlot, is a family favorite.

Tío and Lila sat down on either end of the rectangular dining table. I was at my uncle's right, as indicated by the dark-haired, blue eyed doll that held a small orange and white kitten in one of its arms. Unlike the doll, I was dressed in an authentic Christian Dior royal blue satin sheath, circa nineteen sixty-one, I had bought at a consignment shop. This was one of my proudest purchases, and it fit as if it had been made for me. I also wore the sapphire earrings my father had given me one Christmas; I was told the glittering blue of the stones set off the color of my eyes. My new hairdo framed my face in glossy curls. I felt beautiful and happy.

To my right sat John, looking quite yummy in gray wool slacks, yellow shirt and tie, and a navy blue blazer. Across from me, Frank and Abby Johnson, a handsome couple if ever I saw one, sat resplendent in a dark suit and sequined grey dress, respectively.

Richard was placed to Lila's left and Victoria to her right. Richard actually wore a tie with his shirt, one I had given him for his fifteenth birthday, and he tugged at it absentmindedly. It clashed with the shirt, but at least it was a tie. I can't say what Victoria had on below the neck because I couldn't get my eyes past her hat. It was a large, intensely neon pink, floral thing, jauntily tipped to the side and looking like it had just barely survived an explosion.

Richard and Victoria had married in Las Vegas on that eventful day two weeks before. And now she was part of the family, Mom was getting much better about Victoria's garb. A hardly discernable reaction came from Lila who, upon first seeing the hat, merely downed the remainder of her martini and rang for Guadalupe to start pouring the champagne.

Tío was dressed in the traditional white cotton costume of Vera Cruz, in honor of his father. Tossed over one shoulder was a soft, woolen serape, hand woven in the muted colors of the sea. On his deathbed, my grandfather had presented the serape to Tío, the eldest son. Someday Tío would pass it on to Richard or me or one of our children. Given the history of my love life, I saw Tío glance hopefully toward his nephew's new wife. I didn't blame him.

Lila, of course, stole the show by wearing a deceptively simple, white cut velvet two-piece dress. Her hair was parted on the left with a gold, pearl encrusted clasp holding it to the side. Naturally, she wore her pearl stud earrings. I watched her as she radiated beauty and charm, the Hostess Extraordinaire. My mother was happier than she had been since my father's death, and it showed.

After we were seated and more champagne was poured, Lila stood and said, "Before we begin dinner, I would like to make a toast to the newlyweds, Richard and Victoria, even though I do not care for the manner in which they got married." She raised an eyebrow at her son, who smiled indulgently at his mother before he began his rebuttal.

"Now, Mom," began Richard, "we were in Las Vegas; they were offering a half-off coupon at a chapel close by that included a free bottle of wine and..."

"...And, we couldn't resist a bargain like that," Victoria finished for him and kissed her new husband on the cheek.

"And while we're talking about not caring for the manner of something," Richard said, standing up and staring at me. "There I am getting married, and my sister calls me on the phone to tell me she's going after a killer! *Ay, Chihuahua!*"

"Hey, *el stupido!*" I replied loudly, forgetting I was supposed to be a lady and standing up myself. "I didn't know you were getting married! You could tell someone! Besides..."

Suddenly everyone was talking at once. Even Tío was telling Abby about his hand injury the night I was kidnapped, and Frank was waggling his finger across the table toward me saying something I couldn't hear over the din. Lila picked up a fork and began hitting the side of the champagne flute until I thought it would break. Finally, everyone shut up and looked at her. Richard and I took our seats reluctantly. Mom forced a large smile on her face and stared all of us down.

"Ladies and gentlemen, please! It doesn't matter where or how these two young people got married," Lila said, as if she wasn't the person who started the whole thing in the first place. "What is important is they love each other and are married! We couldn't be happier." She lifted her champagne glass high and said in her best CEO voice, "To the newlyweds. We wish you joy, happiness and long life!"

"*Y Bienvenido a la familia*, Victoria" added Tío.

"*Sí!*," Mom, Richard, and I repeated in unison to a blushing Victoria. "*Bienvenido a la familia*, Victoria."

"*Gracias*," she answered, with a heavy American accent. "*Por nada!*"

We all laughed, clinked glasses and drained them dry. Guadalupe served the food and none too soon, judging by the alcohol consumption of the group. Tío hovered at the kitchen door, making sure every dish was to his satisfaction.

The night's menu included a few of Tío's specialties from when he was head chef at *Las Mananita's*. The recipes were often written up in gourmet food magazines, along with pictures of my illustrious uncle, and I have all of them in a scrapbook I started in my early teens. Tío always made the ice cream the old-fashioned way, and the evening's flavor was mango garnished with fresh spearmint leaves. I must have gained about six pounds.

By mutual consent — actually at Lila's insistence — we didn't discuss any of the details of the murders during the meal, but enjoyed the wonderful food, wine and each other's company. After dinner, Lila announced coffee and brandy would be served in the family room, an absolute first. Usually the family room was far too casual for such occasions, according to her. She usually preferred the quiet formality of the living room. Everyone who knew her noticed lately Lila was full of surprises. That's my mom. Only after settling in and drinking our fresh roasted decaf coffee, the only coffee ever served after eight p.m. in the house, did we begin to speak of the incidents that transpired recently.

"The part I don't understand," Frank said, as he turned to me after he settled down with his coffee in one of the barrel chairs, "was how you knew it was her? Mrs. Wyler had checked out. Her housekeeper gave her an ironclad alibi, for which she'll be spending a lot of time thinking about in jail. Perjury is no small matter. But what made you suspect they were both lying?"

"It was the shoes," I remarked taking a sip of the specially blended coffee. "I remembered the night of the murder, when I found Tugger and brought him to my vet for a checkup, Ellen mentioned in passing it had just barely sprinkled in Palo Alto that night. Then a couple of days later, when I went to visit Mrs. Wyler, she offered to replace my boots ruined by the San Francisco storm and mentioned her shoes had been ruined in the same storm, too. Except she claimed she had been in Palo Alto all that evening...where it had only sprinkled."

Frank stared at me in complete disbelief. "That was it? You chased your mother all the way up to San Francisco, interrupted Richard's wedding, nearly gave me a heart attack, on something as flimsy as that? Maybe the lady got her feet wet from an overflowing sink, for God's sake," he challenged.

"She hasn't been near a sink in years," I replied and stuck out my tongue. "That's what she has a housekeeper for, Frank. It was a lot of little things. Why did she demand I go to see her right after her husband was murdered? When I was there, why did she keep asking me again and again what I saw or heard? I remember she claimed it was because anything I knew might help the police. But that wasn't it. It was because she wanted to make sure I hadn't seen or heard her shoot her husband. She was already heading for a nervous breakdown."

During this oration, I noticed I was beginning to use one of my mother's annoying speech patterns. You know, where one word in nearly every damn sentence is *emphasized*. I tried not to panic about it but vowed I would seek psychiatric help as soon as possible. Richard interrupted my reverie.

"She probably would have shot you then and there if you had mentioned you had seen something," Richard said.

"Richard!" Lila said, bringing her hand to her breast. "Don't even say things like that jokingly. We were almost killed."

"Sorry, Mom," he said but winked at me.

"Another thing," I continued, not pleased I had lost the focus of the group when I was coming to the climax of my story, "was when Richard mentioned Wyler's partner, Ernie Butler, went to a Stanford-Cal tailgate party that night. There wouldn't have been a tailgate party during a downpour. In fact, they probably would have had to cancel the game. It didn't smack me in the face then, but it nagged at me how different the weather was in San Francisco than here, something Mrs. Wyler didn't count on." I noted with relief I had curbed my tendency for the emphasis patter. Maybe I didn't have to see a shrink, after all.

"That's right," said John in an amazed voice. "I remember listening to a commentator say the same thing as I watched the game. I went to Berkeley, you know." He smiled at me knowing I came from a Stanford family, Berkeley's archrival.

"To sum it all up," I said loudly, garnering the attention once more, "none of these things meant much to me at the time they were said, but I guess my subconscious paid attention. Then Mrs. Wyler sent me the replacement boots, and it all came together. Everything revolved around wet shoes, and I knew Mrs. Wyler was in San Francisco that night killing her husband, not in Palo Alto."

"She got rid of those boots, so it's nice Richard got her confession on tape," said Lila proudly.

"Well, yes," Frank answered, "but she still had the murder weapon, and she did plenty of talking to the police when they took her into custody. And all along everybody thought it was the Wong woman," he added, shaking his head.

I smiled but didn't mention the fact my belief in Grace Wong's innocence was what had spurred me on. I had a warm spot in my heart for the beautiful dancer who wanted her family to be together and was willing to do practically anything to make it happen. Maybe it was a fatal flaw, but I've seen worse.

Almost as if reading my thoughts, John said, "Grace Wong has a lot to thank you for, Lee." He stood and poured himself another cup of coffee from the carafe. "You saved her from possibly going to jail, even though one of her brother's eventually came forward and admitted she had been with him that night. She didn't want to admit that because he's an illegal. I think she would have gone to prison, rather than risk sending a member of her family back to China. He came forward, anyway."

Victoria, who had been resting her head on Richard's shoulder, commented, "How sad. Will he be sent back to China?" She sat upright, looking at the INS representative in our midst.

John remained standing as he spoke. "Once the brother came forward, he had to be detained until a hearing can be set regarding his status. Grace Wong has been arraigned and will have to stand trial as an accomplice in the trafficking of illegal aliens into the United States. Due to extenuating circumstances, she'll probably serve a light sentence. She's out on bail at the moment."

"By 'detained,'" I said, "you mean he's sitting in jail?"

"But that's horrible!" Lila exploded with outrage.

"I read somewhere a person might be in jail for up to two years awaiting a hearing and then still be sent back to the native country," added Richard.

"Well, a good lawyer might speed up the process," John responded. "A sponsor is another way to go. Personally, I wish we could take them all in, but we can't," he added.

"What's going to happen to Yvette, Frank?" Lila asked. "Do you know?"

Frank looked down at his coffee cup for a moment. He, too, had known Mrs. Wyler since college and found this difficult. "She's retained one of Palo Alto's best attorneys to defend her. She will be pleading temporary insanity for both the murders and the abduction of you two with intent to commit harm. I don't say she won't pay for it, but she'll probably spend more time on a psychiatrist's couch than in jail."

"What he needs is really good legal counsel, Richard," I said out loud. Everyone but Richard stared at me, puzzled.

Richard, obviously thinking along the same lines, smiled and said, "You mean Brother Wong."

I nodded. "That's something trust funds are good for, don't you think?"

"Well, I've always said you had way too many clothes, and as for me, I've got a working wife now. I've got money to burn," Richard proclaimed.

"While we're at it, I think we ought to see Grace Wong has a good lawyer, too," Victoria chimed in, her hat bobbing with each word she spoke.

Lila gazed down at nothing and finally spoke, "John, how long does it take for an illegal alien to become legal if they have a sponsor?"

John thought for a moment and shrugged his shoulders. "I couldn't say. There are a lot of variables. I know it makes a difference, a very big difference, especially if it's a qualified sponsor. Why?"

Lila looked into the somber and earnest faces of her two children, no, make that three children and said, "Because I think Discretionary Inquiries will become a qualified sponsor, that's why. If Mister Wong can learn a little English, maybe we can finally have a clerical person who will stay for more than a few months. That should make Stanley happy."

I leaned over and smothered her in an embrace. "Oh, Mom, what a great idea!"

"Liana, my hair, dear," Lila said, pulling away and patting the sides of her coiffeur but smiling. "I'll speak with the Board tomorrow and put it into Mr. Thompson's capable hands."

"Yes!" I shouted, as the party began speaking animatedly to one another until Frank's bass voice over road us all.

"All right, all right. If the rabble rousers wouldn't mind calming down, I have a question to ask." He stood and took over the room much as if he was directing traffic on the street.

"Liana," he said standing over me. "Do I have your word you will never meddle again in police affairs that do not involve software piracy?"

Before I could answer, Abby stood up and pointed a finger at the chair beside hers, "Frank, come here and sit down. You are to stop interfering in Liana's life. She's a big girl now. She can take care of herself." She sat down, turned to the rest of us saying, "He does this all the time with Faith, as well. He can't face the fact you both are grown up."

Frank grinned. "Maybe Abby's right. So, I will leave you alone," he said and then added, "for tonight." He sat down comically and everyone laughed.

The party broke up around eleven p.m. Abby and Frank were the first to leave followed by John, who took me aside in the hallway. We made dinner plans for the following night. Tío, who had cooked all day and had an early morning at the animal shelter, went to bed after quick, but warm, farewells. Richard and Victoria began kissing at the door and continued as they walked to the car. Lila, ever the mother, reminded Richard to keep both hands on the wheel while he drove.

Guadalupe had gone home hours before with the promise of an extra day off for all her hard work, so it was just Mom and I. We straightened chairs, picked up glasses and, in general, tidied up. Feeling like a real family for the first time since Dad's death, we sat down on the sofa, kicked off our shoes and snuggled into feather down pillows. We lay our heads on the back of the sofa and stared up at the nothingness of the ceiling. After a few moments, Lila laughed softly.

"What, Mom?" I asked, turning my head toward her, as she still stared upward.

"I was thinking about the first time I ever laid eyes on your father. I knew then and there I wanted to marry him. They say that's not the way it happens, but it did with me. I don't know why I thought of that now but I did."

My eyebrows arched in surprise. "You're kidding. I never knew that."

"Oh, yes. It was his last year in college, my first. It was November. I was with a friend, and we were shopping at the Stanford Track House on campus for Christmas presents." She looked at me, and her face glowed with remembrance.

"We had just stepped outside the building when I saw him. He was coming around the track with several other young men. He and another boy were out in front, when the boy tripped and fell down. Roberto stopped running and helped him up. I remember thinking at the time what a kind thing that was to do and how it was going to cost him the race." She played with the wedding ring on her finger before continuing.

"I somehow found myself standing next to the track fence watching him, from maybe three feet away, when he looked over, and we locked eyes. I'll never forget that crooked smile and those dark, intense blue eyes." She turned and looked at me, "You have the same eyes, Liana. Every time I look at you, I see my Roberto in your eyes." She reached over and squeezed my hand. "It's a bittersweet joy for me."

I couldn't speak, for fear of crying. She leaned back into the cushion again and went on, "He waved at me and helped his friend off the field. I thought I might never see him again. Later on that day, I found him waiting for me outside my English class. Roberto had somehow gotten my name and my complete class schedule in less than two hours. He was a born detective."

"I never heard that story before," I said in wonder.

"I never told it to anyone before. It was always very…personal. Besides, everyone likes to hear the story of how he proposed to me less than two months later on New Year's Eve."

I studied my mother's face for a moment, while Lila stared up toward the ceiling. "Dad was the big love of your life, wasn't he, Mom?" Lila didn't answer but closed her eyes. "That's really nice, Mom, really nice. I hope I have something like that some day."

"You will, sweetheart. He's out there waiting for you. Just don't let what happened with Nicholas get in the way."

I watched Lila's face cloud over. Her body stiffened, and she sat upright.

"What's wrong, Mom?"

"I remember who was with me that day. Yvette! She was with me every step of the way with Roberto. Now that I think of it, I met her the same day, too, just a few hours before your father. Maybe that's why I so stupidly fell into every trap she set. I didn't want to see her as she really was. What a fool I've been." She let out a deep sigh and put her hands over her face.

"I wouldn't be so hard on myself, if I were you, Mom. I mean, when you think of it, you had a little bit more of Dad with you, as long as you and she were friends. It's only natural not to want to let go of something like that when you love someone as much as you loved him."

Mom dropped her hands and looked at me. "When did you get so smart?" She asked.

"Sometime within the last minute or so but don't worry. It'll probably go away just as fast as it came."

Lila laughed. She leaned back again and fixed her eyes on a small crack in the ceiling. "I've decided to donate your father's jeep to charity. It's wasted sitting in the garage, and from what Mateo tells me, the SPCA could use the money."

I swallowed hard. "That's good, Mom. Dad would have liked that."

"I know," she murmured and then asked, "How's that stupid cat of yours, by the way, what's his name?"

"His name is Tugger, as you well know," I replied, but with no recriminations. I put my head back on the pillows. "And he's just fine. He's already 11-weeks old, you know, and got altered yesterday. I brought him home from the vet today." I let out a mock sigh. "They grow up so fast."

"So that means he's carrying a slightly lighter load, huh?" asked Lila wickedly, grinning from ear to ear.

I raised my head and looked at her with wide eyes. "Why, Mother May I! You made a little joke...and an off-color one at that. When did this start?"

Lila raised her head and looked at me. "Maybe you're just starting to get my jokes." We both giggled.

"He's actually quite cute and very personable. Tugger, I mean," Lila said.

"Well, I didn't think you meant John. He's gained four pounds."

"John?"

"No, Tugger."

"Well, John's cute, too, and pretty personable. Anything I should know?"

"Nope. Tugger's in for the long haul, Mom. The jury's not in yet on John."

"Well, you could do worse than either one of them."

"And have," I replied. We laughed long and loud this time. Then we closed our eyes again, lapsing into a well-earned silence.

It had been a good day.

Read on for the first chapter of
Book Two

A Wedding To Die For!

Chapter I
I Love to Cry at Weddings

Mira McFadden was getting married. And I was the thirty-four-year-old divorcee who had introduced her--my best friend--to one of my brother's best friends, who also happens to be my mother's godson. When Cupid's wings start flapping, take cover. And when the groom gets arrested for murder, call me, Lee Alvarez, private investigator.

This all started three months ago. Carlos Garcia, groom and suspect, ran into Mira and me at a Chinese restaurant in Fisherman's Wharf, we having ordered too much lobster moo goo gai pan and chicken lettuce rolls, and he looking as if he could use a good meal. I asked him to join us. It was as simple as that.

Just for the record, it never occurred to me for one moment these two might fall in love. And it certainly never crossed my mind that they would wind up getting engaged. Christ, it was just lunch.

Who would have thought that this Latino playboy, whom I have known since he was gnawing on pacifiers, would have become besotted by a shy and soft-spoken female three years his senior, whose idea of a good time was analyzing the contents of a mound of rocks found in the back yard? Not me, for one.

True, she was drop-dead gorgeous, with one of the sweetest, most generous natures in the world. The daughter of two tall Irish-Americans, she had honey-red hair, turquoise eyes and a glorious ivory complexion covering her nearly six-foot high frame. Even at my own five-foot-eight, when standing next to her I looked like I was parked in a hole. We were a study in contrasts, we two best buds—me with wavy, brunette hair, dark blue eyes and a slightly olive complexion, more exotic than not, and Mira looking like a larger than life water nymph.

Her beauty aside, Mira was also one of the planet's major klutzes. It wasn't at all unusual for her to trip over her own feet in the middle of a room, hurtling her elongated frame to the floor, taking several objects or people with her.

There is even a photo op of just such an event where, on her eighteenth birthday, she fell into her five-tiered birthday cake in front of two thousand people at a fashion show. That was right around the time her father and head of the McFadden Fashion Empire got rid of the illusion that his little girl would become a top model. Yes, she had the physical attributes, as well as being heir to the throne, but when destiny covers you in butter cream icing at the end of a runway and the occasion has been frozen in time by every major newspaper, it's probably better to make other plans. Mira enrolled at Stanford University, obtaining a PhD in geophysics. Good girl.

A few years later enter Carlos, "one of the ten most eligible bachelors in Latin America," as the San Francisco Chronicle liked to say. A scant two months after that, early May to be exact, he threw away his little black book and begged Mira on bended knee to be his bride. I was there. I saw the bending and the begging. Between his hot looks, gentle humor, devotion to her, and ability to sing any love song in Spanish, she would have been a fool to let him get away. In fact, in her excitement to say yes, Mira knocked a chocolate vodka martini onto his pristine, white linen lap. He didn't even care. That's love.

This was all happening while I was on a demanding 24/7 undercover assignment, buoying up my own sagging relationship with the man in my life, Detective John Savarese, and raising Rum Tum Tugger, an adolescent feline, better known as My Son, The Cat. Not that raising a cat is all that tough, but I was feeling stretched pretty thin. All I needed was a wedding.

Between being maid of honor, sister of the groom's best man, and daughter of the godmother of the groom, I was enmeshed in the upcoming nuptials like nobody's business. Everything except the romance seemed to revolve around me. I've said it before and I'll say it again: Cupid has a lot to answer for.

Then Mira came down with the flu during the wedding preparations. High on love, she kept running, jumping and leaping until she collapsed with pneumonia. She was going to be fine, but needed complete bed rest for the next two or three weeks. This made it all pretty intense, as her dream wedding was being thrown together at the last minute due to a sudden cancellation at Stanford Memorial Church, "Mem Chu," for one of the Saturdays mid-June. It was now pushing the end of May. Usually there's a two-year wait for such openings at what some people call "the closest thing you can get to a cathedral this side of Manhattan's East River."

My stubborn friend had had her heart set on being married in this spectacular church, ever since she saw it our freshman year. Postponing the festivities was out of the question. If Mira had to wobble down the aisle in three weeks' time filled to the gills with antibiotics, then wobble she would.

Carlos was to graduate from the MBA Program at Stanford's Graduate School of Business one week before the nuptials. Directly after the wedding, he had to head back to San Miguel de Allende, Mexico, bride in tow, to take over the running of the four-thousand acre cattle ranch, Los Positos de Oros, being temporarily managed by his adoptive mother, Virginia Garcia, who's also my mother's best friend.

So in less time than it takes to grow out your nails, a formal wedding with two hundred guests from the varying worlds of fashion, politics, theatre and society was being thrown together. I hold moo goo gai pan personally responsible.

One recent Saturday morning, I sat at the ancestral dining room table across from my beautiful, ice-blonde, and very put together mother, Lila Hamilton Alvarez. As for me, I was puffy-eyed and exhausted and looking like something my cat had left in his litter pan.

"We should have hired somebody to stuff these stupid things, Mom," I groaned, filling envelopes with yea or nay response cards and a sheet of driving instructions to the upcoming shindig. "There must be a million of them."

"There are only two hundred, Liana, but I want Mira Louise to know that we did this ourselves, that we didn't hire anybody." Mom has a habit of stressing certain words in every sentence she utters, like the word 'ourselves,' which makes me crazy.

"After all," she continued, stressing away, "We're all she has. Her mother is dead and her father is nowhere to be seen, as usual."

"Mr. McFadden did design and build the gowns for the bride and attendants, Mom," I said but paused, realizing that I had imitated her vocal pattern. I mentally slapped myself across the face and went on, "and I think he's still planning on giving her away."

"At least," Mom countered, "he hasn't reneged on that yet."

"True. Maybe this time he'll be there for her. We can only hope."

"Mateo is standing by, just in case," she sniffed.

She was referring to my wonderful 'Tio,' and more of a grandfather to me than an uncle. He's filled in for Mira's father on more than one occasion ever since I brought her home years ago. His is a large heart, with room for us all.

I sat for a moment, sifting through sad thoughts about my friend's childhood. There had been the early divorce, followed by the shuffling between two warring parents, the death of her mother when she was thirteen and then living with an uncaring, narcissistic father. Mira's family experience was so different from mine. Now that my dad was gone, my family was even closer, especially with our having to run the family business, Discretionary Inquiries, a Silicon-based software investigation service.

"You're right," I said. "We are all she has. Don't pay any attention to me, Mom. I'm just tired."

And with good reason. For the past few weeks, I'd been driving back to my pretend day job around midnight. That was after the last workaholic cleared the building but before the scheduled four a.m. trash pick-up. I'd ransack through our client's latest piles of garbage in the hopes of finding some evidence of which employee was stealing top-secret encoding. A couple of hours later I'd drag myself home, shower off bits of pizza and Po' Boys and get a little sleep.

At five a.m. the alarm would go off and it was time to start my day all over again. I could have slept an extra forty-five minutes each day by eliminating my daily ballet barre but that will never happen. Dance centers me. And even though I've had to face that I am, at best, a mediocre dancer and could never make a living at it, I still need ballet in my life. It's the necessary food for my soul, my own pizza and Po' Boy.

Born Liana but known as "Lee" to everyone in the world save a mother who would rather eat broken glass than utter a nickname, slang word or abbreviation, I am half-Latina, half WASP, and one-hundred percent private investigator for Discretionary Inquiries, Inc. That's the family-run business left to my mother, brother, and me by my dad, Roberto Alvarez, a Mexican immigrant who made good, and died unexpectedly and too young, of an aneurysm a little over two years ago. I mourn his loss every day. The family now consists of Lila Hamilton Alvarez, mother; Richard Alvarez, brother; Mateo "Tío" Alvarez, uncle; and yours truly.

When Mom's not around, we refer to Discretionary Inquiries as D.I. It's one classy operation. That's probably because Lila Alvarez, the driving force behind it, is one classy lady. She believes that what really separates us from the rest of the animal kingdom is our ability to accessorize.

If D.I. were a car, it would be a Rolls Royce. I own a Chevy, so I needn't go on. I always get the job done, but I get it done a little differently than anyone else. It's a blessing; it's a curse.

With the help of about twenty employees, we deal with the theft of intellectual property, hardware and software programming in Silicon Valley, often worth millions of dollars. Computer thievery is frowned upon here, especially by the injured company, so this type of skullduggery usually winds up on our doorstep. I am proud to say that D.I. has a recovery/prosecution rate of over ninety-four percent. *We Are Smokin'* should be our motto but I'm sure that Lila Hamilton Alvarez would never put that on a business card.

"I've always sworn by cucumbers, Liana," Mom said, interrupting my reverie. "Use those and you'll be fine."

Frankly, I had no idea what she was talking about, having lost myself earlier in my mental wanderings. I fought to remember what I'd said a good five minutes before. Was it something about me looking like cat scat and my mother looking like something out of Vogue magazine? No, no. I was just thinking that; I hadn't said it. Then the thread came back. Pooped, tired and exhausted. That was me.

"Okay, I'll do that. Cucumbers," I echoed and changed the subject. "Mom, the gowns arrive this afternoon by special delivery. I hope I make it back from the florist's in time to sign for them."

"Why don't we have Mateo keep an eye out for the delivery truck?"

That's the upside of living on the family property in an apartment over the garage. The downside is that you live on the family property in an apartment over the garage. Tugger and I share a two-bedroom, one-bath abode originally used by the live-in chauffeur back in the days when people in Palo Alto had such things. Four years ago, Mom and Dad renovated it as an inducement to my coming home after my marriage had broken up.

"Good idea. I'll give him a call later." Just thinking about my uncle brightened my mood. "Speaking of Tio, the bridesmaids' fittings are at four o'clock. We're going to have a small party afterwards, sans Mira, and Tío made the food." Apart from being wonderful, Tío is a retired chef. Recently, he's been trying to teach me how to cook. So far, I have mastered eating. "Try to stop by for it," I added.

"If I can. What's on the agenda for next week, Liana?" she asked, stacking envelopes alphabetically.

"Mainly, I'll be at my exciting job, delivering mail, emptying trash cans, refilling supplies and being a General Factotum."

I was distracted by a slight smile on Lila's face and one of the flaps of an envelope sliced my finger. Sticking it in my mouth I muttered, "Shit!"

"Liana!"

"Sorry."

"Regarding the job, are you making any headway?"

"Not really."

"That's too bad," Mom said. "And please stop making those sucking noises."

"Sorry." I pulled the offending digit out of my mouth.

"One hundred and forty-three. If we can get these out in this morning's mail, the guests will have almost two weeks to respond in writing. The caterers will like that."

"The caterers told me yesterday that with this short notice, we were going to get one-hundred and fifty Chicken Supremes and fifty Beef Wellingtons and like it."

Mom smiled, saying, "That was before I spoke with them. They understand now that for the type of guests we are expecting, *Saumon Braconne, Canard á l'Orange, et de l'aubergine francais seront plus convenables,*" she rattled off in flawless French.

"Okay, Mom, you're saying that poached salmon, orange duck and boiled eggplant are preferable to the chicken and beef?"

"The eggplant has a few more ingredients than just boiling water," she said, "but essentially, that's what I'm saying."

My finger hurt from the effort, so I stopped stuffing the envelopes.

"Keep working," Mom said, nodding at the cellophane tape nearby on the table. "I think you can wrap some tape around your finger as a makeshift bandage."

She continued sealing the envelopes and adding postage, while I did as she told me and pressed on, like a good little soldier.

"Are you finished with that stack yet?" Lila said and brushed at the sleeves of the soft silk of her lemon yellow jacket. No one wears lemon yellow like my mom. Absolutely radiates in it. When I wear anything in the citrus family, I look like I've got a bad case of jaundice. That's the difference between my mother's Nordic, cool beauty and my Latina coloring.

"Just about. By the way, were you going to meet me at the church at eleven-thirty for the conference with the florist?"

"I don't think so. I need to get back to the office and finish up a few things. Then I'm meeting a client for lunch."

"On a Saturday?"

"Necessary, my dear. As for the flowers," Mom said, "keep it simple but elegant. For the church pews and altar, try white roses, open and budding, a little Baby's Breath, with a touch of Lily-of-the-Valley, for interest. For Mira's bouquet, eight or ten cascading gardenias wrapped in white ribbons. And the attendants might have white rosebuds with colored ribbons that match each dress. Rosebud boutonnières for the men, as well, with Carlos' rose in a sterling silver holder. Virginia is wearing a Givenchy lavender suede and beaded gown. A single purple orchid might do nicely."

Virginia Garcia was known to everyone else in the world except mom as "Tex," due to her love and devotion to the state. The two women had met outside Saks Fifth Avenue in Manhattan when Mom was six months pregnant with me. Tex had been pregnant, too, so a bond was formed faster than usual. Tex lost the baby – hence, adopting Carlos from a Mexican orphanage a few years later -- but the two women's friendship has endured over three decades, even though they are as different as a bottle of Dom Perignon and a tall-necked Lone Star. Whatever void lives inside each of them, the other seems to fill. It's a mystery to the rest of us but makes perfect sense to them.

Mom went on, "As you know, Mira Louise has asked me to stand in for her deceased mother and I have accepted the honor, so I, too, will need an orchid. I will be wearing ice blue, so something in a pale apricot shade should do."

I was writing furiously as my mother talked and would no doubt follow her suggestions to the letter. Neither Mira nor I had a clue about what flowers to order.

I'm not a wedding kind of person, having eloped at twenty-two with the Biggest Mistake of My Life. After eight years of trying to make a faithless marriage work, I finally had the courage to get out. As for Mira, she's more interested in boulders than flowers. If she had to, she could combine some pretty nifty rock formations for the occasion but that might look a little odd, a granite bridal bouquet.

"Thanks, Mom," I said. "This is a big help. Hopefully, Mira's marriage will last longer than mine." I let out a dry chortle. Mom reached over and patted my hand, saying nothing. "I'm sorry. I shouldn't have brought up Nick. Casts a pall over everything."

"You can't help but think of your own marriage at a time like this, good or bad. I know I've been thinking of your father even more the last few weeks." Mom smiled at me.

"Have you? In your case, Mom, that's nice."

"Do you keep in touch with Nicholas?"

"You must be kidding, right?" I said, before remembering that I had never told my family the details about the night I left. It wasn't just the other women, who could hold reunions once a year in Yankee Stadium. It was that when I finally confronted him about them, he hit me. Once to knock me down and then once more to make sure I stayed there. I left him and our marriage as soon as I could get out.

"Nick and I have nothing to do with each other, Mom. I thought you knew he remarried a few months ago in Vegas. That part of my life is over."

"That's good." She smiled and changed the subject. "What more do you have to do? Possibly I can help," she offered.

"Thanks. Let's see." Dragging out a dog-eared, worn sheet of legal- size yellow paper, I read it carefully. "Wow! I don't think there's much more," I giggled with relief. "I signed the contract with the two bands yesterday. One is an eleven piece mariachi band that our very own Richard plays guitar with now and then. He's agreed to play a set with them. I thought that was a nice touch. The alternating band is a three-piece jazz combo. Something for everyone."

"Indeed," Mom responded.

"Allied Arts is renting us the restaurant for the reception, including the outside patios, from five-thirty to eleven-thirty p.m. Do you think ten cases of champagne, plus five cases each of Chardonnay and a Napa cab are enough?"

"That sounds more than sufficient. What else?"

I started counting off items on my fingers. "Bridal shower, next week. Richard is in charge of the bachelor party. The tuxes are ordered. The gowns arrive this afternoon and I have two seamstresses set up for the fittings. I haven't seen a picture or rendering of the designs yet but I'll bet they're incredible. Mr. McFadden designed them himself, something he hasn't done for years. He said he chose a 'theme,' which reminds me, I'll have to get samples of the fabric to the florist. Don't you own one or two of Warren McFadden's dresses?"

"No. I find him a little avant-garde, Liana," Mom said.

"I think they call it cutting-edge now, Mom," I corrected.

"If you say so," she smiled and changed the subject. "Did you find a photographer?"

"Yes, finally. I thought I was going to have to buy a camera and take pictures, myself."

"Who is it?"

"Did you know that the reason the wedding got canceled that was supposed to take place at Mem Chu was because the bride came out of the closet and is now living in San Francisco with her lover, Charlene?"

"Get to the point, dear."

"I thought you might be interested in hearing the lead-in."

"No."

"Oh. Well, anyway, this guy was supposed to be their photographer, so he was available. I've seen his portfolio. He's good."

"That sounds fine," Lila said, somewhat mollified. "What about the rehearsal dinner? Didn't John offer to take care of that part of the festivities?"

"Originally, but he had to bow out due to a heavy work schedule."

"That's too bad."

"Yes," I said, and nothing more. My latest love had been pulling back big-time on a lot of things but I didn't want to admit it or deal with it yet. "However, Carlos took over and got us a private room at that new Japanese steakhouse for after we go through our paces." I looked at the tattered list again with all the checkmarks indicating completion and would have done cartwheels around the room if I hadn't been so tired.

"Mom, I think I've done it. After I order the flowers and take care of the fittings, I'm done," I said with pride. "This wedding is *se fin*, complete, and Good-to-Go."

Five hours later, I stood in front of a mirror, enveloped in what felt like eighty yards of a chartreuse moiré taffeta laughingly called "Whipped Lime." Between the starched crinoline underskirt, ruffled hem of the overskirt and tufted bodice, all in a hideous yellow-green, I looked like a New Year's Eve float depicting baby poo.

I ripped open the other boxes to find matching gowns in different odious colors sporting the names of "Pineapple Fizz," "Mango Madness," "Orange Frappe," and "Passion Fruit Frazzle." Mr. McFadden had created a theme, all right. Jamba Juice Rejects. And in moiré taffeta. When Mom called his work avant-garde, she was being kind.

The phone rang but I was afraid to move. On top of how I looked, any movement sounded like leaves trapped in a wind tunnel. No wonder no one wore taffeta anymore, I thought. Noise pollution. One of the seamstresses answered the phone and slapped it into my frozen hand.

"Hello?" I said.

"Lee, it's me," Mira said. Her voice sounded frantic and as if she'd been crying.

"Mira? Are you all right?"

"No, I'm not," she sobbed. "We need your help. Carlos is being arrested for murder."

"What?" I said, sinking straight to the floor, buried in a mound of taffeta. "Carlos is being arrested for murder?"

"Yes, they say he murdered the thief that broke into our apartment last night. They're taking him away," she wailed.

"Wait a minute. What thief? What murder? Mira, what's going on?" She tried to tell me but between the hysteria, coughing and wheezing, I couldn't understand her.

"Never mind," I interrupted. "Hold tight. I'll be right there." I struggled to my feet and thought that with the groom arrested for murder maybe this Good-to-Go wedding just Got Up and Went.

≈

About Heather Haven

After studying drama at the University of Miami in Miami, Florida, Heather went to Manhattan to pursue a career. There she wrote short stories, novels, comedy acts, television treatments, ad copy, commercials, and two one-act plays, produced at several places, such as Playwrights Horizon. Once she even ghostwrote a book on how to run an employment agency. She was unemployed at the time.

One of her first paying jobs was writing a love story for a book published by Bantam called *Moments of Love*. She had a deadline of one week but promptly came down with the flu. Heather wrote "The Sands of Time" with a raging temperature, and delivered some pretty hot stuff because of it. Her stint at New York City's No Soap Radio - where she wrote comedic ad copy – help develop her long-time love affair with comedy.

Her first novel of the humorous Alvarez Family Murder Mysteries, *Murder is a Family Business*, is winner of the Single Titles Reviewers' Choice Award 2011. The second, *A Wedding to Die For*, and third of the series, *Death Runs in the Family*, received the finalist nods from both Global and EPIC's for Best eBook Mystery of the Year, 2012 and 2013, respectively. The fourth installment, *Dead...If Only*, will be coming out soon!

Also by Heather Haven

The Persephone Cole Vintage Mystery Series

• *The Dagger Before Me*
• *Iced Diamonds*
• *The Chocolate Kiss-Off* – Coming soon!

A 1940s holiday vintage mystery series taking place on the streets of New York City, with a five-foot eleven, full-figured gal named Persephone 'Percy' Cole. A trail-blazing female detective with the same hard-boiled, take-no-prisoners attitude, like Sam Spade, Lew Archer, and Phillip Marlow, but with a wicked sense of humor. A lover of pistachio nuts, Marlene Dietrich pants suits, and fedora hats, this one-of-a kind shamus blazes a trail for all other lady dicks to follow.

• *Death of a Clown*

A stand-alone noir mystery, written by author and daughter of real-life Ringling Brothers and Barnum and Bailey Circus folk. Her mother was a trapeze artist/performer and father, an elephant trainer. Heather brings the daily existence of the Big Top to life during World War II, embellished by her own murderous imagination.

The Wives of Bath Press

The Wife of Bath was a woman of a certain age, with opinions, who's on a journey. Heather Haven and Baird Nuckolls are modern day Wives of Bath.

www.thewivesofbath.com

Made in the USA
Charleston, SC
22 June 2013